LOVE CHANGES

LOVE CHANGES

AYANA ELLIS

www.urbanbooks.net

Urban Books, LLC
78 East Industry Court
Deer Park, NY 11729

ISBN 13: 978-1-60162-297-6
ISBN 10: 1-60162-297-X

First Mass Market Printing April 2011
First Trade Paperback Printing July 2008
Printed in the United States of America

10 9 8 7 6 5 4 3 2 1

Distributed by Kensington Publishing Corp.
Submit Wholesale Orders to:
Kensington Publishing Corp.
C/O Penguin Group (USA) Inc.
Attention: Order Processing
405 Murray Hill Parkway
East Rutherford, NJ 07073-2316
Phone: 1-800-526-0275
Fax: 1-800-227-9604

Acknowledgments

Thank you Father In Heaven for EVERYTHING you have done for me. Thank you for the good and the bad because I know that there is a lesson and wisdom to be gained in ALL that you've done and placed in my life so thank you. I wrote this book 10 years ago as a hobby and am blessed to be able to share it with you all.

This book is dedicated to my sister and all of my girlfriends, from the ones I speak to daily to the ones I barely speak to even the ones that I no longer consider my friends. All of you have inspired me in some kind of way to press on and fulfill my dreams, be it through love and support or through doubt and maliciousness. We all have our ups and downs and differences, but when its all said and done, when the men are gone, when the beauty fades, when negative outside influences have moved on to crush someone else's friendships, all we have is one another, all thats remaining are your true friends, the women that create that circle of trust, that friendship, that bond, that female stability that we all need in our lives no matter how much we LOVE to say "I don't rock with females like that." Deep inside we know we do-more importantly we need to rock with one another and stick together. Sometimes its hard to be happy for your friends when you're not happy with yourself and sometimes your unhappiness is displayed as jealousy when it really isn't. Sometimes it is in fact jealousy and sometimes you just never know. Trust that you are exactly how and where God wants you to be in life and there is no need to lose a true friendship over malicious jealousy. Love yourself and be happy with yourself and if you have true friends, hold on to them. Friendships are not determined by the years you know a person but is determined by who is always there WITH you on the front lines of the war. But as we all know, Love Changes and Best Friends Become Strangers. Such is life. So to the positive women in my life, thank you for your love and please know that I need you all. And to the ones who form weapons against me-just know this: I AM THE ROCK THAT YOU WILL BREAK YOURSELF AGAINST.

With Love,

Ayana

To the beautiful dark-skinned sistas who got passed over for the lighter shade, because a man had no idea how beautiful dark skin was. . . .

To the light-skinned, long-hair sistas who got ahead in life because of their brains not their beauty.

To the "unskinny" women. Big is beautiful, so represent it right, be classy.

To my daughter Nia, I loved you before you were even conceived, I wanted you here, I brought you here for a purpose, and your name means *purpose* . . . nuff said.

To the young sistas who believe that looks will get them every and anywhere, know that pretty only gets you somewhere . . . *half the time*, the other half you're either getting disrespected or coming up short. . . .

True beauty lies within.

Prologue

Many of us women get caught up in peer pressure, competition, envy, jealousy, hate toward other females, videos, but change comes with maturity and finding what works for you.

In my life, speaking for Yaya, life isn't about worrying about what the next person is doing and what they have, it's about dancing to my own song, smiling at my own jokes, laughing at my own mistakes and learning from them, it's about being real to myself at all times, it's about being comfortable in my skin, it's about making the right choices and taking my time in doing so . . . it's about focus, consistency, it's about loving over and over no matter how much pain you're going through, it's about happiness, it's about understanding that happiness is a state of mind that only I can control, it's about knowing what's right/good for me and what's not, it's about taking chances, it's about change and growth, it's about being happy for someone even if you're not happy in your own life, it's about knowing the right dosage to give and take when it comes to your emotions, it's about praying at the end of the night, it's about my daughter, loving her, protecting her, moving the right way so she can follow the right things not the wrong, it's not about competition, it's not about someone getting something and me running out to get something "better," it's not about jealousy and envy but about admiration . . . it's not about being with a man because my friend has one, getting married because my sister is getting married, it's not about making excuses for a man when he hurts me or hurts himself, it's about being smart enough to know that adults *are* and *should be* held accountable for their own actions and that no matter how much good there is in a person, I shouldn't let that be the reason I deal with the "bad" things coming from a person, it's about the people I hang around, the things they say and do, it's about benefiting from my surroundings it's about loving people, smiling at strangers . . . it's about staying strong mentally and not breaking down, it's about knowing . . . it's about observing others, learning from their mistakes and going another route, it's about friendship and understanding those around you who are not like you, it's about me knowing that NO ONE is like me so I can't expect them to understand me sometimes . . . It's about letting go, growing up, moving on, it's about being comfortable in your skin and your decisions . . . it's not about being jealous or envious, it's about being inspired. It's about being okay with what you do, it's NOT about anyone but you . . . it's about my self-esteem and knowing that no matter what's on my back, what's in my wallet, what's on my mind, what's on my finger, what my friends have, what the next woman has, that I am beautiful and nothing or NO ONE can determine my beauty, intelligence, and strength, it's about shining brighter than the woman next to me although she has on diamonds because what I have inside of me is priceless . . . . it's about being real real real, my life is not a facade, my life is not a front, I don't come out smiling and go home crying, this is me all day every day, I don't put on shows, I don't do Broadway plays, I'm not an actress, I'm not trying to win an Oscar, be it bad, good, embarrassing, hurtful, I express it, I reveal it and I get it out of my system and move on, it's about knowing the most put-together woman on the outside can have hell in her heart and home, and that I should not be down on myself because someone else is "doing better" you never know who on the outside is admiring you! It's about home, family, being an inspiration to others without knowing, it's about being attractive but knowing my biggest asset and commodity is my strength. It's about knowing and accepting God and being thankful for the blessings good and bad that he has bestowed upon me, it's about believing that despite the situation, HE is blessing you right now, it's about paying HIM back and giving HIM my all, not a relationship, not a friendship, not a job . . . it's about doing my best and letting God do the rest . . .

Toni

I was always a simple person, didn't want much, didn't ask for much, and didn't pray to God for material things or only when I was in trouble. I always prayed for peace in my mind and strength to endure all that comes my way, good, bad, happy, sad. I always figured that those are the things you would need to make it in life, not the other way around.

I was never really the school type, either. I only went to college for a year thinking it would help me out in my career, but that only lasted a year.

Through all kinds of ups and downs, friends and foes, moving and coming back, heartbreaks and drama, my only friend through it all was Beatrice, but I called her B because I hated her name so much. I met her in elementary school and she was the complete opposite of me although we were alike in a lot of ways. She was sitting at the lunch table looking frightened and I sat next to her and offered her my friendship; just like that we became friends. Beatrice believed in fairy tales, I didn't. Beatrice was a girlie girl, I wasn't. Beatrice was beautiful but she didn't think so. She always ridiculed herself and always outdid herself with the makeup and hair weaves. She always told people what they should or should not do as if she had done any of it for herself. She had a lot of dreams and not enough sleep. We both came from the hood, me growing up in the projects, her growing up in a three-family house right across the street, therefore she didn't consider herself to be from the projects or the hood for that matter. She was the first one to call someone a project chick and would never let on that she used to be right with me every single time, puffing weed in the staircase or flat-out in the street while we were walking to our destination. She was ashamed of where she was from, where as I didn't care, I was an individual and where I was from was not a reflection of who I'd become; if anything, my surroundings as a child made me the woman I am today, strong and knowledgeable, *street but sweet*. We ate, slept, played hooky in one another's houses over the years and stayed up many nights talking about losing our virginity, me finally losing mine to a street cat from Marcy projects that had a girlfriend and her losing hers to her "boyfriend." B would criticize me often for being *trifling* and creeping with him despite my knowledge of him being involved with a chicken head blade carrier named Donna, that had his baby. The fact that I used to have to sneak out of windows at dawn when his baby momma would pop up on him or me having to tuck and roll off of his motorcycle when we'd see her or her friends, me just living on the edge while dealing with him did not sit right with B. Actually, no guy I dealt with ever sits right with B.

She and I grew up together in the East New York section of Brooklyn and we didn't really fool around with the other neighborhood girls. However, we had two male friends that we sparred with regularly, Maurice (Mo) and Quentin. But B wasn't *one of us*, she'd just be B, she'd act too good to be around us. She really didn't feel my whole "man's best friend" approach but yet she smoked more marijuana than I did and did her dirt on the ultra–down low just with a different breed of men. It took up too much energy to be sneaky in my opinion. She was very worried about her appearance. She was a down girl like myself but for some reason she put on a facade and I never understood why. B was the type to make the truth out of a lie. But she was my sister and I was hers. True friends can argue and tell one another the truth and not hold grudges and be mad. That was us. We always looked out for one another when it came to telling the truth, among other things. We got into the most heated arguments and seconds later we'd be laughing about something totally different. B lived in a "hood" in New Jersey but because it was Jersey, you couldn't tell her that she wasn't in the ghetto. All and all she is a good person, has a good heart, and that's what matters at the end of *my* day.

The only thing she and I thoroughly disagreed on coming up was my lack of respect for the glamorous life and men. I pretty much had no desire to spend my check on $350 jeans and thousand-dollar bags and I damn sure didn't have any respect for men. I guess it came from the married men I dated as a young woman, the involved men, the older men, all kinds of men that did what they could, hurt who they shouldn't just to get a piece of my pretty brown round. It was ridiculous how easy men were. They thought they had it all mapped out, thinking that their game was tight enough to get a woman in bed. Little do they know, that within the first ten seconds of an encounter with a man, we know if we are going to sleep with them or not.

Sometimes I would meet a guy and if I dug him I'd sleep with him. Then he'd never hear from me again. Now that I look back, it was cruel but those were never my intentions. I never had what it took to be faithful, not that I gave it thought, I just saw no reason to be with one person only, no matter how much I loved them. I guess that's why an unfaithful man doesn't bother me. I don't expect a man to be with just me. It's physically and humanly *impossible*. He may love and want me the most, sure . . . but he will see and be with other women. An old woman told me once that I was *seasoned* before my time. Then I heard that word again in college from a friend. I lived to know what *seasoned* means. Sometimes being a *seasoned* woman has its disadvantages. The stronger you are, the *least* most men think they have to do for you, so I accepted the fact that because of my strength and independence I could forget about a man doing anything for me so I never dealt with them on that level, I got what *I thought I needed* out of them sexually (because in my mind that's all they were good for) and then I moved on. Hold on, let me backtrack and explain what I mean by *seasoned* woman. A seasoned woman is a woman who has been through it all, has grown in her experiences gracefully. You name it, she has experienced it, to a degree that is worth writing about. She has been through good ships and hardships. So you see, a woman with problems can go to a *seasoned woman* and talk to her about *anything* because nine times out of ten she has experience in that field and she is wise. But not only does she have experience, she is knowledgeable. She hasn't just been through negative things, she has experienced the positives also. But you're not seasoned just because you been through shit. It's like soaking your steak in vinegar and not putting your salts on it and cooking it thoroughly. You can go through things and still not learn how to take it in stride and move accordingly. You can bring your car through the car wash but that doesn't mean it's clean, if you just ran through it and didn't take the time to get scrubbed, pushed around, lathered up, washed off, and buffed. Being a seasoned woman is experiencing all things, learning from them, and living accordingly. You cannot be a *bitter* seasoned woman. It's like eating bland chicken. Can you call something seasoned if it tastes bland or bitter? If you're still mad at the past then you are not seasoned. When you're seasoned it shows on your face and it's in your walk and you attract certain people. If you're humbled and okay and forgiving of past situations, then yes, my love, you have arrived. You are well seasoned and ready to be served upon those who are hungry for your tasty knowledge. *Bon appétit!*

I've seen and done too many things to actually

think there were some decent men out there. But none of these situations could prepare me for Jacque.

Beatrice

I was pretty much a loner unless Toni came around, which was hardly. I didn't miss her, though, because we spoke every day either through e-mail or phone. I moved way out to Jersey because Brooklyn was just too crowded for me, everyone knew everybody and I hated that. Toni loved that, though, she loved the city, she loved the guys, she loved being loved, she loved the thrills, and she loved it all. Toni was a wild chick in her own little way. She just straight didn't give a fuck about nothing, in my opinion. I saw the more passionate side of Toni, which is why she and I got along so wonderfully. She is my best friend. We brought balance to one another. We are ying and yang, Cagney and Lacy, Thelma and Louise.

I worried about my girl sometimes because I can't believe a woman could go through so much and not show emotion. I tried to explain "karma" to her but to no avail. I'd be the first to tell you that her mother wasn't shit—*in my opinion*, nothing like my mother or how a mother is supposed to be. She provided for her and although they lived in the projects, Toni was well kept and so was her mother. The house had nice furniture, no roaches, and always smelled nice. Toni had a queen-sized bed, forty-six-inch screen TV, AC, and carpet in her bedroom, in the projects!. Her mother made excellent money as a deputy warden at Rikers Island so I don't know why they lived in the P's to begin with. Her mother chain-smoked and pretty much did her men the same way, one after the other. Toni followed in her footsteps as we became young women. I think it was her attitude that chased the men away not to mention her weight. Toni's mother had to be 190 pounds, which is bad if you're only five-foot-four. She just let herself go and wasn't the petite bombshell that she was when we were children. I always thought her mother looked like Debbie Allen. I hated going to her house because her mother was always uncomfortably quiet. Toni hung out with guys because they didn't care about the "mean mother syndrome" and I was used to Mrs. Jolly. Funny, her last name is Jolly and she is mean like shit. She never really talked to Toni as far as I could see. Coming up, she'd leave the money on the table with a note and leave for days, which is why Toni is such a great cook. She had to fend for herself. It had to have bothered Toni, although she always seemed upbeat and never talked about it. She never even met her father, who I think helped conceived Toni during a one-night stand. That type of shit must be in her blood because her and her mother is the same way. I'm so thankful to have come from a loving two-parent home.

* * *

I like to think of myself as a woman's woman. I'm very feminine, I like pretty girlie things, I like long hair, I like high heels, I like tight jeans, fitted shirts, makeup, bags, shoes, and costume jewelry. I believe that a man doesn't have to know of any nasty habits you may have, which is why I keep the fact that I smoke marijuana away from them. That's my thing and the kinds of men I deal with don't take lightly to drug use. I'm a one-man woman. I love being in love and I love being in relationships, I have no time to run around and my body is too precious to share with everybody. Growing up, I wasn't a tomboy, unlike my best friend. While she sat outside with the fellas "shootin the shit" as she liked to say, I'd either be on the sidelines waiting for her to finish or I'd be in the house napping, reading, or on my way out on a date with a man that was worth my time, not no project benchwarmers. I had big plans, plans of meeting a rich man, someone who will take care of me while I took care of the house. I was that kind of woman. Working was not my forte but it would have to do for now, so I got jobs that would put me in the position to meet well-off men, which is how I met each and every one of my lovers and although they didn't last, I know what I am capable of getting. It can only get better. There aren't too many females as young as myself that can land a corporate bigwig or a rising exec. That's the shit I'm on. My best friend is somewhat the opposite. She is not out to get paid, she is just out to get laid. She straight doesn't give a shit about a man's feelings, at least that is the image she puts out. But I've seen enough of her doings to know that she doesn't give a damn! I've seen her do some foul shit, I've seen her take men from their wives just to leave them, get credit cards from men and take me shopping because she is not a clotheshorse like me. She'd buy herself nice leathers and some shoes to match, that's it. I've seen her do so many things, it's safe to say that my girl is loose cannon when she wants to be.

But Toni is the best friend a girl could ask for. She is brutally honest. I remember my breakup with Marcus. After she ripped me and him a new asshole she came to my house with two home-cooked meals that would hold me for a week since she knew I'd be too distraught to cook. She even rolled my joints for me. She dropped movies off when she couldn't stay, because she'd be on her way to victimize someone and when she could stay she sat up and listened to me for hours and hours as I talked about the same thing, without judging or intervening. She's a good woman and I admire her strength.

The last time I spoke to her she was talking about some guy down in VA and how smart he is, a future actor, rides bikes, and has her heart. I was happy to know that she was *feeling* some kind of emotion as opposed to someone. She said she had been dating him for six months and that he had not tried anything. I said he was gay, she got upset then told me that he explained to her he had a six-month rule, so she had to wait until this month was over before bedding him. He sounded like the perfect gentlemen but of course that was too much for Toni. She kept complaining to him how she hadn't "had any" in months. It reminded me that I didn't, either, but I was not dating right now so I didn't feel the need to have casual sex, it wasn't my thing. My job at Macy's was tiring enough and although it paid my rent—which was only $585—I needed a more professional gig; maybe I'd go to college too.

I fixed myself a glass of wine, rolled a backwoods, and decided to take a bath, then I'd call my parents who I was proud to say were still together and happily married. I wanted to be like them one day. My eyes glanced across the room at a picture of Marcus that I still kept in a frame after being broken up for a year now. I still loved him even though he dogged me out, which was for the better because I had bigger dogs to accomplish and I wasn't getting that house on the hill messing with him. His money was long enough to take me shopping and buy me things, but I needed more. As I undressed for my bath, I noticed stretch marks on my thighs and gagged. "What the—? My weight had been fluctuating and I had gone from a size six, to a ten when I got on the Depo shot, back down to an eight when I got off, back up to a twelve, now back down to an eight. *Stretch marks?* Ugh. On my stomach too. I had to start working out again, taking care of myself. I turned to each dimension of my body and criticized my flat ass. You could bounce a quarter off of it. I despised Toni's huge butt. But then felt better when looking at my D cups, where as she had small B's, *maybe* a C. I was shaped like a white bimbo. I pinned my long auburn weave up in a bun so that it would not get wet and slid my mahogany brown frame into the tub. I settled in there for about a half an hour and told myself after I ate I'd call Toni, then my parents, but I winded up going to sleep.

1

Tracy made it her business to tell everyone's business in college. She was a gossiper, that's what she did. But Tracy, Toni's nosy roommate from Raleigh, North Carolina always had the necessary information. And for once, Toni listened to her when she spoke because it was about someone that Toni was interested in—his name was Jacque. Toni had been secretly lusting after this guy, who stood about five-foot-eleven, maybe slightly shorter, had a slim build, a chocolate brown complexion, and dark wavy hair. He dressed to kill, majored in theater, and was loved by most. So as Tracy rambled on about everyone, she realized that Toni was not paying her any mind as they sat at a bench drinking water and eating sandwiches. "Who you looking at, Toni?" Tracy asked as her eyes followed her path. Once she saw Toni's target, she commented, "Mr. Jacque, he is eye candy, *isn't he*?"

"He's nice, what's the *know how* on him and

how come he does not know me. Everyone who is anyone knows me," Toni boasted.

"Look, *Mrs. City*, two popular people don't just *know* one another because they too dang conceited to introduce themselves. Mr. Jacque is very experienced I hear, knows the ladies well, just transferred over from Penn State, is a senior and has no kids, no ex-girlfriends on campus, pretty much playing the field."

"How you know all this?"

"My cousin goes to Penn State, told me about a guy named Jacque that was coming this way, told me to try to snatch him up before the vultures do, she described him as contagious and said he left a lot of broken hearts back at PS."

"*Really*, I see him around, who does he hang out with?"

"The Rough Riders," Tracy said with her eyes intently on Jacque.

"Damn, you look like you want a piece of him. So, he is into riding bikes then, yes?" Toni inquired.

Tracy paused before answering. "I would hope it's bikes and not dick!"

"Tracy!"

"Hey, you asked!"

"I *did not ask* and *anyway*, how can I get to know Mr. Jock? Is that a first or last name?"

"First name, Jacque, pronounced *Jock*," she says putting emphasis on her already big lips.

"You shouldn't make that face," Toni says in disgust.

She did it again to annoy Toni. Toni rolled her eyes as Tracy chuckled while checking Jacque out, who was donning fresh Timberlands, a neat button-down shirt, crisp blue jeans, and a cap. He looked very neat and well kept.

"I need to make my way over to him," Toni says, getting up to smooth out her white linen dress.

"I see Nicole over there. Maybe I'll go talk to her and make small talk."

"I'll come with you. Jacque and my cousin were cool so I know him like that," Tracy offered. Toni stopped in her tracks and turned to Tracy.

"Tracy, do not embarrass me, okay? You have a habit of just going off at the mouth. Just be cool, *okay*?"

"Okay, Mother," she clucks.

"You really make me sick," Toni says jokingly. Toni's country roomie followed behind her, towering over her with her six-foot frame and slim figure. The women walked over to Nicole, whom Toni knew didn't care much for her but she smiled at her anyway and approached her.

"Hey you," Nicole says lamely.

"Hey, what you been up to? I don't see you in class anymore."

"I switched majors," she says curtly. She is occupied with Jacque's presence, Toni concludes. Tracy gives Toni a look and Toni gives her the eye, letting her know that she needs her big mouth because she sees that she has competition, but to be discreet in whatever she tells Jacque about her. Tracy smiles at Toni happily, then makes her way over to Jacque. One good thing is everyone knew and loved Tracy. Her personality was big and her heart was bigger. She was loved by many and popular for her sense of humor and height. Toni watched as Tracy started talking to Jacque, who turned around to look at Toni about five minutes later. She put her head down as Nicole smiled at him and braced herself for his "arrival." He walked up to both women, no doubt playing on their anticipation of him and smiled. But Toni knew without doubt that he was coming to talk to her and not *midget ass* Nicole, lil' Nicole, as she was known around campus.

"Hello ladies," he says.

"Hi," Nicole says hungrily. Toni plays it cool as usual and nods her hello. Jacque touches his chest and laughed.

"How you been, Nicole?" he asks her. She gets nervous, shifts to her left foot and answers, "I'm good, how you?" Toni is a bit bothered that they are on first-name basis and she is just now meeting him.

"I'm good, do you mind if I talk to Toni for a second?" *Ooh, slap in the face.*

"Why would I mind?" she asks with attitude now, her smile fading slowly.

"Because you were talking to her and I didn't want to be rude."

"Oh no, I wasn't talking to her *like that*, do your thing," she says and sits uncomfortably on the wall next to them. He puts his back to her and leans on the wall in front of Toni. "So I heard you wanted to meet me," he said.

"And where did you hear such a lie?" *I'm gonna kill Tracy!* Toni thought.

"Your friend said that you were inquiring about me. I'm Jacque."

"Toni," she says, extending her hand.

"What is your full name? Antoinette or something?"

"No, just Toni."

"That's sexy."

"Thank you." *So are you, damn you fine as hell even up close, no pimples, teeth pretty straight, eyes white, gums pink, breath fresh.*

"So, since we met, we can speak now instead of avoiding one another's eyes like we been. I really can't stay too long because I have theater now. But I'd like to see you during my free time. Rough Riders is having something on Saturday, come through, maybe I'll let you ride," he said stone-faced. Toni didn't know how to take his comment or maybe it was just her dirty mind. Whatever it was she smirked.

"Sounds like fun, I'll let you know if I'm available later on this week."

"Good," he says.

They stand awkwardly for a moment waiting for one another to speak. "Well, I guess you better get to class."

"Yeah, so, Saturday . . . maybe." He smiles.

"Okay."

He turns and walks off and waves at Tracy as she walks toward Toni. She yells to him that she'll go check him later.

"So, how'd it go?" she asks once she reached Toni. The two women begin to walk so that Nicole can't hear them.

"He said something about now we can speak and stop avoiding one another's eyes, what is he talking about?"

"That means he been checking you out and he knows you been checking him out."

"How so? I just started peeping him about three weeks ago and I know he hasn't seen me do it, because it's been from afar and I haven't told anyone."

"Well, maybe he try'na mack I don't know! Did you get the digits?" Tracy asked, annoyed.

"No, I'm being cool, but he did invite me to some Rough Rider party on Saturday."

"Oh boy, Mrs. City, you sho' is cocky, anyway, you going to class today?"

"No, I'm going to go to the library, catch up on some reading, hit the mall, hit the gym, then hit the bed. You going to that Rough Rider thing he talking about?"

"Well, you don't want to go alone, do you? I can always go with Deirdre and dem."

"Don't play yourself big, country, you're going with *me*. I told lover boy that I had no idea if I was going or not. I might just show up at the last minute."

"Let the games begin!" she said.

"You know how us city gals do!" Toni laughed.

"And that's why all of you are hardened, scorned, mad, and lonely. You need to give love and get love like us country girls, see, we some seasoned mature gals and we know how to learn and earn and keep a man. Take note, Ms. City."

"Please, yawl Bamma hoes don't know shit. Slow asses. Just watch how I operate. See, back home you didn't know me, you don't know how I get down. But I'm fixing to show you, big country, I'm fixing to show you how I move," Toni joked, mocking her accent.

"Yeah, okay, well, while you're *moving*, I'll be *moving* my tall butt to class. I'll see you tonight. I got classes till six."

"Okay, I'll see you tonight."

2

Toni had been seeing Jacque exclusively now for about a year and things were going well. He was a little different from what she was used to but he was nice. He was very attentive, always smiling, and definitely knew how to separate the woman in her from the friend in her. The only thing that Toni had a problem with about Jacque was that sometimes he would become so distant and quiet and she often found herself asking him what's wrong a million times in a day and she hated that. After she expressed to him that college was not for her, he expressed his disappointment in her not wanting to continue her education. Toni explained to him that in her eyes being a writer took skill, not education, that the college experience was great but it just wasn't for her and with that, she found an apartment not too far from campus and got a job at the *Virginia Tribune* as a columnist. Instead of being on campus, Jacque spent most of his time at her studio apartment.

* * *

Toni wanted to go visit B, so she gave Jacque her keys and told him that he could stay in her apartment for the entire week that she would be gone. Jacque wasn't a rowdy guy although he had his biker friends, so Toni trusted him in her apartment while she was gone. He pretty much kept up with his studies and kept to himself, making him all the more desirable to her. After a nice lovemaking session finally (it was worth the wait) and a kiss good-bye, Toni headed to the bus station to New Jersey to see B, whom she hadn't seen in almost a year.

B picked Toni up in her new car, an old square Acura Legend that she called "Gertrude."

The women both laughed as soon as Toni got in and traded affectionate hugs. "I missed you, girl, and look at you, you look great!" Toni said.

"I need to lose some weight," she complained.

"Where, in your breasts? You look like a size eight!"

"I am and I want to be a size six again."

"Well, how are you doing otherwise?" Toni said, already annoyed at B's persistence in wanting to be waif-thin.

"I'm fine, I don't live too far from here. Let's get to my house so that we can really hug!" she gushed.

They pulled up to her dilapidated building that Toni prayed would collapse while Beatrice was at work or something. Toni pulled her luggage out of her trunk and looked up and down the block. This was a long way from her Virginia apartment and she'd rather go back to the projects than be here. Her apartment wasn't as bad as the building, though. It was actually comfy and pretty nice but B kept it a mess. She was always a messy girl. The kitchen was very clean because B couldn't cook worth a damn but her bedroom was a mess, clothes everywhere. Toni wasn't surprised. B loved to dress up and wear accessories and stuff. All kind of pocketbooks and shoes were scattered about. M•A•C cosmetics cluttered the bathroom sink.

"Put your bag anywhere," she said and disappeared into the junky bedroom. Toni placed her bag in the dining area and sat on the brown futon. "Where the hell am I going to sleep?" Toni shouted out to her. Beatrice came out with a huge blunt and passed it to Toni while toting on her own. "Welcome home, biatch!" she said.

Wondering where Toni was going to sleep quickly faded as the high took over, the music started blaring, and she was in the kitchen cooking a mean salmon while listening to CeCe Peniston's "We Got a Love Thang."

"I like how you had this salmon sitting out just knowing I was going to cook it, you whore!" Toni yelled out over the music.

Over dinner Toni told Beatrice that she quit college and decided to pursue her career in writing. Beatrice as usual was happy for her but was sad when Toni told her she was not moving back to New York.

"New York is the mecca for all things. Why

would you try your hand at writing in a small place like Virginia?"

"Because I am at peace out there and I can concentrate on writing my book and besides my man is there. Maybe once I hit it big I'll get my deluxe apartment in the sky-iye-iye by Central Park."

"And I will be your maid!"

"No, you'll be my assistant!"

"Yeah, that's right, *assistant*, I will gladly assist a bitch!" They both laughed.

"So tell me all the details about Mr. Jacque. That name sounds like he can fuck the lining out your pussy, can he?"

"Yeah, he is good. He can be rather timid sometimes but he is good in bed. I can't complain."

"That's nice, you guys been together some time now, you love him yet? And don't be all hard-core and philosophical on me. Do you love him? It's a simple yes or no question."

"You know what, B? I do. I can honestly say that I *think* that I am in love for the first time."

"I am so happy for you!" B squealed.

"I'm happy too. He is so sweet to me, opens car doors, smiles when he sees me. He's in love with me too."

"Have you guys told one another yet?"

"No, it's kind of the unspoken truth, you know? I think if we said it, it would change things. So what is up with you? Who are you seeing these days?"

"My therapist."

The girls cracked up boisterously after that re-

mark. "You are a nut, girl. For real, nobody tap-
pin' that *flat ass* of yours?"

"Nope, it's been about a year, ever since Marcus and I broke up. I just been laying low, trying
to find out what I need to do with my life. I can't
work in Macy's forever. I'm thinking of going to
business school or something."

"Why don't you come to Virginia with me?"

"Virginia? No, that's too far away from my parents. They would have a fit."

"I don't think so. If it was with some man then
yes, but your parents love me. It will be fun. My
studio is like a one bedroom. You can have the
sofa bed in the living room."

"What about Jacque?"

"He doesn't live with me. He is just always
there but if my homey needs a place to stay then
Jacque will just have to stay at his dorm. It's not
like he doesn't have a place to stay so it's not a big
deal. You can find a job out there and I got you till
you find one."

"It sounds like a plan," she said, smiling. Toni
could tell Beatrice had some things on her mind
but she let it ride. Beatrice never held secrets from
her so in due time she knew she'd break and tell
her.

"Well, I miss you girl, I do!" Toni said and
hugged her. Beatrice reached out and hugged her
back.

"I am seriously considering it. I'll let you know
in about a week, maybe less."

"Wonderful, roll the rest of them trees," Toni
said, flicking the roach into an ashtray.

* * *

As usual, B and Toni had a ball over the weekend. They partied, drank, and visited their parents and old friends, then it was time for Toni to go home and she was glad to because she was missing her baby whom she had never been away from since they met. She had Tracy looking out for her to make sure no foul play was going on while she was gone. Toni created a lot of enemies on campus because of Jacque. Everybody wanted him and the southern girls loathed city girls, especially ones from New York that took their men. Tracy didn't call, so Toni assumed all things were going great as expected.

She called Jacque to come and pick her up from the bus station but couldn't get in contact with him. It was 11:00 at night and she couldn't get in touch with Tracy either. Apprehensively, she hailed a taxi and cursed at having to spend $30 to get home. When she got home the house was quiet; an almost empty feeling as if he did not use her key at all.

Once she looked around she realized that he hadn't. She was hoping Jacque would be there waiting for her, missing her too. She called his cell phone when she got in and he answered, sounding half-asleep.

"Hey baby, I'm back," Toni said, putting down the last of her bags.

"How was your trip, baby?" Jacque asked with sleep in his voice.

"I had a good time with B as usual, why don't you come over? It's been a while since I've seen you. Seven days is a long time," Toni flirted.

"I'm very tired, Tone, but I will see you first thing in the morning, okay?" he whispered.

"Okay, I tried. I'll talk to you later," she said and hung up. She had no intentions on letting Jacque go that easy so she showered and got dressed and headed to his dorm to surprise him.

It was so dark outside and the guards were strict so they immediately asked Toni for ID before allowing her on the campus grounds. After realizing that it was her under the cap and hooded sweater they smiled and let her in. "I see you creeping up on that fine young man. I don't blame you!" a female guard said and winked. Toni smiled too and headed to his dorm.

The hallways were desolate as it should be at 2:00 in the morning. Toni knocked on the door lightly and butterflies took over her gut. She was sure that Jacque would be so happy to see her. When a short, chubby light-skinned guy answered the door, Toni stepped back to make sure she was at the right place. "This *is* two-oh-four, right?"

"Yes," he said with an attitude. Toni stepped in and looked around the room, wondering why this faggot was in her man's room. "Where is Jacque?"

"He stepped out to get some juice from the vending machine. Who are you?"

Toni looked at this guy who was flat-out gay.
She looked around the room briskly for any signs
of anything, but found nothing.

"I'm Toni."

"Toni *hew*?" he said, emphasizing the *who* by
leaving his lips in the "o" shape.

"Who are *you*?" Toni asked.

"I'm Jacque's friend."

"You got a name, *friend*?" Toni still asked light-
heartedly because the guy seemed comical to her.

"Leslie. Now back to you. I never heard of a
Toni, now *Tone* maybe, would you be that Tone?"

"I don't know about Tone. Jacque does call me
Tone sometimes, so yes, that would be me, I guess."

"So you're the one that he was just talking to
about an hour or so ago?"

"Yes, as a matter of fact, I was just on the phone
with him, why? Where are you going with this?"

"That lying sack of wine!" Leslie threw his hands
up dramatically and huffed around the room.
Toni watched with her eyebrows frowned in disgust. "He told me that you were an ex-boyfriend
of his and that he did *not* do fish. I can't believe he
is seeing *a fish* behind my back!"

"Excuse me, who are you calling a fish, *faggot*?"

Just then, as if on cue, Jacque entered the room.
He stopped cold when he saw Toni. He was
standing before her, shirtless and not smiling.
Toni's heart was breaking and her eyes were beginning to burn.

"*Please* don't tell me you do fish!" Leslie said as
soon as Jacque closed the door.

Toni spun around and got in Leslie's face. "You

bitch-ass homo, shut the fuck up! This is between me and him, shut your punk ass up, *bitch*!"

"Bitch? No, *you's the bitch* and you needs to get outta my face with your breath all stank."

Jacque came between them, still holding the sodas.

"I wanted to tell you, Toni," he said.

Toni put her head down. She couldn't even look at him. She thought about how she was a fool to think that she wouldn't get hurt. Men were selfish dogs. She knew this all along, what made her think that he would be any different?

"How long has this been going on?" she whispered with her voice choked up with pain and anger. She stared directly into Jacque's eyes. He held her stare.

"All my life," he said openly and honestly as Toni wondered why he couldn't be this open and honest from the gate.

"Uh, me and him have been doing our thing for about a year and a half now off and on, if you must know. Hell, where you been, cause he been with me all weekend?" Leslie asked.

"I was out of town, visiting family," Toni mumbled humiliatingly, looking at Jacque.

"I'm sorry," was all he had to offer.

"Sorry . . . wow, you ruin my life and all I can get from you is a *sorry*."

Jacque put the sodas down next to his computer and leaned against the desk. He reached for Toni's hand. Her heart allowed him to hold it.

"This is why I waited the six months to have sex with you. I wasn't sure if I wanted to go back to my old ways. I'm so sorry, Toni, I do love you, I do. This in no way has anything to do with you so I don't want you to get all fucked-up behind this baby."

"What about the times we didn't use condoms?" Toni asked, snatching her hand away from him angrily.

"I assure you I am in good health. I'll go with you for testing. I am always safe, even ninety-five percent of the time with you. Tone, I'm sorry."

"You have been calling me Tone so that this bastard could think I was a man? You played me, Jacque. How many people on campus know that you're a faggot?"

"I'm not a faggot. Don't say that," he said, getting up. He could feel Toni getting heated.

"Okay, so what are you, then?"

"I'm a man," he said walking to the other end of his room. Leslie sat on the bed drinking the sodas that Jacque brought back. Toni followed behind Jacque barking.

"A man? How dare you even disrespect the likes of a real man by saying something like that? You are a pig, you're disgusting. You mean to tell me, that you would rather have some big hairy man wrap his arms around you at night than a woman? How do you two get along? *Yo son, pass me the remote, thanks son,* then you tap him on the ass? You fucking faggot!"

"Stop calling me that, I know you're upset—"

"I should have known, what man majors in theater? How does it feel to have a dick in your mouth, Jacque? And with a name like *Jacque* I should have double-checked your story any god-damn way, so my bad! *Un-fuckin'-believable* is what it is," Toni said and put her hands in the pockets of her hoodie. She then began pacing back and forth like a madwoman. Jacque stood off to the side, praying that she didn't begin to go buck wild.

"Toni, can we talk about this in private? I want to tell you all about me and why I didn't tell you sooner."

"Are you serious? Okay, so you think that you can explain to me *now* or make it clear to me why you hid the fact that you are a pillow-biting, dick-sucking, cock-getting, faggot, baggy asshole, bitch-ass homo! After I put my mouth on that dick of yours and you done had it in some nigga's ass? Let me ask you a question, you on top or the bottom?"

"Definitely on top!" Leslie said. Toni turned around and without a second thought pounced on Leslie and began clawing at his face. He screamed like a true bitch until Jacque pulled them apart. Toni snatched herself away from Jacque, then slapped him.

"Tell me, how many people knew?" she inquired.

"No one out here, only my family back in Pennsylvania."

"No one here knows. You sure?"

"Yes, I'm sure."

"This is ludicrous, absolutely ridiculous. A homo, *my, my, my* and you know something? I always said, damn Toni, you done been through it all. The only thing you have not experienced was a man lying to you about his sexual preference. I thought I'd be able to tell, but you hid it well. You had me fooled. Wow, that explains you loving doggy style more than the average man."

"That has nothing to do with it, Toni, stop it, okay? Stop it with the stereotypes and the name-calling. It's not going to change what happened here today."

"You always seemed distant, deep in thought when around me and I thought it was me, then I chalked it up as it just being you, you seemed like a laid-back kind of guy. But now I see what it is. The secret of being a faggot was kicking your ass, huh? Tone . . . calling me Tone. It turned you on to call me Tone, huh?"

"Don't make this harder than what it has to be, Toni, it's not your fault, so don't beat yourself up behind this."

"Whatchyou think? I'm going to go home and slit my wrist? You don't know me very well. I'm *definitely* moving on already. Fucking faggot, can't believe it. This is the kind of shit that people get killed over. How could you do something like this to me? Why didn't you just tell me from day one, listen, I used to fuck with dudes, I don't any-more, not sure if I will again; I mean, *I know* I wouldn't have dealt with you after that, but how dare you make the choice for me? How dare you put me at risk? How dare you allow me to give you my heart when you knew how hard it is for me to do that, I told you how hard it is for me to give my heart, and knowing that, you turn around and do some shit like this? If that isn't the most insensitive shit to do, to me! You know how hard it is to give my heart. Why would you lie to me, Jacque?"

Leslie interrupted Toni as she was on an emotional rampage. He was in the corner, clapping slowly and sarcastically.

"*Ms. Loranda*, save the Broadway production, love, it is what it is, *he's gay* and he don't want you, so can you *please* take your act to another stage so my man and I can continue doing what we do? I mean, he did get the sodas because we were quite thirsty. We were *so* not done here. Two more condoms to go!" Leslie sang. Toni took a deep breath and decided not to cause bloodshed and before she let a man see her cry, *a faggot nonetheless*. She turned her back and headed out the door. Leslie was right, he was gay and there was nothing she could do.

3

Toni was so burned she walked home, which took a good forty-five minutes and when she got in, B was on her machine checking to see if she got home safe. She couldn't call her right now in all her embarrassment and fury, so she called Tracy instead, who sounded wide awake. Toni was so mad, mad more than she was hurt for letting her guard down. She knew better. She knew that in this world a woman has to think and make moves like a man but on the outside present herself like a woman. *I slipped*, she thought out loud.

"What are you doing up this time of the morning?" Toni asked.

"Never you mind, Ms. City, what you doing up calling me?" Tracy drawled. "How was ya trip?"

"It was good, what did you do while I was gone besides miss me?"

"I did miss you, Ms. City. I didn't do much, but tonight I went out to some place called the Sugar Bar with Deirdre and them. I'm just getting in. It was okay, the dranks was better than the men. Some real lames out here."

"And faggots."

"Tell me about it. All this down low shit going's on. Anyway, I know you must be up either waiting fo' yo man or he must have *just* left," Tracy giggled.

"Actually I just left him, literally, he's a faggot."

"You two arguing?"

"No, he's a faggot, for real," Toni said, then proceeded to tell her what happened.

"Why you ain't stop by my room? You should have come to get me, we could have whipped some ass tonight!"

"I was so mad I had to get out of there. I can't believe it," Toni said, fighting back tears as the reality came down on her.

"Aw man, I feel so bad. My cousin never mentioned to me that he was no homo or anything. I'm so sorry, Toni."

"Yeah, me too. Just when I thought I found someone I can grow with and trust."

"You going to bed anytime soon?" Tracy offered.

"Naw, I'll probably call B and tell her and I'm sure we will be up for a good three hours discussing it."

"Okay, well, I'm on my way, okay?"

"Yeah, thanks Tracy, bring me some water. I ran out."

"Don't mention it, see you in about a half hour or make it fifteen minutes the way I drive," she said, laughing.

"See you."

* * *

Beatrice looked at her clock and it read 3:15 AM. She saw Toni's number on the caller ID. She was home safe, B concluded, so she decided not to pick up the phone. Toni kept calling back so she knew that she had something to tell her and knowing Toni, it would be something off the hook.

"Hello," B said in an exaggerated tired voice, hoping Toni would decide to call her back tomorrow.

"B, you up?" Toni whispered.

"I'm up now, what's going on." B continued to act overly tired.

"You will never guess what I found out."

"You're pregnant."

"Nope! Jacque is a homo."

"For real?" B said unenthusiastically. She knew how Toni was with her lies. She would have B going and then say something stupid like *psych, I was just playing*.

"I am *so* not playing, B. I went to his room after I dropped my luggage and this gay-ass guy opened the door and had the nerve to be raising up on me talking about Jacque was his man!"

"You better shut your mouth, Toni, you serious?" *There is no way she could be serious and remain this calm.*

"I swear to everything I love."

"Well, you don't love anybody so try again."

"I'm serious B, I'm so serious right now."

For the first time B heard a hint of emotion in her voice so she knew there was some truth to what she was saying.

"Shut your piehole! You're serious!" *Oh wow, she is serious!*

"As cancer."

"So what happened, where was Jacque?" B asked now, sitting up in her bed. Toni went through things that you couldn't make up. Unbelievable.

"So what did he say?"

"Sorry."

"That's it?"

"Yeah, sorry and I wanted to tell you but not now and all this other crap. I cannot believe it, Beatrice. You see why I'm not quick to love these men? It's always some shit, always, but I never thought it would be this shit here, not in a million years."

"I can't believe it, either! Well, how are you feeling, sis, I feel so bad!"

"I'm okay, I guess. I smacked his girlfriend up a few times. That bitch-ass nigga kept going off like a true flaming faggot, it was horrible. I was too torn to really do anything else, I just left. I'm waiting for Tracy to come now. I know once she gets here she is going to go off, she was drinking too. It's about to go down," Toni said, managing to let a chuckle escape as she dug in her carry-on for the joint that B gave her as a departing gift.

"Damn, another one bites the dust. I'm sorry to hear this, I really am, because I know you loved him a lot. Well, how are you really feeling, honey?"

"You know me, moved on already," Toni said as her fingers touched the joint in the dark. She smiled to herself. She lit it and hit it so hard, it took her about ten seconds to respond to what Beatrice was saying because she was pulling.

"Toni, it's okay to admit that you're hurt, you know," Beatrice said softly.

"Yeah, of course I am hurt, but, I mean it is what it is. The things men do doesn't surprise me at all. I can add this to my list of fuck-ups," she said as smoke came out of her nostrils.

"Not all the men you dated were bad, Toni, what about Byron?"

"Who, Byron with the little dick?"

"He was still nice, though, Toni. I mean, damn, you act like he tried to punish you with his dick."

"He was a compulsive, habitual liar. He lied about his earnings among other things. Next!"

"Okay, what about Kip?"

"Oh, Kip, who forgot to mention he had a daughter? Next!"

"Okay, Samson," Beatrice said, turning her bedroom light on.

"Ah yes, how could I forget Samson *the pimp*."

"That was just hearsay," Beatrice said, knowing he really was a pimp.

"Bullshit, he was a pimp and you know it." Beatrice had to laugh when she thought about Samson being a pimp and how Toni pimp-slapped *him* when she heard about it.

"Remember how I slapped the shit outta him?" Toni laughed.

"I was just thinking about that! But I got one for you. Raymond. You fucked-up big-time on Raymond."

"Okay, Raymond was okay but he was too soft."

"Too soft? You better stop messing with those thugs and get you a sensitive man!"

"Yeah, so he can sit back and watch someone go upside my head! Or better yet, he can be nice and sensitive like Jacque and turn out to be a faggot, no thank you. Let's face it. Niggas ain't shit."

"There are some nice, good men out there, Toni. I mean, could my view be different because of how I was raised, you know, seeing my dad at home?"

"Could be, I won't deny that, but I am also open-minded, you know that. Now I know you live in this world where men are good because you want to get married and all of that. But what is marriage? I mean, I know what marriage is *supposed* to be but in this day and time, it doesn't stop a man from cheating! Look at the married men I done laid up with! Marriage is just an excuse for a man to have his cake and eat it too," Toni snapped.

"How do you figure that, *Toni?*" Beatrice asked, exasperated. She was not up for a debate but she knew once Toni got her words running there was no stopping her until the last minute. She loved to hear Toni analyze because she always made perfect sense whether she was wrong or right but you had to be in the mood for her. Toni took another toke before talking.

"You smoking?" B asked.

"Yeah, why?"

"Well, then you are in a different state of mind. Hold on, let me join you," B said, reaching over to her nightstand and relighting her joint.

"Men know how most women believe in the constitution of marriage so they get married, mess around on the side, and when they get caught, they talk all that *let's work our marriage out* shit and nine times out of ten, a woman will *not* leave her husband if he cheats. So the man gets to keep his wife *and* his mistress. And if a man is married and not cheating? I guarantee you either his wife is younger than he is by a significant amount of years, so he is open and/or he has erectile dysfunction of some sort."

Beatrice began laughing hysterically and Toni joined in.

"Well, that's not all men, Toni, let's be realistic here. There are some good ones and bad ones."

"But even the good ones are turning bad because that is what the times call for right now. The way relationships are, how men treat us, how we treat ourselves is all a trend."

"I see what you're saying and I agree, Toni, but there is that handful that stays real to what's right."

"Yeah true, but where are they? I thought Jude was one of those keep it realers. Remember Jude that I used to deal with?"

"Oh, how can I forget him?" Beatrice said, walking to the kitchen for a glass of water and a snack.

"I assure you I had no hidden agenda on making this man cheat. Now this is a grown man, fifteen years my senior, he knew better. But he is a prime example of shit happens," Toni said, blotting her joint in the ashtray.

"Well, what does this have to do with the structure of marriage?"

"Remember when his wife found out about me, cried a river, threatened divorce and all he had to do was throw in the speech about how many years they been together, the kids and the vows, put that heavy dick on her, cry with her, say sorry and bam, the next day where was he? Up in the Marriott with his head in my pussy, pulling money out of his pension to pay for us to go away, telling his wife he was away on business and in my bed while his wife was recovering from the birth of their second child. If I didn't cut him off he would still be around. When I call home my mother said he *is still* calling."

"He is?" Beatrice asked, shocked.

"Yes, he still is, and what about Derrik? Married one week when I met him, *one week* and was already cheating and let's not talk about Tyrone who was in my bed the *morning of his wedding*! He took a shower and put his tux on at *my* house. What kind of shit is that?"

"Yeah, I can't believe you would get down like that. Now T, admit that you were foul for that. That was so wrong."

"How was I foul? Listen, I didn't owe his wife any respect, that was *his* job. Then he told his wife to have an abortion because he wasn't ready for a child so soon in the marriage, because I was pregnant and he wanted *me* to have his *firstborn*, not his wife. Ain't that a bitch? And what about Robert, who named his son Tony after me!"

Beatrice started laughing. Toni joined in.

"Yeah, like how do you explain that to people? Your name is Robert and you name your son Tony? Where's the logic in that?" B said and began laughing harder at the thought of it. Toni joined in then finished her rampage.

"I'm telling you, half the women don't even get married for the right reasons, they get married just to say *my husband*, or because their friends are married, or because they can't find nobody else, because of the children, because they getting old, because it's cheaper to keep him or because of some kind of security, they can't pay the damn rent or mortgage alone. And you think these men don't know it? They know that shit so they do *whatever* they want 'cause all a woman gon' do is fucking complain and threaten to leave, *maybe* step out to shake the nigga up, make him act right but he is going to return to his same shit once he gets hip to her game. No woman wants to struggle, so what we do? We sell our soul for cheap, stay in a miserable relationship so this bastard can go half on the bills instead of doing it on our own. And we think we're getting over. Ha! The men are getting over, not us. Nobody gets married because *baby I love you, we are compatible spiritually and emotionally, you're my soul mate.* Motherfuckas can't stand one another, don't even sleep in the same bed, or be engaged for a million years then have a 'fuck it' wedding."

B had to laugh at that one. Toni had a way with words.

"Yeah, you're right, Toni, times have changed from when our parents were doing it," Beatrice said, still laughing.

"Right! Which is why everyone is cheating and carrying on. Good men? Good men my ass, and half these bitches ain't shit either, I know because *I ain't shit*!" Toni barked then laughed.

"There are good men out there, you just have to be patient. Look at my dad, for example. My father is a provider, takes care of us the way he should and he keeps my mother happy. I would love to marry a man like my father. He pays all the bills, he works, he comes home every night, him and my mother barely fight, he takes her out, I can't remember him ever not being around," Beatrice bragged.

"Yeah, okay, your dad is from the old school of knowing how to treat a woman, so he knows how to provide and put his woman first and all that but that's because he's an OG, but don't tell me you are *that naive* to believe that your father has not stepped out on your mother the *entire twenty-five years* they have been together."

"I believe he has been faithful. My parents come from a spiritual background of fidelity. Southern people have that upbringing," B said adamantly.

"*Wow*, I don't know, B, I really think you should tap into your realistic side every once in a while. It's *unnatural* for a person to be with just one person for so long. God created us to be attracted to one another. Your father goes out *faithfully* since I have known you *every single Saturday night*, just like Jude used to. He gets dressed and he is gone, *religiously, just like Jude*. Jude used to make plans with me every Saturday night, no ifs and or buts, telling his wife he is with the boys. Either his wife is dumb or she had her own agenda. Where in the fuck does he go? I mean, there were times when you called me and told me that you and your mom were worried because your father hadn't come home. Then he'd pop up and say some wild shit like he got drunk or cops raided the spot he was in and he had to spend the night in jail. Now how the hell you get locked up on a Saturday night and come home Sunday afternoon?" Toni said and laughed. "If you paid attention to the streets and stopped denying your background you would know that his ass would be locked-up *over* the weekend. All those locked-up relatives of yours, girl please, stop acting like you don't know the judicial system like you know your last name."

"So you think my father was with a woman? Toni, you can't be serious, my parents are above and beyond that cheating crap."

"No offense, but your mother is also very timid, almost like a Chinese woman and you act just like her."

"That doesn't mean she is dumb or naive, she just knows how to present herself like a lady! Maybe your mother would have a man if *she* got a lil' timid!" B said, getting pissed. Her goal was to offend Toni like Toni had done to her but to no avail, which always pissed B off even more.

"*True*, I tell her that all of the time, but, let me ask you this, how come your mother *nor you* have any idea where this *spot* is?"

"Look, this isn't about my father, Toni, so chill. This is about you being upset because you have bad taste in men, that's all it is."

"Jacque, very smart, good-looking, mannerable, educated . . . gay! I'd like to think he was one of my not-so-bad choices."

"You win, Toni, you win."

But Toni wouldn't let up, she knew B was just trying to shut her up so she did the opposite. "These men are selfish assholes. The good ones are gay or involved. It's no hope for the future."

"You shouldn't be so pessimistic, Toni. You just move in the wrong circle."

"And what circle might that be?"

"Well, okay, for starters, the guys you dealt with in the past were all . . . you know, street guys. What can you expect from that kind of man? The streets are their first love, money is their second love, and a woman is their third. They have too much time on their hands so they can get into any amount of shit, there is no stability cause they are either going to wind up dead or in jail and what real woman has time to be on some bus for six hours going to see some jerk who is not coming home, when she could be at work making money or sleeping or with a new man that is worth her time for six hours, hell that's a flight to Vegas and halfway back! What kind of future can you possibly have with a guy that sells drugs or makes any kind of illegal living? I'm sorry, but I'd rather be with a lame-ass square than a drug dealer. I'm not the *hustler's wife* type. That shit is not for me."

"When have you *ever* seen me get serious with a hustler? The only hustler I ever dealt with was Lyte and he was *not my man*, nor was he a hustler when I met him, he was a long-term fling, every guy I ever dealt with seriously had a job, good jobs. Jude was a Correctional Officer, Brice worked at FedEx, Raymond worked . . . damn, don't know, but they all had jobs, so what are you saying?"

"They were still ghetto as hell," B said.

"Ghetto *how?* No more ghetto than you and I, you forgot where you from?"

"I know where I am from but that doesn't mean I have to be a product of my environment messing with some cat that has baby mamas or spends his savings on a Lexus before he buys a house or after work he sits on the corner with his button down and his tie! See, that's the shit I'm on, Toni, you may call it saddity but I call it smart," B said finally.

"Okay, since you're on this square-biz kick, what about Travis? Travis was a young promising attorney and when he found out where you lived he said you were too ghetto, Jonathan said your hair wasn't long enough and what you do? You start rocking weaves, then you switch over to Michael, the rising Wall Street investment banker and what do you find out at an office party? That he was banging his boss and had a coke habit. What do all of these men have in common? They were square. Now no ghetto brother as you call them would diss a sister because she lived in the ghetto or had short hair. And Mark, let's talk about the man you were *in love with.* Mr. Brown Brothers, who you just *knew* was going to buy you the house on the hill, not only did he bust your ass whenever the wind blew too hard, but he left you for his assistant! Square-ass Mark was punching you square in your face!"

"Let's not go there, it's a different situation and it only happened like three times 'cause he was drunk."

"You always have an excuse for shit when it's about you. Why can't you just agree with me sometimes, B? Agree that the men out there are trash!"

"I *don't* agree with you, Toni! Who the hell says you're always right?" B shouted at her.

"You keep going off about ghetto guys this and me moving in the wrong circle and all this shit, let's talk about *you* for a second, missy poo! I can admit my mistakes and my faults, hell, I'm not ashamed of anything I go through. I learn from it and I try my best to do better the next time. Now you go get you a square guy thinking you're safe from the infidelity and bullshit that so-called *street guys* have to offer. And every day you drilled in my head what a good man you have, how he comes home every day and all he does is sleep, how you guys are engaged and getting married and how you're house shopping and how I need to leave the roughnecks alone and get me a nice guy, an older guy, how your man is too tired from working to run the streets and when he *does* go out you know where he is so you know he ain't cheating. That was you, right? Constantly trying to make me feel bad about whatever my situation was at the time. That was you, right?"

"You can't be serious, Toni, make you feel bad about what? If you were a little insecure or jealous about what I had going on in my life then that's you. If I'm happy why can't I share that with my best friend?"

"Don't go there, B, because you know I don't have a jealous bone in my body for *anyone*. All I'm saying is when things aren't going your way you make it your business to front and I don't understand why you have to front for me? I'm your sister and I have never been anything but honest with you."

"Why are we having this conversation, Toni? If

you want to date ghetto blue-collar workers, then fine."

"See? There you go. Okay, so let's continue with the white-collar brothers you were dealing with! He leaves you for his assistant! How you love that, B? You right! He was coming home every day. Every single day, giving you half his check for you to shop and do your thing, like a good man should, he had you controlled, not to mention he was ten years older than you."

"So what? All the guys you dealt with were that much older than you too Toni!"

"Like I was saying, he knows you like to shop so he controlled you with Bloomingdale bags, coming home *eh-day* like a good man should and was always *tired* from fucking his assistant, excuse me, I mean *working hard*. And what you do? Just to maintain this happy-go-lucky image you hung on to him just so you can maintain a certain lifestyle, did your hair like his assistant, started acting white, started fasting and hitting the gym, started to bug the fuck out and eventually you got tired of fronting and what did you do? You started cheating on him and he used that against you and said that *your infidelity* was the reason *he* was leaving *you*. Never mind the white chick he left you for, never mind the black eyes, never mind the receipts from hotels and shit. But he was a good man cause he provided and offered security, right? What about being your own security, buying your own house, taking care of your own shit so that we won't have to put up with any man's nonsense and try to convince ourselves that it's not that serious or that we are the ones getting over?"

"Why are we having this conversation again, Toni?" Beatrice said.

"You're right, I don't even know why we are having this . . . Oh, we were talking about my faggot-ass man. I'm telling you, this is why I treats 'em like I treats 'em, better them than me!"

"I refuse to give in to your negativity, Toni. You're a bitter woman and I pray that you change one day. You really need to experience love in order to understand what I am talking about," B said. She was hurt that Toni brought memories up that B thought she had buried. She always had a way of cutting deep. Making reality 3-D.

"Love? There you go, that's a whole *other* can of worms for another day. Love? It takes a fool, B. I just called to tell you the latest chapter in my life story. I'll let you go now. I guess I'll be coming back to New York sooner than I thought. I feel too humiliated here. It's time to come home anyway."

"Call me in the morning should anything happen," B said with salt in her voice.

"*Will do*, rest up," Toni said, sounding vindicated by her argument and hung up. B lay in bed seething over her past that had gotten thrown at her while she wasn't looking.

4

Toni was sitting in her small office that was housed in her two-bedroom condo, thinking of an idea for her second book when her phone rang. It was her mother, wanting to know if Toni wanted to go with her out to Riverhead, Long Island to go shopping. Knowing that she hadn't spent much time with her mother over the past few months, she told her she couldn't go anyway. "I can't, Ma, I got things to do but I'll call you later and I'll come over," she said irritably and hung up. The day wasn't long enough for her to do all that she needed to do. She was still waiting on B, who as usual had to be fashionably late. She assumed that she was probably catering to her latest square, Stephen, who Toni could not stand although no one seemed to care. B had been with him for the past two years and thought that he was God's gift since he was a computer geek that made $185,000 annually and lived in Montauk out in the Hamptons. That's all B talked about, how she lived in the Hamptons with Stephen, what they bought, and what celebrity was renting the beach house next door.

Toni looked at her watch impatiently and tapped her foot on the hard marble floor and thought about the changes she wanted to make in her condo that she had just bought a year ago after clearing up her damaged credit. She sought assistance through government funds to purchase her place and as usual her mother came through financially and gave her a few dollars toward the closing costs. She was proud of it. Even though it was small, it was hers. It was big enough for a single woman such as herself. Toni's favorite amenity in the condo was her bathroom. It looked like a hotel bathroom. It had a huge wall-to-wall mirror over the sink, a deep clawfoot tub, and on the other side it had a stand-up shower. Both of the bedrooms were equally large, even bigger than the living room so Toni decided to make one of the bedrooms her living room and make her living room her office. In her office she had a huge black leather chair she loved to sit and spin on that she called Idris, named after the actor Idris Elba, who played Stringer Bell on HBO's *The Wire*, adorned by an even larger desk that belonged in an office building. Toni needed to be comfortable while she worked and not cramped up. She had a stereo system and most of her CD's, candleholders with ready-to-be-used candles in it, and a wine rack to ease her mind before she began writing. Her living room was pretty simple with a small aqua-blue sectional that she bought from IKEA, a beige chaise, an end table with magazines, a six-foot artificial plant, her forty-six-inch television that she brought from when she lived at her mother's house, and another stereo system as Toni loved music. She had a few pictures around her house, one of her and B last year at a Patti LaBelle concert, posing with Fantasia Barrino and Gladys Knight, one of her and her mother at her first book signing and one of her male friends from around her way when she was a younger woman, when she first moved back to New York ten years ago after Jacque had broken her heart. Tracy made sure that everyone on campus found out his dirty little secret, and after she did she said women and men alike were going nuts because they had slept with him. She was thankful to be in New York by then. She packed and left the next day but didn't feel bad after she found out that Jacque had slept with Nicole on the down low. *Joke's on that bitch*, Toni figured when she found out. She shuddered at the thought of Jacque and was thankful that over the years she had tested negative for HIV.

Toni stepped out into the sunshine and stood in front of her Jersey City high-rise building and waited *ten* minutes for B's *two-minute* arrival. She looked at her watch again as she always did when she was nervous. "Fucking girl, man," she cursed. Beatrice pulled up alone in a silver Ferrari without Stephen and Toni was thankful. She couldn't stand looking in his cockeyed eyes that he tried to hide behind designer frames, his sleuth foot walk, his pissy yellow skin or his skeletal frame. Stephen was a hot mess and although looks were not everything, B was taking it way too far. On top of everything else, he was an arrogant fool because he was half white and she pretty much knew that he was the reason why B didn't hang out with her anymore. Toni wasn't upper-class enough for Stephen's taste but what the hell made Beatrice good enough?

B met Stephen when he was shopping in Saks for his mother's birthday gift. B helped him pick out a Dana Buchman suit and the rest is history. With attitude, Toni walked to the fancy sports car and slid in. "It's in the city by the Jacob Javits Center, we need to hurry."

"Well hello to you too Toni, get the wild hair out of your ass. This car will get us there in five minutes."

Toni ignored B, who was sitting next to her looking like Mary J. gone white, with a long platinum blond weave making her beautiful mahogany skin look fucked-up, huge Jackie O glasses, a tiny white scarf around her neck, and a baby blue mini sundress. She looked a lot thinner than what Toni remembered her to be a month ago when she saw her last. "Have you been eating?" Toni asked, disgusted.

"Yes, just eating right, you better start paying attention to what *you* eat," B said, looking at Toni over her glasses like an old lady. "That ass of yours is getting real black."

"What do you mean *getting* black?"

"Big, Luke dancer, black! You got a fat ass, girl!"

"You are such a sellout Beatrice, I can't stand you sometimes. What is up with Bill Gates?"

"He's wonderful," was all B ever said about Stephen.

"Wonderful, well, what took you so long?"

"I'm coming from the *Hamptons*, Toni, not my apartment," B boasted. "Well, you were supposed to be coming from the *Hamptons* two hours ago, thank God I lied about the time or I'd be late," Toni said, mocking Beatrice.

"I'm here now and that's all that matters. So what is this seminar about again and *why* am I coming?"

"Because you are my best friend and—"

"Your *only* friend and let me guess, you must need a ride, right?" B cut in.

"The seminar is about the art of writing the perfect book and getting paid."

"I don't know why you bought that condo, thinking you were going to get paid from that first book you sold. You should have waited. Now you're struggling."

"I resent that! Who said I was struggling?"

"Well, you must be! Stephen said that you should at least be able to put down a thirty percent down payment on your property to avoid paying costly monthly fees and I know you didn't put down thirty percent."

"You don't know what I put down, first of all and secondly, I'm good and I still have a lil' suttin suttin from the profit of my book. It didn't do too well but I still got a little something for it and I needs to push this new one along so that I can get paid, because I need to quit this part-time gig I have, it's depressing."

"Okay, if you say so. Anyway, how long is this seminar because I have to pick Stephen up at six-thirty."

"You'll be able to pick him up. As a matter of fact, you don't even have to come, just drop me off and I'll get back to Jersey," Toni said, turned off. She was tired of B's half-ass friendship, always putting Stephen first, but let B tell it, Toni was jealous so after she made that comment she never showed her true emotions about Stephen and B again.

"Nonsense. You know I'm going with you," B said as she whizzed through traffic, blond weave interfering with Toni's vision.

"Well, when you feel the need to leave, please do not hesitate," Toni said as she moved the hair from her mouth.

"Someone is being shady! You need a man, that's your issue, you know that, right?"

"I need a man like I need a hole in my head," Toni replied.

B shook her head empathetically. "They are out there, girl. Stephen has some very wealthy friends and you need to get with the program, maybe your books will become a bit more interesting."

"No thanks, I don't do the cornball thing."

"Oh that's right, you're still in search of your intelligent hoodlum."

Toni decided to stay silent and stare out the

window as B continued to ramble on. "You know Stephen and I have this wonderful understanding of one another, it's beautiful, not to mention he makes a great living."

"Then you should feel bad about only bringing home thirty-four thousand dollars a year, when he is bringing home more than triple that. What do you do? Buy the napkins and toilet paper for his house? And what is up with your apartment anyway? You still live there?"

"I keep it for emergency purposes but I much rather go to bed on the beach looking at Puffy run laps," she said and laughed smugly. "Stephen and I come into the city together on the Hampton jitney."

"And he goes to Morgan Stanley while you go to Papaya's to serve hot dogs, must be nice."

"First of all, my job at Saks is not as tedious as you would like to believe, at least I manage my own floor and I don't see you being featured in *Essence* as the number-one bestseller *either*. I don't have to bust my ass to be superwoman and independent woman. The *S* on my chest stands for *spend*, not *superwoman*. Shit, I rather not work up the sweat but to let my man take care of things for me," B said and laughed to herself.

"I just want to see you do more. God bless the child who *holds* her own," Toni responded.

"How bout those Knicks?" B said, using a phrase that Toni uses when she wants the subject changed.

* * *

After driving in silence for the duration of the ride, Toni pointed to the address where the seminar was to be held. "Right there," she said as Beatrice turned into the parking lot.

Not even thirty minutes into the seminar Beatrice was tapping her foot impatiently and looking at her watch. Toni was pissed. "You said you don't have to pick Doogie up until later."

"What is a Doogie?

"Doogie Howser, remember that show?" Toni said laughing and whispering.

"At least I got a man, *lesbian*."

"That was low, you fake-ass Mary J."

Beatrice laughed loudly and drew attention. Toni joined the onlookers and looked at B in dismay.

"Eh-hem, excuse me," Beatrice said and put her head down as the lecturer finished her conversation. After twenty more minutes, Toni decided that there wasn't anything going on that she wanted to hear. "Let's blow the joint," Toni said, grabbing her purse.

"I got a better idea," B said.

"What?"

"Let's blow *him*," Beatrice said, pointing to a short, stocky brown-skinned guy in a suit.

"I can tell you right now, that is a Ralph Lauren Purple Label suit and it costs a whole lot of money, you hear me?"

"That's very nice, but no thank you. He's too short for me," Toni said, getting up and heading out the door.

"You wonder why you can't catch a man,

damn, you could have felt the brother out!" B said as she slid in the car.

"No, I'm not interested, and who told you that I wanted a man so bad?"

"The last time I was in your bedroom your vibrator jumped in my purse and begged me to save it and your pillows are tired of you squeezing them at night, they need to breathe too!"

"My vibrator is just fine and so are my pillows, I am fine, thank you."

"You haven't dated or been with anyone exclusively in a long time, Toni. I know I tease you but I'm serious, Toni, you need a man or a companion. You've been single for so long, no sex or anything!"

"And I'm okay with that," Toni said, strapping on her seat belt.

"Are you? Who was the last man standing? Jacque had your ass fucked-up for a while, then you get with Ross, and after him you had a few flings to get through Ross, that was all four years ago. You gotta be horny as a nigga who just came home," she said, laughing before she even finished her statement.

"Sometimes I'm not. I mean, I have my moments but I'm so used to being alone that it's like second nature, it's really not that serious, Beatrice."

"I can't see myself without some male companionship."

Toni started to comment on that but decided against it.

"I mean, don't you want to feel a man's arms

around you at night? A smile across the dinner table, dressing sexy to go out, to go to bed, a compliment, conversation. You don't even talk on the phone with anyone."

Toni took a deep breath, leaned on the window, and looked at B. "What is your fascination with my single life?"

"Girl, I think you're gay! There, I said it!"

"What?" Toni said, laughing.

"I don't know a woman that can go so long without sex. It's been three years for you! You got to be gay."

"Don't you think I have my hormones under control by now, B? I'm not some thirsty teenager that needs it all day every day."

"Right, you're an *old bitch* that needs it every day!"

"You are so foul, my time will come. I'm not even sure what I am looking for anymore and I am so busy with this book I'm writing."

"Well, your clock is ticking, Miss Toni, and you need to make me an auntie."

"Why don't *you* make *me* an auntie? You're the one that has such luck in finding a man, ones with good jobs and benefits at that. How come you and Mr. Wonderful haven't gotten hitched or pregnant yet?"

Beatrice drove in silence for a few seconds thinking about Stephen's reaction to her getting pregnant last year. He lost his mind, told Beatrice not to even think about a baby or marriage and that if she wanted this lifestyle with him she'd have to take it as he dished it out. He said he wasn't trying to give up half his check to alimony or child support and for her to abort the baby immediately or else it was over. She could never tell Toni that. She shook the thought off and said, "Maybe next year. We are just having fun!"

"Well, me too," Toni said.

"It takes two to tango."

"And it takes *one* to have *fun*. I'll be fine. I get a new toy once a month."

"Stephen has some nice wealthy friends, girl, you need to get up on it."

"I told you, I don't do the dickhead scene, I can't. I'm a grown woman, yes, but I just can't vibe with a corny brother."

"Do you ever wonder why you are single? You need to broaden your search, explore other things, other kinds of men and stop stagnating yourself to this one specific kind of man."

"Um, how 'bout those Knicks?"

"Yeah okay, what are you doing tonight? You want to hang out with me and Stephen?"

"You know damn well I do not want to hang out with you guys. Okay, where you guys going?"

Beatrice laughed. "Dinner maybe, dancing, visiting friends."

"You know what? I am due for a night out. Call your man and make sure you let him know that I am coming. I don't need any attitude."

"Why do you think Stephen dislikes you so much, Toni? He really has nothing against you."

"I have a good sense when it comes to these things. He doesn't care for me, which is cool because I don't care for him, either. Just let him know that I am tagging along—oh, and I want to go home and change."

"Oh, but of course!" Beatrice said as she dialed Stephen's number for the fourth time. The last time she left a message telling him that she and Toni were meeting him at the Roman Candle by 9:00.

5

He had just stopped by the Roman Candle after a long night at the office and decided to have a drink or three before heading home to his wife to whom he was legally separated from. He knew he'd have to hear her mouth, begging him not to leave but she knew it was over long ago, she just didn't want to risk leaving behind the glamorous life she had grown accustomed to since she had been with him. He offered to give her whatever she wanted to maintain her lifestyle but what she wanted was *not* to get a divorce. She loved the whole fairy-tale image of being married to a powerful man. She'd be nothing alone no matter how much money he gave her in a settlement and she knew that. Besides, he made her sign a pre-nup so she was only entitled to a drop in the bucket compared to what he was worth, and the way she spent, that money would be gone in days. He didn't believe that she loved him that much and besides, he wasn't in love with her anymore. He needed a woman that had her own life, was smart, had goals that she was achieving not just dreaming about, something more than beauty. He didn't care how much she was making as long as she had a passion for life. His wife was beautiful but all she had was her looks. Besides she was in love with the money and the lifestyle, not the man. He knew she had plans on leaving him years ago but once the money came rolling in she stayed. That was a huge sign that he ignored because he loved her so much . . . *back then.*

He continued to watch this other woman. There was something about her that made her stand out in this crowd. She wasn't glamorous, she was just there, looking around the room as if she was waiting for someone. She looked wonderful in an all-black jumpsuit with sparkling earrings and silver stilettos. Her short boy cut showed her beautiful oval-shaped face. It took a confident woman to cut her hair off and show her face. The more weave his wife wore the more he began to appreciate the natural-haired woman. He stood on the sidelines sipping his wine, watching her. She smiled delicately at passersby who nodded their head at her in acknowledgement. After some time, she finally accepted a drink from the tray that the waiter offered to her for the fourth time as he passed. She sipped it lightly, looked around, then guzzled it. He was tickled. He watched her for a little while longer, wanting to see how she moved, how she laughed, if she had nice teeth, was she feminine, stuck-up, loose, uptight. He wanted to know if she was with someone tonight. He tried to watch her but the four glasses of champagne that he had was urging him to go to the bathroom so he disappeared into the men's room.

Toni had no idea where she was suppose to sit so she stood at the doorway waiting for Beatrice who was running around looking for Stephen. Her nervousness got the best of her so she snatched up a flute of chardonnay and guzzled it. Just as she schemed on the waiter to take another one, Beatrice walked in and grabbed her elbow.

"I don't know where he is but he better get here before I get *black* on him. Let's sit over here," B said, leading the way, stomping like a true diva, lips pouting and all.

"What do you mean, get black on him, Beatrice, you are already blacka den a motherfucka, you get any blacker someone is going to drive their car over you or draw a yellow line down your ass!" Toni said and cracked up.

"I'm serious, Toni, he knew the plan was to meet me here."

"He'll be here, lighten up. In the meantime let's have some fun and liven up this dead place," Toni said, looking around.

"I'm not here for that, I eat, drink, socialize, powwow, and go home."

"For damn near one hundred dollars a plate? You do know you're treating, right?"

"Fine."

"Fake-ass baller. You know you can't afford it," Toni mumbled loud enough for B to hear. Beatrice was too busy looking for Stephen to come back with a usual witty line.

"I'm going to get a drink, you want something?"

"The waiter will come around to us, Toni."

"I do *not* want to sit here and see that miserable face of yours. I rather go get it myself. What do you want?"

"Scotch on the rocks."

"You even drink like him," Toni said and headed to the bar.

Just as he hurried out of the men's room to continue keeping an eye on his prize, she came walking his way. He stood in the shadows and bit his fist when she turned her back to him showing her small bare back and thick round buttocks. She was a small woman and one would never know from seeing her coming that she was so thick. He watched her order her drink, check her watch, look up at the sky, and take a breath. He concluded that she didn't want to be there, had a lot on her mind or was waiting for someone. He noticed that she had small delicate hands that were neatly polished in an iridescent pink shade—no ring. Her hair looked as if it was just done and he noticed how thick and shiny it was, which meant she ate right. He learned that from his mother. She yawned and he noticed her dimples. He walked up next to her the minute the patron next to her got up. "Hello," he said, then looked at the waitress. He then ordered a drink.

Not thinking that she would find a half-decent brother in here, Toni was shocked at what was sitting next to her. Handsome with broad shoulders, cologne and dress-down attire was enough to intrigue her in such an uppity place. He appeared to be average height and had a nice brown complexion. She heard him say hello but when she looked his way he wasn't looking at her so maybe he was talking to someone else. As she turned her head away, they made eye contact and he smiled politely. Truth be told, Toni had been in dire need for a friend. She wasn't talking to anyone on the phone, hadn't met anyone, and didn't see anyone that she liked. She was going to be thirty years old in a few months and had no one to call her own. She believed she served her time, got rid of all negative things and outlooks on men, got past the hurt and pain she had endured and dished out, and was seasoned enough to get her a good man. She looked at this guy and remembered the kind of place she was in and she was sure the minute he opened his mouth he would say something about his Benz being parked outside, his stocks and shares and pay for his *one drink* with his platinum MasterCard so she changed her mind about giving him the time of day and waited for her drink. The bartender brought her drinks over along with his. He pulled out a few crumpled twenties and placed two on the bar. "That should cover hers and mine," he said and got up.

"Thanks," Toni said.

"You're welcome," he said and got up to walk away. Toni lingered at the bar for a second and sipped her drink. When she realized that he was just being a gentleman by paying for her drinks and had no real interest, she got up and headed toward Beatrice, disappointed.

"I'm Preston," he said.

"Toni," she responded, trying to hold in her excitement.

She left it at that and kept walking. He stopped her again. "I noticed you when you came in. I was on my way out but had to wait to see if you were with someone."

"So you were stalking me," she said as a statement rather than a flirtatious question.

"No, just hanging around to see if you were with a male friend. I'm assuming you're not?" he asked shyly.

"Maybe."

"Well, if you aren't, I would like to see you again."

Toni smirked. *This guy is really smooth, huh?*

"What are you doing in a saddity place like this? It doesn't seem like your style," Toni said, looking him dead in his eyes.

"Networking, catching a few drinks before I go home."

"The wife annoys you that much?" Toni said.

"No, the wife has yet to be found," he said with a serious look on his face. He threw back the rest of his drink and put down a tip. He smiled and winked at the waitress and said he'd see her next weekend. She blew him a kiss.

"A regular here, are we?"

"Yeah, I like the place, it's quiet, a bit of a break from the norm. Toni, if it is at all possible, may I get your number, I'll give you mine also. I'd like to get to take you out."

"I'll take your number for now," Toni said. He smiled at her. She blushed.

"Fine with me, I'll take it any way I can get it," he said and asked the bartender for a pen. He wrote down several numbers and handed it to her on the back of a bar receipt.

"My cell, my office, and my home phone. I hope you call me soon. Enjoy the rest of your night," he said and touched her shoulder before walking past her.

For lack of anything else to say, Toni just nodded her head real cool and said "nice meeting you too."

"Well, what the heck took you so long?" Beatrice said, reaching for her drink before Toni could sit down.

"I met a guy."

"You did! Who, where is he?" Beatrice said, doing an *Exorcist* move in her chair, scoping the place out.

"He was on his way out," Toni said as she sat her drinks down.

"Okay, so *whom* does he work for?"

"I don't know, damn, can I call him first?"

"Did he give you a card? What did his business card say? That should tell you something!"

Toni took a sip of her drink before answering, "He didn't give me a card, *deary*, he gave me a piece of paper, the old-fashioned way."

B began sipping her drink while wagging her finger *no*. "Hated it! He's broke, never mind," Beatrice said and fanned Toni off. Toni chuckled at Beatrice and gave her a *you're something else* smile. "How do you figure he is broke?"

"Real men, with real money have business cards."

"Oh, is that right?"

"Oh, hell yes," Beatrice said and sipped her scotch some more.

"Did you find Mr. Wonderful?"

"Yeah, he is over there someplace, he should be here shortly," Beatrice said excitedly.

Toni guzzled her Grey Goose and orange juice and headed back to the bar for another one before Stephen got there.

On the way back from the bar, she could see Stephen's long head. He was laughing like wild with this woman as Beatrice, looking like the third wheel *to them*, laughed hard too, and definitely tried to be noticed. Toni guzzled her drink and ordered another before walking back, making this drink number four in less than an hour. She headed toward the table and sat down directly in front of Stephen, smiling extra hard at the woman he was talking to. "Stephen," Toni said and nodded.

"Toni, nice to see you," he said, as phony as a three-dollar bill.

"Likewise, hello!" Toni then turned her attention to the woman.

"Hello," the white woman said.

"I'm Toni, a friend of Stephen and Beatrice," she said, extending her hand for a shake.

"I'm Claudia, nice to meet you," the woman said and stood up.

Toni's eyes followed the woman up to five-foot-eleven. She stared at the woman then at Stephen, who was annoyed. But if B wasn't going to put an end to the shameless flirting she would. Beatrice sipped her drink, her eyes glaring at Toni who ignored her kicks under the table.

"Good night, Claudia, nice meeting you," Toni said, dismissing the woman. Claudia looked at Stephen, unsure.

"Um, what do you think you're doing, Tonay," Stephen said.

"Tonay? No, my name is Toni and your friend needs to excuse herself so that you can flirt with your woman. Did you ever meet Beatrice?" Toni asked Claudia.

"No, I haven't."

"Claudia, I'll see you around, um, give me a few," Stephen said politely. Claudia smiled awkwardly and disappeared. Toni smiled.

"Dag Stephen I mean flirting right here right now? 'Sup with that?" Toni asked Stephen.

"I was not flirting. Ugh, anyway Beatrice are you okay, you look a little parched," Stephen forced.

"Fine, wonderful, honey you wanna dance?" Beatrice asked with attitude toward Toni.

He flicked her off and said no. He had his legs crossed, sipping on a Samuel Adams beer. "Your woman wants to dance, stop being so stiff," Toni said, jokingly serious.

"Come on, honey." Beatrice beamed and pulled

him up by his hand. He got up and put his beer down reluctantly. Beatrice dragged him onto the floor but after his fifth beer his stiff ass was loose and Beatrice had to leave him and sit down.

"I don't know how you do it," Toni said as a tired, sweaty Beatrice sat down and drank the ice that was floating in her scotch.

"He is not that bad. His dancing is okay." Beatrice laughed, looking back at Stephen.

"Not the dancing, the flirting!"

"It's not that serious, Toni, it really isn't. And if I may say so, you were out of line for embarrassing us like that."

"So *that's* not serious?" Toni said, pointing to Stephen who had his head buried in some woman's bosom humping her.

"He's drunk and they're dancing," Beatrice said and brushed it off. "Gotta let a man be a man. He's coming home to me and taking care of me and that's all that matters."

I bet you learned that from your mother, Toni thought as she rolled her eyes at Stephen. *If he was my man I'd go upside his head right now! But then again, if he was my man he wouldn't disrespect me like that, either.*

6

Preston couldn't concentrate on the ride home. The buzz from the champagne and the high he got upon meeting Toni was messing with his senses. He had never stepped out on his wife no matter how bad things had gotten and Toni was the closest he ever got to infidelity ever. He reached home in one piece and for a split second forgot about his marital woes. His wife was up, he could tell because her "dressing room" light was on. She was probably in the mirror combing her weave for the umpteenth time, painting her fingernails clear and checking to make sure her *silly cone* breasts were still attached to her body. He had forbid her to get fake breasts and begged her not to get a weave but she insisted. One of the many reasons he wanted to leave her was because she wasn't an obedient wife and she just didn't seem real anymore. Her full C cups were fine and he loved when she wore her hair in a choppy honey-brown bob, now she wears it in a jet-black long tangled greasy mess. He took a deep breath and began to undress in his den. He sat down in his chair and closed his eyes as he heard his wife coming down the stairs.

"Baby, you home?" she asked. He didn't respond but kept his eyes closed and tried to ignore her fake sweet baby-doll tone.

"Honey," she called out. He snarled. He hated her voice. She popped up in his den smiling.

"I thought I heard you pull up, how was your day?" she said, sitting on his lap. She pulled his arms and forced him to wrap them around her.

"I'm tired, my day was long as usual."

"So was mine," she said.

You didn't do shit all day! he wanted to yell out but instead chewed his tongue.

"Biting your tongue, I see. What's wrong?"

"Other than the fact that you seem to ignore the fact that I want a divorce and it annoys the hell out of me? Nothing."

"We have been married for twelve years. Why do you want a divorce? Am I that bad of a wife?"

"Yes!" he wanted to say but instead said, "You know why I want a divorce."

"We can work it out," she pleaded.

"I don't want to hear this right now, please," he said, lightly pushing her off of him.

He wanted her out of his face so that he could get back to his thoughts of Toni but was interrupted by his wife's mouth on his penis.

"Don't . . . do . . . that, stop it!" he demanded but she persisted. After a few seconds he relented then ejaculated in his wife's mouth. She got up and tried to crawl on top of him but he was having none of that as he suspected she was now trying to get pregnant. He got angry when he thought about how much he used to be in love with her, begging her to become pregnant years ago and she said no, she was too young, wanted to have a life and concentrate on her. Kids would ruin that along with her figure, her words exactly.

"Stop," he said firmly.

"Honey, you haven't had sex with me in months, three to be exact."

"Which is how long it's been since I brought up the divorce, no?"

"Honey . . ."

"Please stop it with the honey and the whining. Stop it! I said no, now please go to bed or let me go to bed, please?"

"Fine," she said with tears in her eyes. She got up and headed back up the stairs. He didn't flinch, he adjusted his chair, kicked his legs up on the navy-blue suede ottoman and fell comfortably asleep thinking about Toni.

Stephen had gotten exceptionally drunk and Beatrice tried her best to maintain a smile and not be embarrassed. But after a few attempts to help Stephen straighten up, Beatrice got upset and pulled Stephen up by his collar. "You are embarrassing me," she growled. Stephen smiled at her. "Come here, blackberry," Stephen said to Beatrice. Toni picked up her purse and wished she had a way home other than driving with Stephen's obnoxious self.

"It looks like you're driving," Toni said to Beatrice as she stomped back to the table.

"Stephen doesn't drink so when he overdoes it, these are the results," Beatrice said, looking at Stephen who was laughing hysterically with another male.

"I'm ready to go," Toni said. She rolled her eyes at Stephen in disgust and shook her head in pity at her best friend who would sell her soul to the devil for a pair of Pradas or a "lifestyle."

Beatrice walked up to Stephen and gently touched his arm and probably told him let's go but he yanked away from her and kept talking. Toni watched the debacle from afar. Beatrice, who remembered she still had the keys to the Ferrari, told Toni to come on as she headed out the door, not caring how Stephen was getting home.

"He can get home how he got here," Beatrice mumbled as she hit the alarm to the car. Toni opted to stay quiet about Stephen, who was half-white, taking more to his white side and seemed to be prejudiced from time to time depending on whom he was around. She remembered one day when she told Beatrice that she saw Stephen a little too close with a female at a restaurant while promoting her first book and Beatrice went off on her.

"You don't know him like that to judge him, Toni!" Beatrice yelled.

"I don't need to know him but I know you and I know you're not acting the same and I know I saw him with a woman."

"Worry about you and your loneliness and stop trying to get me to join you."

"Are you implying that I am miserable or jealous of you?"

"Yes, I am so tired of you talking crap about Stephen. He is my man, not yours, and I love him regardless of who doesn't approve."

"You love him after three months? Honey, it takes that long to find out a nigga last name and you love him already, like that?"

"Like I said, you have never experienced love so I don't expect you to understand what I am feeling."

"Beatrice, you have been kicking that same line for years and if the love is all that then how come this is relationship number nine for you?"

"Like I said . . . jealous."

"Okay, fine, have it your way, B. But I am not jealous of you and Stephen so please stop saying that. I just see a negative change in you is all."

"Put it in your book, I don't want to hear it," Beatrice said nastily.

So with that thought lingering in her head she decided to not bring up Claudia or the woman on the dance floor. The ride home was quiet as Toni lay her head back thinking how soon was *too soon* to call Preston White.

Beatrice walked in her four-and-a-half-inch stilettos into the department store where she had been head of sales for the past three years. She hated her job. She longed for something where she didn't have to be on her feet all day, where if she didn't feel like smiling or being friendly she didn't have to. Better than that, she longed for the day that Stephen or any wealthy man of some sort would marry her so that she could quit her boring job. But here she was today, on a mission, scheming to catch an even bigger fish than Stephen, since he adamantly said marriage was not in his future, she had to find someone else who would marry her and then she'd dump Stephen once she said *I do*. In the meantime, she'd reap the rewards of being with him. Today her face was done to perfection (as usual) with Bobbi Brown cosmetics, honey-blond weave with platinum streaks, tight and layered perfectly past her shoulders with light wispy bangs, $399 Gucci slacks that she only paid $119 for with her employee discount plus a sale that fit her tiny ¾-frame like a glove, a tight black lycra shirt and a sea-green bolero to match her eye shadow. She strutted into her office today, not ready to be a fake and always in a good mood as her jealous coworkers always believed her to be. Beatrice had a lot on her mind. For one, she was not feeling Stephen like she used to. She doubted if she ever did. He was disrespectful and insensitive, but she convinced herself that no man was perfect and if she was going to be with *any* man, it would have to be one that can provide her with the comfortable lifestyle, that she could not achieve by making $34,000 a year. She knew in her heart of hearts that his wallet was bigger than his manhood and she hated to lay down with him just as much as she hated his pissy yellow skin. He was the total opposite of what she was attracted to. She knew all she had to do was put it on him and then put her hand out and he'd give her one of his cards and send her about her business. She hated how he acted "too white" barely acknowledged his blackness and always called her things like his house pet and "Kizzy" thinking it was funny when it was not. More so she hated when he called her chocolate or anything relating to darkness because coming from him it sounded racist. When she met him and he opened his wallet to charge his mother's suit, she saw all of the credit cards and took notice of the $5,000 he spent with no problem. So on that note, since she was tired of her one-room shack in Jersey City, which she basically used as a closet and mainly slept at Toni's, who lived in a small but beautiful condominium complex twenty minutes away, she flirted and smiled just a little bit and he fell for the bait. She was also tired of driving her broken-down Camry. She assumed she looked much better in a BMW but to her sweet surprise Stephen owned a Jaguar and a Ferrari. The rest is history. Then, she was tired of her mother calling her and crying about the affair her father was having. Beatrice herself had been in denial all this time though deep in her heart she knew her father was not being faithful. It dawned on her when she was in her early twenties. The preciseness of his schedule over the years was a dead giveaway. The Saturday nights that he *faithfully* went out, the change of style from rugged to smooth, always conscious of how he looked. He would always come home at least an hour late and never eat dinner, signs that he had already eaten now that Beatrice looks back. For the past three months, her mother Ava had been calling Beatrice with tales of woe about her beloved daddy whom she refused to look at like the rest of the men. But last week's conversation in particular hurt Beatrice as her mother had only assumed up until now, then calling Beatrice with proof. She had just gotten home from work and went to her Jersey apartment instead of the Hamptons because Stephen was not home and she had forgotten her key. Ava called her as soon as she walked through the door.

"Baby, is this a bad time?"

"No, Ma, what's on your mind?" B asked as she kicked off her shoes and sat on the sofa, ready to listen to her mother sulk about what she *thinks she knows* about her father.

"I got some bad news."

"What happened?"

"I'm afraid that my suspicions have turned to reality, my dear. Your father is seeing another woman, someone he has known from long ago."

"Who, Ma? How do you know?" Beatrice said sitting up, giving her mother her full attention now.

"Well, Saturday night he went to his *spot* and I decided to follow him, so I find that his *spot* is in Flatbush on Avenue D at a woman named Ebony's house."

"Did Daddy see you?"

"Well, what happened was I sat back and watched him go in. I sat there all night till he finally decided to come up for air," Ava said in her sweet southern voice.

"So then what happened, Ma?" B asked softly.

"Well, the woman walked him to his car in her robe, and they kissed for a long time, it was about three-thirty in the morning. I sat in my car and just watched. You know, baby, your mother is not a dumb woman. I just love your father so much, we invested so much time into one another and I know your daddy loves me, I know he does, he is just a man . . . you know?"

"But Ma, you're his wife, he is a grown man, Mommy, Daddy is fifty-seven years old! He should know better!"

Ava sighed heavily. "I know, baby, but when you get married you'll see what I mean. Marriage is a vow before God."

"Yeah, okay, but so is honesty in a marriage. So he cheats and you stay because of vows? What about his part? What happened next, Mommy?" B asked, aggravated with her mother's naïveté.

"Well, after he left, I went and knocked on her door. She answered saying 'yes baby did you forget something?' She opened the door and saw me. I smiled at her and asked could we talk. She knew who I was."

"How?"

"I told you she is a woman from his past. So I say to her, how long have you known my husband? She tells me that she has known him since you were five and has been seeing him on and off since then. That's when it dawned on me that she was the woman your father used to deal with many, many years ago. She put on a lot of weight but then again we were teenagers then. She tells me she's been in my house, been in places where we have been and we didn't notice her. She says your dad takes good care of her and that Saturday is not the only days he sees her. She tells me that they have a child together . . . a son named

Raymond who has been in prison for the past seventeen years. She says she sees him just about every day. I ask her how, she says every night. I ask her how so when he works nights. She said no, he works days. So your father has been out at night with her, me thinking he is at work and he isn't."

"He has a son? Mommy, you didn't know about this other child? And where is he during the day?"

"I'm at work, baby love, I have no idea where he is. I'm thinking he is at work. I guess he is at home resting, acting like he has been working all day. He works for sanitation so I only call him on his cell, baby, it's not like he works in an office. And no, I had no idea about this child."

"Do you believe the woman, Ma?"

"She has no reason to lie to me." Ava sighed heavily.

Beatrice was hurting for her mother and she couldn't believe her father would go to such extremes to cheat on his wife who was so loving and sweet, let's not forget attractive and attentive. Her father was living a double life, something you only saw in the movies or heard about in R. Kelly songs. Ava's heavy sigh brought Beatrice back to the conversation.

"So did you say something to Daddy?"

"Yes, your father is actually in the hospital right now."

"What! What happened?"

"Well, I came home and confronted him and he tried to lie. I told him all that I knew and I got so enraged when all he could say to me was . . . sorry. So I hit him with the same stick I beat her with," Ava said still in her sweet feminine low tone.

"Ma . . . come again, you beat the lady up? And did Daddy admit to the son?"

"Yes, he said that he would have never told me because he didn't want to break my heart and he dealt with this woman so that she would never tell. She knowingly committed adultery with my husband for many years. I feel she deserved the four whacks upside the head with my tiny Louisville slugger. She had the nerve to say to me it's about time I smartened up and paid attention to my husband and that I should have *been known* he was cheating and that she wasn't the only one he was seeing. That's when I hit her once, then twice. She stumbled into her apartment then hit the floor. I hit her twice again, once in the jaw and once on the top of her head. I only stopped because she begged me to. I told her that I'd be sending Benny over to her and that I hope she can give him room and board cause he was getting out of my house. She's sobbing, talking about she doesn't have the room."

"You didn't hit her with my tiny bat, the one I used to keep under my pillow for the boogeyman, Ma," Beatrice said in shock.

"Yes, that one. I'm anticipating the police any day now. I'm sure she is going to press charges on me," she said and sighed. "So your father . . . I got in one too many licks. Someone called the cops when they saw me chase him out of the house and him holding his bleeding head. Baby, you have your own problems, I'm sorry to be burdening you with this."

"It's okay, Ma, it's okay. Listen, you want to come stay with me for a while?"

"No, I'll be fine. I already packed your father's things. He has got to go. He made a fool out of me over the years too many times, this is the last straw. You forgive a man once, okay, but that's it, anything after that is abuse. It tears at your soul to sit back and allow a man to mistreat you, so what he is your husband? Never let a man treat you with any thing less than respect," Ava said and began to cry.

"I probably didn't set the best example for you, honey, letting your father run amok. But trust me, I don't want you to be like me. You're a good woman, Beatrice." Ava sniffled. Beatrice hung up because she couldn't deal with her mother's pain and she knew she was a fool, just like her mother. That was the last time she spoke to her mother and that was over a week ago.

Here she was now, listening to her messages from work, Ava calling a few times asking if her daughter was all right, her father kept calling, saying he needed to talk to her and that he loved her. She was over her father and had nothing to say to him right now and then there was Toni calling just to check in and Marcus calling to say hello. . . . Marcus? The sound of his voice made Beatrice cream her panties. She replayed his message. *B, hey, just calling to say hello, hope all is well, was thinking about you, I was moving into my new house and as I was cleaning, I came across an old photo of us in Mexico* [he pauses] *made me think about you, Honey B* [he chuckles]. *If you want to say hello, here is my number. Your mother gave me your number by the way. She still sounds sweet. Anyway, hope all is well, take care of yourself, if I don't talk to you. Later babe.*

Beatrice saved the message and suddenly she felt like smiling and being a fake at work.

7

"Mark? What is up with him?" Toni asked as she walked down the Avenue of Americas, talking into her cell phone.

"So are you going to call him? You *don't know*? Marcus is trouble you know that . . . you're right, you're a grown woman, so call him, just be careful and don't go showing your teeth or better yet *your goodies, I know how open you get over that fool* . . . so what? It's been *years* for me! Anyway tramp, I have to go, I have reached my destination so I will call you later . . . none of your business where I am, I'll call you later, good-bye," Toni said and flipped her phone shut. She had long since decided to keep her business away from Beatrice until she felt it was necessary, which was always a good thing. Beatrice will analyze things that didn't exist and make a mountain out of a molehill. If she were to date *any man*, she wouldn't tell Beatrice about him until she got serious enough to *not listen* to anything negative from anyone. It had to be in stone before she told

Beatrice, no matter what the situation was. She was nervous as she was seeing Preston today for lunch, for the first time since they met some weeks ago. He was in the city and off from work today. She looked around and realized she got there first, so she went into the bathroom and checked herself. She sprayed a little bit of perfume on her neck and wrist, touched up her gloss and checked out her outfit. A denim blazer, white top, khaki capris and mules, her hair freshly done, and a cream clutch purse. She felt good about her outfit. As usual she kissed at the mirror, winked, then headed to her table. As she sipped her French vanilla latte, she saw Preston walking toward the restaurant. He was nice-looking and the cream polo shirt he had on hugged him just right. He was taller than she remembered and also darker, which was *so fine* with her. She sipped her latte as he walked in and asked a waitress if Toni had arrived. He was escorted to his table where Toni was sitting. She stood up upon his arrival and extended her hand. "Hi," she said and smiled. She shook his hand strong and firm like he was a prospective employer. He smiled and kissed her hand to soften her grip. "Hi, nice seeing you again, you look lovely."

"Thank you, so do you . . . I mean, you look nice also."

He smiled, she noticed his chipped front tooth that gave him character and his dark curly lashes. He had eyes like Tupac. "So do you know what you want to eat yet?" he asked.

"Yes, I'm ready to order."

"Good, can we have a pitcher of water with

lemon and we are ready to order," Preston said to the waitress.

The waitress smiled at Toni and waited for her to order. After that Toni sat back uncomfortable because she didn't know what to say, as it was her first date in years.

When Toni realized that Preston was way more nervous than she was, it kind of made her feel more at ease. He fumbled with his eating utensils a lot, stuttered and could not look in her eyes, something Toni mastered with people no matter how nervous she was. She was a stickler for eye contact. She wouldn't hold this against him, though, not tonight at least. Finally, after digesting their food and ordering a glass of red wine, both of them seemed to be opening up. Preston looked at Toni, who was looking at him while sipping her wine. "You have the most beautiful eyes I've ever seen on a person," he said.

Toni only believed him because she had heard it before. "Thank you, I was thinking the same thing about you."

"They are so black and deep. Make a brother not want to lie to you!"

They both shared a laugh. "Well, I hope you don't plan on lying to me," Toni said.

"I'll try not to. So what is it that you do, Ms. Toni?"

"I'm a novelist." She smiled. She felt proud upon hearing the words come out of her mouth.

"A novelist? Ah, interesting. Any books out yet?"

"One that flopped, it's called *Behind her Smile.*"

"I think I know someone who was reading that

book," he said of his wife who he knew read the book and loved it. "They actually loved the book."

"I did too, but apparently it didn't do too well, now I'm working on another one. I'm taking my time, though. I was younger when I wrote the other one so it didn't appeal to a mature audience. This one will, though, I'm a big girl now."

"That you are," Preston said and winked. Toni gushed. "So what is it that you do? And how many children do you have?" she asked him.

Preston laughed. "No children and I am a banker."

"How boring," Toni said and sipped her wine.

"I know but it's a generation thing. All of the men in my family are in banking or law."

"Interesting. So, are you close with your mother?"

"You ask some wonderful questions."

"I'm just getting started. I like to find out what kind of relationship a man has with his mother."

"My mom passed away when I was in high school. Yes, we were very close. She was my girl."

"I'm so sorry to hear that. What happened to her?" *Dammit I went too far.*

Preston took a deep breath that made Toni wish she hadn't asked. "My mother cheated on my father. Things weren't going too good at home, she stepped out on him. When she decided to work things out with my dad and leave her boyfriend, he killed her and . . ." Toni was expecting to hear she died of cancer, or maybe in a car accident but nothing as dramatic as this.

"Preston, look, I am sorry, this looks very painful for you."

"It's okay. I don't talk about her much and when I do it helps me deal with the pain. It's okay."

Before they knew it, it was dark and they were drunk, the both of them laughing and walking hand in hand down Sixth Avenue, Toni wondering what kind of affect his mother's death and the reasons it had on Preston's behavior toward women.

Toni noticed that Preston had not checked his watch once since they been out and he wasn't nervous, which made her comfortable. *He doesn't have anyone to run home to.* It was she who got uncomfortable once she realized that she was holding hands with a stranger. Before she could pull away, Preston was pulling her into an electronics store.

"I always wanted a portable DVD player. One of the simple things in life that I forgot about," he said.

"So buy it!" Toni said. Preston continued to hold her hand and drag her around the store like a kid. She let his hand go so that she could look at an iPod. "Damn, I want an iPod, this one holds five thousand songs!" Toni squealed.

"Now why would someone need five thousand songs?"

"Because, you never know what you want to listen to. It's good to have, especially for me since I use public transportation," she said, examining the $499 gadget. Preston made a mental note of it then headed to the register to pay for his DVD player. While Toni looked around the store he noticed she also looked at the price on a pretty chromed cordless phone. He instructed the salesman to get the phone and iPod from the back and ring it up without Toni noticing it. The salesman smiled and did what he was told. Once the gifts were wrapped up, Preston gently touched Toni on her waist and told her he was ready. They continued walking and decided to sit down in Bryant Park in front of an ice cream truck.

"Do you like ice cream?" Toni asked.

"Yes, butter pecan is my favorite. Can I get you some ice cream? I see you salivating," he joked. Toni laughed. "Yes, chocolate with chocolate sprinkles."

"You got it," he said and got up to buy an ice cream. Toni's phone began to vibrate. She saw that it was her mother. "What, Ma!" she said before answering the phone.

"Hello?" Toni asked.

"Hi Toni, it's your mother, you *do* remember me, right?"

"Yes I do, how are you, mother dear?"

"Fine and you?"

"Can't complain."

"Good, listen, I'd like to see my only child this week if she isn't busy."

"I think I can arrange that."

"You think you can? How about I make it an order, not a request. I have some things that I need to discuss with you so make sure you find the time."

"You're okay, right? You're not sick or anything, are you?" Toni asked.

"I'll see you some time this weekend."

"Mommy, don't play with me, woman, are you okay?"

"Bye," her mother said and hung up. Toni flipped her phone shut and waited for Preston to come back with her ice cream. He walked toward her lapping up his ice cream so it wouldn't drip and she couldn't help but to think perverted thoughts as she watched his tongue lick the vanilla ice cream. He handed her a cone and continued lapping up his ice cream until it stopped dripping.

"Damn, this ice cream is good!" he said and devoured it some more. Toni was trying to be careful with her ice cream but out loud she said *fuck it* and dove headfirst into hers also so that she wouldn't make a mess. She had chocolate ice cream dripping all down her hands and Preston used his tiny napkin that was wrapped around his cone to try to help clean her up. She continued lapping up her ice cream as he wiped her hands. Once they were done they both looked at one another and blushed.

"I felt like a kid just now," Preston said.

"Preston, what is your full name?" Toni asked him out of nowhere.

"My full name? Why do you want to know?"

"Because I think it's necessary when you meet someone to know their entire name. My name is Toni Jolly, that's it."

"Toni Jolly, huh. Well, my name is Preston Pierre White."

"Pierre, I like that, I can't stand the name Preston!"

"Say what now? You can't stand my name? Well, I don't like Toni!"

"So call me T then because I will be calling you Pierre, it sound so grown and sexy. Sometimes I may call you P, cause I can be hood like that."

"That's not hood, that's just *lazy*, so where are you from?" he said, laughing.

"Brooklyn, born and raised, and you?"

"I'm a southern man, I'm from Jonesboro, Georgia born and raised, and moved to New York City because my company merged. I have been living up here for about five years now. I still have my home in Georgia, though."

"Nice, nice . . ." Toni said, licking her ice cream.

"So what do you like to do? How old are you?" he inquired.

"I'm twenty-nine going on forty, I love to write, as you know, and just relax. I love listening to good music and eating good food, and you?"

"I like smoking cigars, sipping fine champagne, good conversation with smart people, laughing and eating, anything low key and humble," he said.

Toni had a brief thought of him lapping up the ice cream and fought to suppress a smile.

"So you're a simple man."

"Simple but complex."

"Same here. But you still didn't tell me your age."

"Thirty-nine. Do you have any crazy exes or anything?" he joked seriously.

"No, none at all. I've been single if you must know for about four years, celibate for three."

"Really? That's great!"

"Is it?"

"Um, hmm" he said, thinking dirty thoughts as a man would.

"I don't plan on changing my status for just anyone," Toni reassured because she knew what he was thinking.

"Well, I hope in time I can be more to you than just *anyone*."

"Ball is in your court, so play hard . . . brother."

He laughed.

"Come on, you ready to walk some more?" he asked, grabbing her by the hand.

"Yes," Toni said, allowing him to lead the way. She liked how Pierre was so sure of himself, so confident without being arrogant or cocky, or maybe he just felt the same good vibe that she felt from him. It was as if they had known one another for a long time.

The night began to wind down and before they knew it, it was after midnight and they were standing in front of the garage where Pierre's car was parked. He walked to the parking attendant and handed him his ticket. The attendant soon appeared in front of them in a shiny silver BMW. He handed the attendant a crisp $20 bill and walked to the passenger side, holding the door open for Toni. She sat in and immediately reclined her seat back and began to fiddle with the complicated stereo system, unfazed by the expensive vehicle she was in. When Pierre sat down in his seat, he laughed.

"What? These new cars are so damn complex. Whatever happened to just one button? What is all of this RTwo-DTwo shit going on?" Toni cursed. She looked at him and rolled her eyes playfully. "I can't figure this out, I'm sure it has a remote, so where is it?"

"You obviously never heard of the rule of thumb."

"What rule?"

"To never touch a black man's radio. I like how you just take control of things . . . off . . . my stereo please," he said and gently pushed her hand away.

"Okay, well, can you put it on Power one-o-one, I know the slow jams are on by this time."

"You in love?" he asked.

"No, I just like feeling mellow. Slow jams do that to me. Have you ever been in love?"

"Once," he said, changing the station.

"What happened to her?"

"Nothing, I just fell out of love, stopped loving her, saw what she was about."

"And what was that?"

"Money."

"One of them, huh. Sorry to hear that."

"No, don't be, it was just poor judgment on my part. I know now to be more careful. So what's your story?"

Toni took a deep breath. "Well, you want to hear about the ones that matter or *all* of them?"

"Let's start with the one that matters," Pierre said as he made a left toward the Holland Tunnel.

"Well, his name was Jacque, I was in college, some ten years ago, my first time in love, first relationship against my better judgment and I find out that he is gay."

"Ouch! Straight out of a movie, you can't make stuff like that up."

"I know, right? I came home from visiting my sister and I decided to pop up at his dorm. His man friend opened the door, we had an argument, and there were condoms and wine bottles lying around," Toni said and grew sad at the thought. "Yeah, so that was it. Then there was Ross, met him not too long after and he said I wasn't over my past, I wasn't affectionate enough, I didn't smile enough, wasn't tall enough, wasn't flashy enough, wasn't feminine enough, shall I go on?"

"Please, please do."

"Well, I was with him for about two years. But it just couldn't work out. I was scared he might be gay too or something was going to go wrong. I couldn't give him all of me like I gave Jacque because I was afraid of the heartache. He was my last relationship, four years ago."

"You say you been celibate for three years, so what happened during that one year?"

"You sure do pay attention, don't you?"

"When I'm interested in something, yes."

"Well, I wasted a lot of time sleeping with ex-boyfriends who didn't care about me, married men and men with girlfriends. I played a lot of games and tried to love 'em and leave 'em, you know, payback. Then I said, who am I paying back? It dawned on me that I was just hurting myself, that no one really cared. I shut down and I have been celibate ever since."

"You seem like a nice woman. I can't imagine why someone would want to hurt you."

"So you mean to tell me you haven't broken a heart or two?"

"Well, let me be honest. No. The only heart I broke was that of the woman whom I said I should have had better judgment with and it wasn't my fault. I fell out of love with her because of *her*. So technically no, I'm thirty-nine years old and I've been in three relationships including the last one. The first one, she left me because I wasn't hoodlum enough for her, the second one left me because I spent too much time trying to start my own business, the third one was a rebound and I was too blind to see what she was really about, hence the breakup."

"Your résumé sounds good Pierre, but, um, you ever interviewed an employee, and they do all that they have to do to get the job and when you hire them, you find out that they are not as good as the résumé says?"

Pierre smiled at her analogy.

"Oh, I have plenty analogies, Mr. White, plenty for ya."

"You know something?" he started.

"I know a few things," Toni spat back.

"Seriously . . . you know something? Never mind."

"What? I hate when people do that. Say what's on your mind."

Pierre wanted to tell her that he knew for a fact

he was going to fall in love with her but he didn't want to scare her away, so he decided to keep his mouth closed.

"What, P?"

"Nothing T, nothing," he said thinking about his yearning for a regular woman in his life. Not a gold digger, not someone too hood, not someone too prissy, just a regular down-home woman like the one sitting before him.

They drove silently for the next fifteen minutes, then they were at Toni's complex. "This is you?" he asked.

"Yes."

"Very nice."

"It's okay."

"It's yours, so you're good, trust me," he said, thinking about his wife who couldn't even pay attention without him let alone pay for her own condo. "Can I walk you to your door?"

"I'd like that, come on," she said and hopped out. They rode up in the elevator in silence, then reached apartment 22R.

"High floors, it's an aphrodisiac," Pierre said.

"Oh, is that right?"

"Yup."

Toni put her key in the door and stepped in. Pierre handed her the bag from behind his back.

"What is this?" she said, smiling, accepting the bag.

"Have a good night, call me when I cross your mind," Pierre said. He leaned in and kissed her cheek quickly then headed down the hall.

"Goodnight," Toni said.

She closed the door and opened the bag, finding her iPod and cordless phone. She smiled. She started to run behind him and say thank you but opted to call his cell phone instead. It went straight to voice mail so she left him a message.

8

Toni walked down the street listening to her iPod, smiling like a child when she bumped her head dead into the chest of a stranger. They looked up at one another to exchange "sorrys" when she recognized that he was one of her old friends from around the way.

"Mo, is that you? Mo?" she asked rhetorically.

Maurice laughed and hugged her tight. "Toni!"

Toni took her earplugs out and stepped back.

"I cannot believe this. I haven't seen you in so long!" Toni yelled and hugged Mo around his waist as he was a really big, tall guy. "How have you been?" she asked, still hugging him and looking up at him.

"No, how *you* been, Ms. Big-Time, my woman loved your book, she loved that shit, her and her little sister. You got that penthouse on Central Park West yet off of that book?"

"No, not yet, just a small condo in Jersey City facing the Hudson."

"Good enough. So you have any kids yet, a man? You look real good, Toni, real good."

"You know me, still sticking and moving, how are you, how's the fellas?" Toni asked as they walked toward her mother's building. Maurice filled her in on everybody except the one person she wanted to know about. She could tell Maurice was waiting for her to ask about him. "So, how is he?"

"Who?" he asked and smiled.

"You know who, Quentin."

"Your boy Q? He's good."

"I'm sure he is married by now with children."

"Nope, single, no kids."

"That's nice, tell him I said hello," Toni said and changed the subject.

"You know he lives in Queens now, he was living in Maryland with some chick for about four years but it didn't work out so he's back up here now. He's doing really well too. He has his own shop, cutting hair and he opened up two more since he was doing so well, Sharp Corners is its name."

"That's wonderful," was all she said.

"So your mother still here?" Maurice said, looking up at the building.

"Yeah, unfortunately. So what are you doing here? I thought you moved out of this dump."

"Oh, my daughter goes to school over here so I was killing time, I'm about to pick her up."

"Your daughter? Hold up, Mr. Money over Bitches? A daughter? God did you dirty!" Toni said and laughed.

"Yeah, man, makes me regret all the women I dogged out, for real. I'm such a good man now."

"You always were, just young. We were kids."

"Yeah, I want you to meet the missus. I talk about you all of the time and she loves your book. How long are you going to be here?"

"A minute so give me your numbers and I'll call you when I'm done with my mother, okay, hon?"

"Sounds good. I'll be over here at my grandmother's. Make sure you call me!" he said as they exchanged numbers. "I will, baby, I will," she said, smiling at the memory of old friends.

Toni still had her key but knocked, not knowing if her mother would be walking around naked. She hadn't seen her mother in months and realized now how messed up that was. Her mother never did anything bad to her, she just didn't know how to be maternal. She loved her mother dearly and knew her mother felt the same. She knocked again just as Ms. Jolly opened the door, revealing her new size twelve body. Toni stepped back and covered her mouth. "Mommy! Is that you?" Toni said, stepping in and examining her mother. Ms. Jolly did a slow turn, then smiled at Toni.

"Yes it is, come on in!" she said and hugged her daughter. She was smiling, something she didn't do much. Something had her going and when Toni looked down the hall she saw exactly why. "Ma, who is that?" Toni whispered loudly with a smile.

"Thomas, this is my baby, Toni."

Thomas was a very tall strong dark man. He looked like a chocolate God. He looked like Shaq compared to Toni's mother, who was only five-foot-four.

"Nice to meet you," he said and kissed her hand.

"Same here!" Toni said and smiled and looked at her mother approvingly.

"So, mother dear, tell me all about him!" Toni said, grabbing her mother's hand and Thomas's and running to the couch like a kid. Thomas laughed and sat next to Toni.

"I heard so much about you, it's nice to have finally met you," Thomas said.

"Well, how long have you two been dating and where did you guys meet?"

"We've known one another for a while. But Thomas was involved, so you know I didn't cross that street, but the minute he became free, we began dating. We have been serious now for about eight months."

"And you're just now telling me?" Toni asked, smiling happily for her mother who seemed so peaceful.

"You have been so busy and all and besides, we chose to tell you now because Thomas and I are going to get married."

"Married? Ma, this is so wonderful!" Toni said, hugging her mother around the neck. "And Mommy, I am speechless as to how happy and good you look, oh God bless you, Ma, I think getting married is a wonderful idea, I do."

"Yeah, you think so?"

"Of course, I mean, look at you, Thomas is doing something right!" Toni said and tapped Thomas's shoulder.

"Yes, he is very good to me."

"I love your mother very much," Thomas said.

"Ma, this is great."

"Will you be my maid of honor?"

"Of course, of course," Toni said, smiling.

"Okay, well, we have set the date for May sixth, that's eight months for you to get it together."

"So where is the honeymoon going to be?"

"St. Lucia," Thomas said.

"I thought we were going to Hawaii," Ms. Jolly said.

"We can go to Hawaii anytime," Thomas said sweetly.

"Okay baby."

"Look at you, pet names and all, well I'll be damned!" Toni said, hugging her mother again.

"I'll be a size eight like I used to be by the wedding."

"I need my woman to have some meat on her bones, you are fine just the way you are." Thomas smiled.

"Okay, a ten at least?"

"I'm a big man so I don't need anything smaller than a ten," Thomas said.

"Another thing, baby, after we get married, I'll be retiring a year after that. Thomas and I are thinking about moving to D.C. or Atlanta. We are buying a house!"

"I couldn't be more happy for you, Ma. I swear. Over the years you were just so torn down, excuse me for saying this in front of Thomas, but

Thomas, you have brought my mother back to life. Thank you."

"Thank you so much honey, I love you, you know that, right?" Ms. Jolly said.

"Yes, Mommy, I've always known that."

"You're a good daughter and I am proud of you," Ms. Jolly said with tears in her eyes.

"I know, Ma."

"So when are you going to write the million-dollar book?" Thomas asked.

"I'm working on it now, maybe I can buy you that house out of town."

"Sure! Save my damn money." Thomas chuckled.

After catching up, Toni decided it was time to leave. She called Mo and made plans to meet him shortly, and while waiting for the elevator, she thought about how love had changed her mother so drastically. She was happy. Although Toni was content with her life she realized that if her mother could find, appreciate, and open up to love, then she could too. She just didn't want to wait until she was fifty years old to find *him*.

9

Beatrice tossed and turned for most of the night. She couldn't sleep knowing Stephen was not home and had not called. She knew he was okay because someone would have alerted her long ago. The last time she spoke to him he said that he was going out to lunch. She hadn't spoken to him at all since. She woke up at 3:00 in the morning in a sweat, looking around frantically. She went downstairs and he was not there. There weren't any blinking messages on the phone or missed calls on her cell. She even called her voice mail at home, nothing. Finally she broke down and decided she should call the one place that she knew he'd be.

Preston came home on cloud nine after his date with Toni. She was all he knew she'd be and more. She was funny, smart, and just down-to-earth. When he came home, the house was empty. He looked at his watch, it was late, after 2:30 AM.

Part of him wondered where his wife could be at this hour, the other half didn't care. He wanted to get to know Toni better so he made the decision to move into his Central Park West apartment as soon as possible, until things got settled. He heard his message indicator beep on his phone and wondered how he missed a call. He figured it would be his wife telling him about her whereabouts. It was Toni, thanking him so graciously for her gifts. He smiled and figured he'd wait a day or two before calling her back. He didn't want to crowd her space or seem too eager. With that plan in motion, he slid out of his clothes and for the first time in months, he slept peacefully in his own bed.

Beatrice knew that she could count on Lola to condone her foolishness. Toni would just tell her what an idiot she was for stalking Stephen, knowing he was with another woman. She found out about Brandy by accident. Assuming she was asleep Stephen went to his car for something and left his AOL screen up, allowing B to read enough to know that he was messing around. She got Brandy's full name then Googled her. For the past four months he had been dealing with this woman. She never told Toni because . . . well, she was Toni and she knew that Toni hated Stephen so that was all she needed. Lola was already out visiting family when she got the call from Beatrice to come over. Not having anything else to do she drove over to Beatrice's house since she wasn't that far. Beatrice was crying and looking a mess when

Lola arrived. "Pull yourself together, honey, this is so not you!" Lola said, stepping into the house. If only Lola knew, this *was her* all day everyday until it was showtime. Beatrice wiped her face and tousled her weave like a white girl. She had to remember to ask Lola where she purchased such beautiful, natural-looking hair.

"So where is the man at?" Lola asked.

"Guess."

"Brandy's house?"

"Yes."

"How do you know?"

"I called and he answered . . . again."

"When are you going to stop playing games and let him know that you know about Brandy?"

"Why, so he can blow up on me and put me out? I can't go back to Jersey City, no way!"

"Well, honey, I have news for you. You guys are *not* married unlike myself. See, my husband can't do anything but be mad because he knows I can take half his shit," Lola said.

I can't wait for her husband to get rid of her fucking ass and see if she talks this shit then.

"Stephen said marriage is not in his plans, a baby either," Beatrice said, putting her head down. She sensed her end was near but where would she go? Who could she deal with that was financially well-off like Stephen? *I knew I should have had a plan B nigga.*

"You need to find you another sponsor then, someone you can control a little bit, have something over. That Stephen is a real asshole when he is ready. Besides, is he even a millionaire yet?"

Beatrice shrugged her shoulders. "You need to step your game up then," Lola said, concluding that he was not unlike her husband.

Beatrice took a deep breath. "He is over there right now, what do I do?"

"You know what it is, B? You act too meek. You need to blow it up, like, nigga, I know you're out there fooling around, bring your ass home and I'm not going nowhere! Get all in his face and demand that respect. Men love that shit, they love it!"

"So you think I should call now?"

"Oh hell yes, tell him to bring his narrow yellow ass home now and if she picks up, you let her know who you are, but very ladylike. Go on, call!" Lola said, handing Beatrice the phone. Beatrice dialed the number slowly, unsure if she was doing the right thing. It was too late to turn back once Brandy answered.

"Yes . . . hello," she said, sleepily. Beatrice was already jealous of her voice, she sounded like a young white girl that didn't have any problems in the world.

"Hello, is this Brandy?"

"Yes, who's speaking?"

"Hi . . . my name is Beatrice."

"Yes, how can I help you?"

"You can help me by explaining to me why my man is in your bed?"

"Your man? Who, Stephen?"

"Yes."

"Just a minute hon okay?" she said, sweetly. *Hon? Is this bitch trying to patronize me?* Beatrice heard muffled conversation, then Stephen got on the phone.

"Yes, hello."

"I know that you have been dealing this woman for some time now and I do not appreciate it. Stephen, what is going on?"

"What are you doing calling here this time of the night or morning, shall I say?" he said, irritated.

"Why aren't you home in bed with me is the question."

"First of all, how did you get this number?" he asked calmly.

"Don't play games with me, Stephen, bring your narrow yellow behind home *now*. You got it?"

"Listen, I'll talk to you maybe tomorrow if I have time after work."

"What?"

"That's my house you're in, *capiche?* Now get some rest, we have things to discuss tomorrow anyway, it's time that I make some changes. Until then, don't call here any more. I'll see you tomorrow," Stephen said and hung up. Beatrice stood there with the phone in her hand in shock.

"So, how did it go?"

"Not like I planned," B said, telling Lola everything.

"Isn't he something?" Lola said.

Beatrice shrugged her shoulders. Lola plopped down next to her and rubbed her back while yawning. "Get some rest, tomorrow is a new day. You want me to stay?"

"Only if you want to hear the sounds of me breaking down."

"It's okay, that's what friends are for." *Besides, I won't hear you, I'll be too busy breaking down myself,* Lola thought.

10

This was date number four that Toni and Pierre were going on and she was thrilled that things were looking good, but she knew she had to be on point. She could be a rebound right now for all she knew. He seemed like a nice guy but so did Jacque. Not wanting to be pessimistic, Toni fixed herself a glass of Asconi red wine and began working on her book some more since she had time to kill. Pierre had seen her in casual clothes all of this time and aside from the first night they met when she had on that black jumpsuit, he had never seen her really dressed up. The October chill wasn't cool enough for Toni to cover up completely so she dressed in a navy-blue boat neck cotton dress, complete with reversible shawl, navy-blue shoes, and small diamond studs. She wore her hair pushed back and very slick with a traveling part on the side. Her lips were clear and glossy and her eye shadow looked like satin giving her the smoky look. She looked like she needed to be lying across a piano singing the blues. When the doorman called her to let her know she had a guest, she walked to the mirror and gave herself a once-over, did her signature kiss and wink, and headed to the elevator.

Pierre was waiting in the lobby looking debonair, donning a black and beige cardigan set, beige pants, and black alligator–style shoes that looked very expensive, Toni noted, with a bouquet of yellow roses. When he saw her, she took note of how his dark skin turned red. He tried to suppress a smile but couldn't. "You look . . . I mean, you switch up nicely. You're versatile, *I like*."

"Thank you, you clean up nicely also," Toni said and pulled her shawl a little tighter around her.

"After you," he said and let her out first. He was especially interested in her now, after the doorman let him know that since Toni moved in five years ago, no man or woman has come to visit with the exception of a close girlfriend. Pierre asked the doorman if Toni might be gay and the doorman laughed and told him no, Toni was a nice woman, seemingly quiet and always came inside at decent hours, not scarlet hours. That was good enough for Pierre. He tipped the doorman $100 for his information right before Toni got off of the elevator.

Toni and Pierre were headed to Long Island to a place called Garden of Jazz where musicians played jazz barefoot in a garden while waiters walked around with trays of different wines for you to taste. Pierre hoped that Toni liked jazz or was at least open to listen to it. As usual the place was nearly packed but Pierre had reserved a VIP area so that they could be almost secluded. The VIP area was for couples only and held about seven couples for $150 per person. Since it was October, they had the tent up, which went well under the moonlight and sparkling rooftop. Pierre could tell that Toni loved it. She looked around and smiled a lot. "This place is remarkable," she whispered in his ear while holding a glass of wine.

"So are you."

Toni winked and sat down as he held her chair out for her.

A night of jazz, wine, and mingling with educated classy folks was what Toni needed. She sat back and basked in the ambiance as Preston excused himself and went to the bathroom.

Pierre was flying high. He knew she was having a good time and was feeling him. He laughed out loud to himself as he headed to the bathroom. "Gonna make her mine!" he sang to his own tune.

"Get a divorce first," a voice said. Pierre turned to find his wife's cousin standing there with her husband.

"Tracy!"

"Who's the woman?" she asked immediately.

"Tracy, I think you should stay out of this," her husband said.

"He is stepping out on my cousin and you want me to stay out of it? Who is the woman?" Tracy said, putting her foot forward.

"A friend," Pierre said discreetly, looking around.

"Does your wife know you're out with *a friend*?"

"Tracy, let's not act like you don't know how bad things are at home," Pierre said, fixing his sweater.

"I know my cousin isn't stepping out in public!" she snapped.

Yeah, not in public.

"She is just a friend, that's all."

"Let me get a good look at this heifer!" Tracy said, walking toward Toni. Pierre pulled her arm. "Tray, please, *please*."

Pierre wished Tracy's husband would step up and save him and make her cut it out.

"You must like this woman, you all *beggin*, get off me!" she said, snatching her arm away.

"I know my cousin has foul ways, but that doesn't give you the right to be out in public embarrassing her like this. You know how the community talks. If I don't tell her, which I won't . . . someone else will, you don't know who's watching you right now."

"I agree. Tracy, things aren't going too well at home, I moved out and we are getting a divorce soon."

"Dang, she didn't tell me all that, she just said that you guys were having problems, nothing major."

"It's major. I won't say any more because I still do have respect for our privacy and if she wanted you to know things she would have told you, but

I lie to you not. Things aren't right. Have you ever known me to step out and be that kind of man?"

"You're right, this just caught me off guard. But when my husband said you walked in with another woman I just saw red. Don't you think you guys should get a divorce before y'all start coming out in public with other people?"

"Tracy, please. I just want to go enjoy my night. I'm really not trying to think about all that other stuff, with all due respect."

"Just get out of here before I change my mind," Tracy said, fixing her black fancy shawl.

"You need to stay out of it and as a matter of fact, Pierre, brother, I wish you the best of luck in your marriage or lack thereof, Tracy we got plans, so let's go!" Tracy's husband intervened.

"The man has spoken," Tracy said, grabbing her husband's hand.

I didn't know this fool knew how to talk all these years, Pierre thought.

"It was good seeing you," Pierre said, thankful her husband finally spoke up.

"Um, hmm," Tracy said and walked off. Pierre almost forgot he had to use the bathroom. He quickly used it and headed back before Tracy decided to go and see about Toni.

11

Nestled in the nook of his shoulder, Toni lay back and enjoyed the sensuality and freedom that jazz music privileged her with. She was listening to the music but not really seeing the musicians. She was busy envisioning her and Preston dancing under this tent alone with a single bluesman, playing the sax, barefoot as they danced wearing midnight blue as the summer rain melted into their bodies, leaving a sweaty appearance to their skin. Soon her eyes were closed; she was swaying happily to the music inside of her head. Preston looked at her and wanted to just make love to her while assuring her he wasn't gay like her ex, he wasn't a womanizer like other men, he wasn't going to break her heart, but he couldn't. He had to get a divorce from his wife because it was already too late to tell Toni that he was married. He could tell that she wasn't the kind of woman that was going for that. Not after dating for two months.

* * *

Two hours later the show was over and Toni and Preston held hands as they walked to his car. "The night is still young, you want to go someplace else?" Toni asked, feeling high and sexy off of the champagne. As bad as Preston wanted her, he didn't want her intoxicated. He wanted her full attention, mind and body.

"What do you have in mind?" he asked.

"I don't know, let's ride out to Jones Beach, are we far?"

"No, it's about a half hour, if that. But I have a better idea than getting sand all on us. Let's go back to my place."

He could tell Toni got uneasy. "No, I'm not being fresh, I just want to relax, talk to you, extend this romantic night."

"How far do you live?"

"Central Park West."

"I hate you! I'm still building my dream penthouse in my mind on Central Park West."

"Really? It's overpriced and overrated if you ask me."

"Must be expensive to live there, what did you say you did again?" Toni joked.

"It's expensive, but . . ." was all Preston said, as he was leery about discussing money with women. To keep the momentum going all the way to Manhattan, Preston put the radio on, where they were playing "A Ribbon in the Sky" by Stevie Wonder. Toni kicked her shoes off and hummed the words as Preston drove, smiling.

* * *

They parked in an underground garage and took a small freight elevator to the eighth floor. Upon walking in, Toni was greeted by a decent-sized foyer that made way to a huge living room that was festooned in barely touched white furniture. She followed Preston through two more dining rooms until they reached another living room with safari-green furniture, a fireplace, bar, flat-screen television, and entertainment system. To the far left was a small set of stairs that probably led to heaven. "Let me take you for a tour," he said.

"Sure," Toni said and followed him. He reached for her hands and led her up the stairs.

"Here," he pointed, "is the guest bedroom, over here is the guest bathroom, right here is the main bathroom, another small kitchen, the main one is downstairs, and my bedroom," he said, pointing to a room that was the size of her entire condo. Toni could see her and Preston rolling around in the huge double king-sized canopy bed.

"What is it you do for a living again?" she joked.

"I'm leasing this for only four thousand dollars a month," he lied, knowing he paid a whopping $4 million for it.

"*Only* four thousand dollars a month?"

"My company pays for over half of it. They had to offer me this to move to New York City."

"Oh, okay, that sounds more like it! It's beautiful, though. Don't you sometimes wish you could afford this, I mean all the stars and white millionaires live like this like it's nothing. This has been my dream home since I was a kid," Toni said, looking around.

"Yeah, mine too, if only I had the funds."

"Well, at least you can dream while you're here. Just don't piss your boss off!" she joked.

"Tell me about it."

As she headed down the small set of steps he grabbed her hand and walked down with her. "More wine or you're good?"

"Um . . . one more won't hurt."

"You hesitated knowing damn well you wanted more," he teased her.

"I'm no lush, you know."

"Coulda fooled me!" Pierre joked. Toni watched him as he quickly poured wine at the bar so that he could get back to her side. *He is too damn good to be true*, she thought as she watched him. *Something has to be wrong, stop it, Toni, don't be so cynical, stop it!* she fought with herself, smiling as he came and sat next to her handing her the wine while placing the bottle down in front of them.

"So Ms. Toni, with your bad self. Why don't we have children? Do we want kids?"

"I never really thought about it, I mean I guess I haven't found the right man to make me want to have babies."

"Fair enough," he said, sipping.

"So what about you?"

"Never came across a woman that made me want to have kids."

I hope he isn't a wack lover, lord it's been too long for me!

"You're no spring chicken, what are you waiting for?" Toni cracked.

"But *you are*, so when you're ready you can have all three of my babies."

"Three? One is fine with me, honey."

"One? That's just selfish, at least two, two and a dog."

"Um . . . okay, a small dog, though."

"No doubt . . ."

"Two boys, girls are trouble."

"Women are precious, I need at least one girl so I can name her Tamara after my mother."

"Um, no offense, but Tamara would have to be a middle name. I like Sienna."

"Sienna? We gon have to sleep on baby names, I'm not really feeling Sienna."

"You name the boys, I name the girls, fair enough?"

"Okay, that's better."

"Pierre?"

"Huh?"

"Why are we talking about baby names?"

"Because" . . . *I want you to have my babies* he wanted to say but said, "it's no harm in that, right?"

"No, just talking, I don't know you like dat to be havin' yo baby!" Toni joked. The wine had her feeling real easy. Pierre enjoyed her company.

"You want to hear some more jazz?"

"Yes, please," She replied, as she tucked her feet cozily underneath herself.

12

When Pierre returned from his stereo, Rachelle Ferrell was serenading the penthouse with her deep, throaty voice. The two of them sipped their wine uneasily both feeling the sexual tension rising between them. "I don't want to have sex with you, I want to make love to you," he said out of nowhere. Toni stared at him and took him in for a few seconds before she answered, "So go ahead." *It's been so long and I want you so bad oh my god!*

"No, 'cause I don't love you. Not yet. But for now, can I just rub your body, please?" he whispered. Pierre made a promise to himself that he would not have sex with Toni until his divorce fell through. He'd have to hold off on making love to Toni until then.

"After a night of jazz, wine, dancing closely, and talking about babies you're going to just rub my body? That's criminal." Toni hissed. Pierre leaned in and kissed her full lips then undressed her inch by inch. He took a good look at one

breast at a time. "Perfect," he whispered. He undressed her down to her black silk-and-lace bra
and boy short set. "Damn, this is art. Lay down,"
he said. Toni took a swig of her wine then lay
down, her body was tense and going wild inside.
She had to say silent prayers to herself to stop
herself from coming without being touched. "I
know it's been a while for you. I want you to try
to relax, Toni," was the last thing she remembered
him saying.

Toni awakened in a king-sized bed, surrounded by pillows, bright sun, and cold air that
caused her to suck her teeth and have an attitude
if only briefly before she snuggled under a huge
white down comforter, losing herself in feathers.
She took a deep breath and opened her eyes wide
under the sheets. *I spent the night at this man's
house?* she thought and slowly uncovered herself.
With only her head peeking out, her naked body
was still hidden under the army of pillows and
comforters. The October morning air was cooler
than usual. The room was so huge she had to
pinch herself to make sure she was not in heaven.
She got up quickly and looked around for her
clothes. There were no signs of blue fabric amidst
the white sea of sheets, drapes, towels, tiles, and
carpet. Toni passed a mirror and took time to look
in it. Since her hair was short, it was still neat although a little messy, her face was glowing and
she looked relaxed. *Morning breath!* She gagged
and grabbed a white towel and headed to the
master bathroom next door where she took a

long, hot shower and brushed her teeth, then gargled. She wrapped herself in a fresh towel and headed back to the bedroom and crawled in bed wondering where Pierre was with her panties.

Pierre was lying on the sofa downstairs wondering if he should awaken Toni who looked so beautiful even when she slept. A woman of scarce stress and issues, she slept with a peacefulness that you only see on deceased people. Her healthy skin and radiant short hair was as sign of a woman that lived comfortably. Pierre cooked breakfast then headed upstairs to serve her.

Toni was laying in the bed even more comfortable than she was before, from the shower, smiling as last night's events slowly came back to her. Pierre appeared in the doorway with breakfast.

"This looks so good Pierre," she moaned with hunger. He placed the tray of toast, egg whites, and bacon in front of her.

"You're not going to eat?" Toni asked as she munched on the bread.

"I'm feeling like fruit, a mango maybe," he said.

"Sounds refreshing. Can you bring me some too?"

"I'll be back," he said and left out the room. Preston entered the room again with a silver tray with sliced mangoes on it.

He took her breakfast tray away and seductively placed a slice in her mouth. She ate it and didn't look at him.

He laughed inside at her coyness. He peeled the sheets off of her and began dripping mango juice all over her body.

"I got a taste for some fruit," he said and began relieving her of the mango juice. "You smell so nice, you took a shower?"

"Yeah," she said, trying not to give in to what he was trying to do with the mango juice.

He began to drip the juices on her privates.

"The sheets," Toni moaned.

"I don't give a damn about the sheets," he said as he squeezed juices in between the lips of her vagina then began sucking it off.

13

"I have been calling you for like two days, Toni, where have you been?" B asked, upset.

"Busy, I *do* work!" Toni laughed as she sat at her desk at home. She was feeling high and happy, the happiest she been in a long time. She had love on her mind . . . again.

"Well, you were *not* at work when I called you yesterday so tell me what is going on?"

"I was at my mother's house," Toni said as she proofread a chapter in her book.

"You don't expect me to believe that, do you?" Beatrice said with her arms folded. It was amazing to Toni how Beatrice really and truly became enraged when she could not find her.

"I was at my mother's house, ask her, she is getting married, I met her husband and oh, you're a bridesmaid, she is getting married in May."

"What? Ms. Jolly found love? Before *you*?"

"Hey, anything is possible. So that's where I been. Her husband is fine and my mother is a size twelve now! She is so happy!"

"That is blessed news, it really is."

"And guess who I saw. Maurice."

"Who the hell is that?"

"Mo from around the old way."

"Oh! How is he?" Beatrice said, unenthused. She wanted to separate herself from that life back in Brooklyn so bad and Toni always found a reason to go down memory lane.

"He's good, he has a daughter now."

"What? You see how karma works now watch the hell he gets with his daughter."

"Yeah, I know but he looks good, his daughter is beautiful and so is his lady."

"Is she from the hood?"

"No."

"Good for him."

"So what's going on with you?" Toni asked, taking her glasses off and rubbing her eyes.

"Oh nothing," she sighed exaggeratedly.

"Okay, talk to me, what's up with you, everything okay?" Toni asked, now walking to her bedroom for her slippers.

"Yeah, *well no*. What are you doing today? Can I get some quality time?"

"Sure you can. You want to come to my house or do you want me to come to yours, what are you doing in Jersey anyway?"

"I'll come to your house, I'll call in sick."

"Okay, I'll just work on my book until you get here. Do you have any special requests?"

"As far as?"

"You know, do you need to get your *head* right, *mind* right or you know . . ."

"Oh, oh *hell yes*. I need my head right. You're going to need yours right too from listening."

"Okay, be on your way."

"I'll be there in an hour, smooches," Beatrice said and hung up.

Toni could tell that B was in need so she created a comfortable environment for her and Beatrice to talk. She lit vanilla-scented candles, she ran out and got finger foods for them to munch on, she fried wings, made a cheese salad, popped open a bottle of Moët and put two ashtrays on the table for them to drop their joint ashes in. The spare room that Beatrice used to damn near live in was hers for the taking if she needed it tonight or forever. Toni had enough time to finish up some more of her book, then the doorman buzzed Toni to tell her B was on her way up. Toni opened the door and stood by it, smoking her joint and chewing on cheese as she heard the bell from the elevator. Beatrice came off of the elevator with a small tote, Jackie O glasses, weave pinned up, no makeup, and a sweat suit. *This is serious*, Toni thought as she passed the joint to Beatrice and grabbed her bags without saying anything except giving Beatrice an air kiss on each cheek. "Go in the living room," Toni yelled out as she put B's things in the spare room. When she got to the living room, B was already pouring Moët and stuffing her face with Cheez-Its and salad. "I have chicken too," Toni said.

"Hook me up a plate, will you, sis?"

Toni came back with two hefty plates and

placed one in front of Beatrice. They sipped wine and smoked haze until Beatrice was ready to talk.

"All these years, who would think that my father was really cheating on my mother? Do you know that my dad has had a mistress for the past twentysomething years and a son in jail?"

"What?" Toni exclaimed. She knew that Mr. Benny had a mistress, she had been trying to open Beatrice's eyes to that for years. But an outside child?

"Oh my goodness, what happened?"

Beatrice broke down all of the events that had taken place and informed Toni that her father moved out of the house and in with Ebony, his mistress.

"I am so sorry to hear that, how is your mother doing?"

"Actually, she is doing much better than I thought. But then again I'm not there at night when she is lonely. I can not believe that my father could be so selfish."

"Have you spoken to him?"

"No! I have nothing nice to say to him so I rather he keep his distance because I really don't want to hear the *baby I'm sorry* or the *let me explain* or *your mother and I stayed together only for you* or any other bullshit excuse men come up with."

"Damn. I totally don't know what to say."

"Start with *I told you so*," Beatrice said and took a pull off of her joint.

"No, I wouldn't say that. Not at a time like this."

"Aw come on T, you have been telling me this for years and although I hated you for it, it was just because I wasn't ready for the truth. You have a way of forcing people to accept and see the truth way beyond when they are ready to. I love and hate that about you. You're persistent and relentless when it comes to that."

"I have a gift and I see it this way. Why waste years living a lie when you can find out the truth right now and deal with it now."

"You're right. I hate my father so much. I can't believe he would stoop so low."

"Me either, the son thing is what gets me."

"Yeah and then that woman, she knew all this time he had a family and she just laid back in the cut like a snake in the grass. How can people be so unkind and selfish?"

"It's what keeps the world balanced. If we all were the same and had the same beliefs, morals, and things of that nature, imagine how quiet this place would be. Hell, me and you wouldn't be friends because our friendship is based on our hunger to disagree with one another," Toni said laughing and sipping on Moët.

"Oh hell yes!" B agreed.

"So . . . without prying, how's Mr. Wonderful?"

"Not so wonderful," Beatrice answered more so because she was high and intoxicated. She really didn't like to discuss Stephen with Toni. Toni, not wanting to pry, didn't bother to ask what was going on in the Hamptons, so she instead said, "Did Marcus call you?"

"No, he is waiting for my call that he may never get. I would like to say hello but I don't want to open a can of worms."

"Why is it that we love the men that are dangerous for our souls?"

Beatrice sipped her champagne and rolled her eyes at Toni. "We will talk about *that* later, for now, though, I need to talk about what's on my mind. I need to talk to you without feedback. I know you're a great listener as well as adviser. You think you can play therapist today?"

"Sure, hold on," Toni said and disappeared. She came back with her glasses on and a small notepad. She relit several candles that had blown out and instructed Beatrice to lie across her sofa where she sat across from her in a plush armchair. "Close your eyes for a while and think of something positive, I'll interrupt you shortly and I want you to say what is on your mind."

After counting to thirty, Toni began to speak. "So Miz Washington. Please feel free to discuss with me what is on your mind so heavily," Toni said and reached for her glass and a piece of chicken.

"Well, for starters, I want to confess that I really do not love my man. I love more so the lifestyle he provides. He is a pompous jackass that is way too light skinned and narrow for my tastes. And I am looking for a new man to provide me the same lifestyle, just someone more likeable."

"Do you think that he loves you?"

"No. Not really and I don't care. Honestly, I think he is about to replace me."

"Why is that?"

"He has been cheating on me with some woman named Brandy for the past five months. I read their e-mails and even called her house the other day because he didn't come home and my gut told me that he was there, so when I called he answered. He had the nerve to be calm, comes home the next day and tells me that it's his way or the highway. He told me basically I could stay there as long as I keep my mouth shut. He then of course bought me a bunch of expensive mumbo jumbo and then told me that he was interested in a three-way encounter with me and her."

"What? I mean . . . how do you feel about that?" Toni said, trying to remain professional.

"Disrespected."

"What is wrong with going home then or staying with a friend?"

"Because I have dreamed of getting out of the ghetto since I was a kid. Finally I have someone who is capable of doing this for me. I can't mess this up."

"Why not be capable of doing it on your own so that you won't have to compromise your self-respect?"

"It's easier this way."

"God bless the child who *holds* her own."

"Sounds good but I'm thirty years old. There is nothing I can do quick enough to keep me out of the ghetto except team up with a wealthy man. I have this friend named Toni who is a power driver if you will. She is single so I think that affects her sanity."

"How so?"

"Well, she is way too independent, doesn't like to open up her forum to receive help or take advantage of what life has to offer. She wants to do everything on her own."

"I see nothing wrong with that."

"I do, I believe that is why she is lonely. At least let a man *think* you need him so he can do things for you."

"Who says she is lonely? And what if your friend doesn't like playing games with men? And what if she feels that if she does things on her own she won't leave herself open for disappointment?"

"Life is a game and you have to play to win and survive. And she is lonely. I can tell. I know my sister, she hasn't had a date let alone any kind of contact with a man for years. What kind of life is that?"

"Well, maybe your friend is just waiting for the right time, maybe she has compromised enough of herself to where she feels as if she wants to be alone."

"Sounds good but I just can't get with that. She always has an opinion like she is Dr. Love yet her ass doesn't have a man and can't keep one it seems."

"Enough about your friend, let's get back to you. So this Stephen guy . . . he's cheating openly, is there anything good about him?"

"Aside from him being financially generous? No. Anyway, look, I rather let a man with money mistreat me then some broke ass."

"How about *not* letting a man mistreat you no matter *what* he has?"

"How about getting a man?"

"How about I don't want one?"

"Yeah, that's like saying you don't want a million dollars."

"Okay, how did this turn on me? Stephen is an asshole and now I have *reason* to not like him. I feel good now that I have a reason . . . finally. So how long are you going to allow these shenanigans to go on, B?"

"Until I find someone new."

Toni shook her head in disapproval. "You can't keep paper chasin', B."

"I'm not a gold digger if that's what you're saying. I'm just not messing with any broke niggas."

"Listen to how you sound. There isn't anything wrong with getting things on your own."

"Nor is there anything wrong with letting someone get it for you."

"Yes there is if you have to compromise your pride, self-respect, and dignity for it!"

"You know my friend Lola? She does not want to be with her husband. They have been legally separated for a while now. But whenever he brings up divorce, she performs, acts like she cares and wants him so much. They got married years ago and she thought it was a big mistake. He made her sign a pre-nup right before they got married. She did not understand why. Just when she was about to leave him, she learned of how good his company was doing. Almost overnight he became a multimillionaire. She has been used to her lifestyle for some time now. But guess what, if they get a divorce, she gets nothing accept some bullshit alimony, if that. So now, she is trying to get pregnant. I mean, imagine living like that after being with a multimillionaire for so long. I never even see her husband, but the way she talks about him, I would hope he looks like Denzel."

"How come you have never seen him?"

"Because he doesn't come to any functions, he doesn't mess with her like that. Him and Stephen used to be close but all of a sudden they just stopped speaking. I've never been to her house or anything."

"Why does he want a divorce?"

"She never really said why, irreconcilable differences, I guess. But if she gets pregnant then she'll be straight."

"So she is scheming on this poor man."

"It's a dog-eat-dog world out there, Tone, you of all people should know this. Since when you sympathize with the men?"

"Because there are some good men out there, Beatrice."

Beatrice sat up erect and stared at Toni. "Is there something you want to tell me? Because unless you have good man that you're hiding, I can't see myself listening to you sing about the good men, especially after you've been dogged out so many times."

Toni took a swig. "B, it doesn't matter what I've gone through, I never put myself in a position to need a man and I never will. Shit, I hate the fact that I have to pay bills on my own but I love the fact that I am able to and if someone comes along and offers assistance, fine, but if they leave I won't be unable to pay my bills alone. Help is fine as long as you're not depending on it."

"Yeah okay, I guess you like paying bills and all that. Not me, and I'm going to either reel Stephen's ass in deceitfully or find someone new."

"Nothing good is going to come by you if you go about things that way, B."

Beatrice shrugged her shoulders. "Well, maybe this is why you're lonely, because you ran through so many niggas back in the day, now you're alone. There is nothing wrong with what I'm up to. Look, Stephen is cheating on me, what should I do?"

"You don't seem to care about him at all, so why does it matter?" Toni was pissed. Beatrice always tried to drag her down or into her bullshit.

"Because I feel disrespected regardless. I am supposed to be his woman!"

"Do you want me to talk to you as a counselor or friend?"

"Doesn't matter," B said, rubbing her head.

"Do you need an aspirin?"

"No, I'm fine, my eyes just burn."

"Beatrice. There are other things you can do to occupy your time. A real man doesn't care what you have or where you live, he will accept you for you as long as he sees that you're serious about your life and your goals. And he will help you become a woman to capacity if he cares about you. He will help you grow. You can go home, you have a place, and you can stay here if you hate your neighborhood. You have options, Beatrice. Don't settle for this man who is trying to use money to control you."

Beatrice took a deep breath. "I just don't know which way is up right now, Toni."

"Pray on it, B, the answer will come. But please don't do a threesome."

"That is not in the plans, trust me."

"Please don't do that, Beatrice," Toni said again knowing that Beatrice would stoop to the lowest of levels to please or keep a man. "Always maintain your self-respect and that is from woman to woman. It's all we have in this dog-eat-dog world and if we don't think like men on the inside and present ourselves like women on the outside, our asses are grass."

"How can you be so strong?"

"I'm not that strong. It's hard work, and trust me I'd give anything to be a damsel in distress, just for a little while, but I don't trust anyone enough with my life or my heart."

"As you can see, I packed my bags. I plan on staying here for another two days. I'm playing the *let's see if he'll miss me* game."

"And what if he doesn't miss you?"

"I don't know. I just wish I had a plan B, another man with some cash and maybe I wouldn't give a shit."

Before Toni spoke another word she looked at Beatrice. She was lost. There wasn't but so much Toni could say to her friend to let her know that this was not the way to live. She began to even feel sorry for her. Toni got up and sat next to her friend. "We have come so far, B. Think back. Don't go back to having men run all over you. You're a good woman. I've been noticing that you go through so many extremes to be what each man wants you to be."

"I'm not trying to be something I'm not. This is me."

"If that helps you sleep at night. But you are going to get tired of running from yourself and you will have to face your insecurities sooner than later. Why not confront your demons now?"

"I have no demons, just a cheating man, and a bastard of a father. Would I be a fool to call Marcus?"

"What do you think you're going to get out of calling Marcus?"

"He knows things, he was always good to talk to. I just need something different from Stephen right now, you know how it is. It'll be innocent, I promise."

"Don't promise me, promise yourself."

"What is up with Maurice and Quentin?"

"Well, I heard Q has a few shops that he opened and he is doing well."

"So when do you think that you'll be ready to confess to me that you and Quentin had a fling and you were in love and you miscarried his child?" Beatrice said, getting up.

"Where do you get this stuff from?" Toni laughed nervously.

"So . . . when are you going to talk to me about this? It's been eleven years now since I've waited to hear this from your lips, not someone else's."

"Beatrice, I don't do mind games, Q and I liked one another and we never told one another, that is as far as it goes."

Beatrice sighed heavily and folded her arms. "I can't be mad, I too have kept secrets. But if you confronted me about one that was true, I'd tell you all about it," Beatrice said, desperately wanting Toni to ask her what her secret was so that she could finally get it off her chest.

"Beatrice, I assure you, what you heard was false. I don't know why people make things up."

"Okay, okay," B said, putting her hands up in a surrendering fashion. But she knew Toni was not telling the truth but if she told Toni for sure how she knew, it might ruin their friendship . . . for good.

Toni was on the PATH train this morning racking her brain trying to figure out how Beatrice knew about her and Quentin. She called Maurice several times but couldn't get through to him but she did not leave a message. She knew Mo or anyone for that matter would not have told Beatrice anything. Furthermore, if B knew something like that, why didn't she confront her? That left her with a not-so-good feeling in her stomach. Reaching her stop, she forgot about it momentarily and walked off of the train. She bought the *Daily News* and continued her thoughts. She remembered Quentin and his girlfriend. She remembered her well because she'd come to Toni for advice. She trusted Toni. She knew Toni was that one girl that the guys were cool with that she didn't have to worry about. Somehow Toni fell in love with Quentin and he in love with her. Toni could never tell Beatrice about this because the relationship was a bit sacred to her so she made up a name for Quentin when she told Beatrice about things, his alias was Haman. Somehow Toni wound up pregnant, foolishly wanting to keep it. Quentin, being scared, disappeared for a month, maybe three. Stress caused a miscarriage, Quentin resurfaced after finally telling his girlfriend that he was in love with Toni and that she was having his baby, he then approached Toni only to find his child was dead. Quentin was heartbroken and disappeared for some time. Toni went to college. Quentin's girlfriend Miriam harassed Toni, sent threats, did everything but leave a headless chicken at her doorstep. The pain she caused Miriam haunted Toni for years until Jacque came along and caused a new kind of pain called karma. She cried on Maurice's shoulder when she came home from college and told him about what happened. She never let on to Tracy and Beatrice how hurt she really was about Jacque being a homosexual. He comforted her, it was hard, Quentin was his right-hand man and Toni was like his sister. Once Quentin got wind that Toni was back in town, they had a brief affair, but unbeknownst to Toni, he was back with Miriam. Once Miriam found out about Toni . . . *again* she left Quentin for good, but not before trying to kill him. What Toni didn't understand was where did Beatrice fit in this equation when she always thought that she was too good to be around them.

14

Beatrice sulked around Toni's apartment for at least three days before she gave in and went home. Stephen had not called her at all. When Beatrice arrived home, she had a surprise waiting for her. Stephen had all of her belongings in a small box with a note for her to call him when she got in. When she called him, he did not speak but instead told her he'd talk to her when he got home, which would be within the next hour or so. Beatrice looked through the many closets and did not see any of her mink coats, shoes, and bags, not even her perfumes or jewelry. Her underwear and even her Bobbi Brown and Chanel cosmetics were gone. "What the fuck is this about?" she asked herself with her hands on her hips, looking around the room dumbfounded.

An hour later, Stephen entered the house whistling. He saw Beatrice, nodded his head at her and began to loosen his silver tie. Once he did that, he took off his gray Salvatore Ferragamo shoes and placed them neatly at his side. He undid his cuff links and pulled his shirt out of his trousers. He then crossed his hands and cocked his head to the side, looking at Beatrice who was trying to ignore him by watching television. "I won't be ignored in my own home, as you can see your things are packed."

"My things? I think my things consist of at least thirty more boxes. What is that?" she said, pointing to the box.

"That is what you came here with."

"Excuse me? You did not buy everything that I own, Stephen."

"I beg to differ. You can't afford the shit I buy you on your salary. Now let's make something clear here. You want to stay here, don't you?"

Beatrice wanted to tell him to fuck off but where would she go now with two outfits and a pair of Nine West shoes that she thought was the bomb until Stephen purchased her first pair of Pradas for her. She thought she tossed out her old shoes. She saw now that Stephen kept them as a reminder.

"Hello, earth to Beatrice."

"I heard you."

"So answer me. You do like it here, don't you?"

"Yeah."

"I thought so. So why do you think that you can play games with me like this? This is my house. I take care of you and those things that I took from you were bought with my money, honey, mine. Saks can't pay you enough to get the shit that I get you. Right?"

"Right," Beatrice mumbled.

"I suggest you get your act together. I want you to go home for a while, do something until I call you. You're on time-out."

"I'm a little confused, Stephen. What do you mean, time-out?"

"I mean I want you to learn to appreciate what I do for you. You need things to be taken from you in order for you to truly appreciate how lucky you are to have a man like me, because I know no other man would be dumb enough to take you in and keep you up like I do. But I can see the hunger in your eyes. You want this life, you crave it. But you can't get anything in life without working hard and it looks like you put on a few pounds, what have you been eating, sister? You've been at Toni's house?"

"Yes."

"You need to leave that low-class working bum alone. She is not in your caliber. She can't snag a well-off man such as you can. If you ask me, I think she's a lesbian. She hasn't had a male friend since I met her. She is probably feeding you all kinds of fuck-Stephen speeches so that you can be alone and miserable like her. Hell, if you played your cards right you wouldn't have to work, but you just won't let this black woman independent thing go now, will you? Following Toni. Is she buttering your bread?"

"No."

"Milking your coffee?"

"No."

"How about putting clothes on your back, keeping your weaves tight, getting hair imported from Europe and shit. Your weave costs more than her damn rent. Ain't that about a blip." He laughed wickedly.

"Stephen, where am I going with just two outfits? I had more than that when I met you! I wasn't a slouch, you know."

"*Let you tell it.* Anyway, those things are gone. And you will be too, if you don't shape up. Anyway, have you thought about what I proposed to you?"

"What."

"You know, the threesome," he said, getting up and taking his shirt off.

"No, I'll pass."

"No? You're still being defiant, huh?"

"No, that's just not my forte, Stephen, feel free to recruit someone else," Beatrice said, getting up to retrieve her things. She knew once she said no he'd make her leave.

Stephen grabbed her arm as she tried to walk out. "I'm not asking you, B, I'm telling you."

"Telling me what?"

"That you will do as I say or you're a goner."

"I don't have to deal with this shit, Stephen, you don't own me."

"Fine, I can get anyone to do it if I name the right price. You're dumber than I thought, Beatrice. All this and you're going to let your pride fuck it up. You black women, boy, I tell ya. Then you wonder why black men go to other races. You bitches got too much shit with you. I hope some jailbird in your hood can do a better job of taking care of you."

Beatrice snatched up her box and sifted through

it. She knew she had at least two weeks' worth of clothes and things at home but she hadn't near a variety like she had at Stephen's. She didn't get paid for another four days and she had to pay her rent and car insurance on a car and apartment she barely touched. Lucky for her she had a whole makeup case and another five outfits with shoes and underwear in the luggage that she left at Toni's house. Taking that box would be an insult so with just the clothes on her back, as Stephen pretended not to be watching her, sifting through mail, she walked out of Stephen's house and headed for the Hamptons jitney although another bus wasn't scheduled to leave for another two hours.

15

Toni was excited as she was nearing the end of her second book and she was very impressed with what she had written so far. She decided this time around to use her own money to press her book so that if anything went wrong she would have no one to blame but herself. She needed start-up money to launch her own publishing company but she'd worry about that some other time. Her credit wasn't A1 but she was sure she could get some kind of small-business loan.

She was done with her last chapter for the night and after proofreading it, she shut her computer off and decided to watch some television. It was pretty cold outside, she could feel the air coming through her window. She put on some warmer house attire and while she was up, decided to fix herself a cup of coffee. Her mind ran across Preston who hadn't called her in a few days. She was sure that he was playing cat and mouse. He had no idea how good Toni was about not giving a fuck. But for some reason a small aorta of her cared about Preston so she figured before she drifted off into a deep slumber she'd call him and say hello.

Toni laid across her chaise enjoying her French vanilla cappuccino and the movie *Heat* when her phone rang. The expensive phone displayed an unknown number to her. She recited the number in her head, trying to figure out whom it belonged to. Finally she answered.

"Hello."

"Hello, may I talk to Toni, please."

Still trying to catch the voice, she said "this is she."

"Hi, how are you."

"I'm fine, who am I speaking to?"

"This is Quentin."

Toni's heart skipped several beats as she sat up and fixed her clothes as if he could see her. "Quentin, how are you?" Toni was excited to be on the phone with him. It had been a long time and a part of her wanted her friend back but so many things including years had come between them she didn't know where to begin.

"I'm doing well. How are you?" He smiled. He was done with his last head for the night and was sitting in one of the barber chairs toying with a set of clippers with one Air Force One Nike up on the dresser.

"I can't complain. I'm assuming Mo gave you my number."

"He said you wanted me to have it. Sorry I'm just now getting back to you. I'm a busy man these days," he said, brushing his dark caesar and deciding to shape up his light goatee.

"That's wonderful, so what can I do for you, Quentin?"

"Nothing Toni, I was just calling to say hello and check on one of my favorite people."

"I'm okay, I can't complain."

Quentin laughed, noticing her curt answers. "Is this a bad time? I can always call back."

"I'm not doing anything that can't be put to the side for a few minutes. So how's the family?" *Girl, talk to him like you know you wanna talk to him, stupid.*

"Everyone is good, how's Ms. Jolly?"

"She's good, getting married in a few months."

"Oh, that's good, that's real nice. I'm glad she found someone to make her happy. What about you?"

"I . . . I have someone."

"Is he making you happy?"

"He's trying. And you?"

"Single."

"What's wrong with you?"

"I just been working, focusing on getting this legit money. I don't have time for a woman. You know you can't get with a real woman with your shit half-ass. I rather be complete when I step to mines."

"I hear you."

"You still sexy, short haircut?"

"Yeah."

"You put on weight?"

"About twelve pounds since you've seen me last."

"Nice, nice. How's B?"

"She's good, out in the Hamptons now."

"Got her some rich white guy, huh?"

"He thinks he's white and he does well for himself."

"I am not surprised, that's B's style. Tell her I said hello."

"I will," Toni said, being reminded of the secrets that B knew about. She was debating if she should ask Quentin now about it. She decided to keep him on the line a little longer to see what kind of conversation they could conjure up.

"Yeah, that B is something else. You two guys didn't talk much, though."

"Well, she pretty much was on some other shit, a little stuck-up, you know, she wasn't like you." *And I mean that literally.*

"Is that right?"

"Yup . . . so anyway, you still writing? Your last book was dope, Toni. I don't do chick books but it was raw, man. Real raw."

"Thank you."

"You're very welcome. Do you have anything new coming?"

"I'm working on something now, actually. Something a bit more seasoned, if you will."

"That's good, writing is your thing. I still have all of those sweet letters you used to write me. I wish you the best of luck."

"Thank you."

"It was good talking to you, Toni. Maybe one day we can go out or I can come over or you can come over. I'd like to see you."

"Same here."

"Maybe soon, then."

"Maybe."

Quentin laughed. "Okay, so this is my number on your caller ID. Do not lose it."

"I won't."

"I know yours by heart already."

"Oh really," was all Toni knew to say.

He chuckled. "*Still Toni* . . . I'll give you a call sometime again. You take care."

"You too, hon."

"Bye," he said and hung up.

Toni jumped up and began swinging at the air. "Stupid, stupid stupid!" she yelled. "Damn you, Quentin, damn you!" she said and fell out on the sofa like a teenager. She grabbed a pen and jotted his number down in case it got erased. She then put it on top of her refrigerator. She took a deep breath and began to settle down. She was still smiling ridiculously hard. "Relax, chick!" she said to herself then chuckled nervously. She then turned the television off, drank her coffee in silence, and daydreamed about Quentin until she fell asleep.

16

Beatrice's apartment was desolate to say the least. Her clothes were neatly laying across her bed with the plastic covering from the cleaners on it. She stuck to her guns and decided not to go back to Stephen but it was hard. It had been two months since she seen him let alone talk to him. She borrowed $1,000 from her mother so that she could go shopping but it was nothing like what she was used to with Stephen. She hadn't spoken to Toni in a while as she was busy working on her book and into whatever else she was into. Beatrice decided to do something she wanted to do long ago. She broke down and called Marcus. Her loneliness was killing her. As fate would have it, he didn't answer so she decided not to leave a message. She returned to putting her clothes away when the phone rang. "Hello," she said with attitude.

"Hi!" Marcus said, chipper.

"Marcus?"

"Yeah, how you doing, Beatrice, how's everything?"

"Everything is good, how are you?"

"I'm fine, I mean although it only took you two months to call me."

"I'm a busy woman, what can I say, so, how are things . . . really."

"I'm doing good. I bought a house in Mount Vernon, work is good, money is good, I can't complain and yourself?" Marcus said knowing all the right things to say to get Beatrice to come flocking.

"I'm doing well for myself."

"I'm not surprised, but listen . . . we aren't new to one another and the truth is I miss you, Beatrice. I made a lot of mistakes in the past. I hurt you, I did dumb shit but we were young."

"I was young, Mark, you were a grown man."

"Well, now I'm a grown-up for real."

"That's nice to know."

"I want to see you, Beatrice, lunch, dinner, dancing. Unless of course you have a man."

"No, I'm single, actually." *Damn that was too eager. Fuck! Too late now.*

"I figured you'd been done ran off with some millionaire and had babies by now."

"No, not me."

"Not yet, huh?"

"I guess not, so when do you want to hook up?"

"As soon as possible, say the word."

"I'm free this weekend. It's my weekend off."

"You still in Macy's?"

"No, I'm in Saks now. I manage my own floor too."

"Look at you, boss lady now, huh?"

"Yeah, I had enough of being told what to do, you feel me on that?"

"Yeah, I feel you. So how's Friday night, I pick you up from work?"

"Friday night is cool with me."

"Okay, honeybee, I can't wait to see you, what time do you get off of work?"

"Six."

"I'll be there waiting for you. What floor are you on?"

"Third floor, just go to any register and ask for me, they'll call my extension."

"Sounds like a plan, see you then," Marcus said, rubbing his hands together eagerly.

17

At 5:45, Beatrice was a nervous wreck when her phone rang at work and the cashier told her someone was there to see her. She hadn't seen Marcus in about ten years. She wondered if he was still tall, dark, handsome, and suave. Of course he was. She checked herself out in her full-length office mirror. Her weave badly needed to be tightened but she was able to put a silk Chanel scarf around the front that matched her navy-blue tight pinstriped suit and stilettos. She lightly sprinkled perfume on all of her joints and glossed her lips. She opened her suit jacket and perked up her large bosoms under her fashionable corset. Marcus loved her breasts so much. The thought of him touching them warmed her insides. She grabbed her black clutch and turned off her office lights.

She spotted Marcus sitting in the waiting area watching two little girls play hide-and-seek behind a clothing rack. He was something for the eyes. His hair was now full and curly, his suit was expensive and dark like his skin, his shoes, big and long like his penis and his bracelet, thick and heavy like his lips. He sensed her coming and turned her way. "Damn, my, my, my, look at you," he said and stood up. She took in his massive six-foot-seven frame. "How are you?" Beatrice said, trying to keep her excitement under wraps.

"I missed you, baby," he said.

"I missed you too," she said, not sure if she meant it but it felt like the right thing to say. They embraced warmly as he swallowed her tiny five-foot-three-inch body in his suit jacket. He then grabbed her hand and pulled her along. They walked four blocks until they reached a parking lot where his Lexus SUV was parked. "I have a nice, quaint place for us to go to," he suggested as he hit the alarm.

"I'm following your lead," Beatrice flirted.

"Good, I like that," he said and pulled out of the parking lot unaware of the unfinished business that followed him in an unmarked car.

She was livid that after all he had put her through he had the nerve to be stepping out. He said that he wasn't seeing anyone, but the way he greeted this woman told a different story. The look in his eyes was the same look he once had when he'd look at her. All the years they had been together, the marriage, the vows, and he could just walk out because he felt that he needed a "time-out" to get his head together. There wasn't any such thing as a time-out in marriage. She was having none of that, not after cosigning on a house and car for him, not after taking care of him when he lost his job until he found a new one that was paying him six figures. All of a sudden when he got what he wanted, after all these years, he decides he needs a time-out, swearing it wasn't about another woman. She was more so mad at the fact that she had to go to this extreme to find out on her own what was going on. But she wouldn't blow her cover just yet, she had to find out who this woman was and how well she knew Marcus.

The day was beautiful with a crisp spring air sweeping through the tents that were put up in the botanical garden in case of bad weather. But by the looks of the clear blue skies and puffy cotton clouds, there was no sign of bad weather on this lovely eighty-one-degree day. The bridesmaid's gowns were lovely peach ballerina-style dresses that stopped below the knee with satin shoes to match. Toni looked like an actress as she sauntered down the aisle alone in an identical dress as the other bridesmaids, except her dress was form fitting. As she marched down the aisle to Angela Winbush and Ronald Isley's "Hello Beloved", she had thoughts of her own special day. She glanced over at Preston's seat and he was sitting there smiling as if she was his bride. She winked softly then joined the wedding party as her mother and her husband-to-be exchanged vows.

* * *

"So where is Mr. Man and I cannot believe you kept him from me all of this time!" Beatrice said, hitting Toni on the arm. "I wanted to make sure it was getting serious before I introduced anyone to him. My mother hasn't met him, either, but she will tonight." Toni beamed. She knew that her mother and Beatrice would be impressed with Pierre's looks and professional status.

"I am not your mother, missy poo, I am your best friend. How is it that you have been dating someone for a week, let alone months, especially after your drought and I'm just now meeting him?"

"It's no big deal. I told you all about him," Toni said, looking around for Pierre.

"Yeah, after seeing him for months! Anyway, you never told me what he does for a living?"

"He works."

"Don't be a smart-ass." Beatrice said, fixing a glass of champagne for herself and Toni as Ms. Jolly walked in.

"So you are now Mrs. Thomas Wadley, go Ma, go Ma, go Ma!" all of the bridesmaids chanted. Ms. Jolly blushed then with her hands signaled them to be quiet. "I just want to say thank you, ladies, you all look so beautiful."

The crowd broke out in oohs and aahs. "And I want to say thank you, especially to my daughter who has been such a patient, forgiving child. I love you, Toni."

"I love you too, Ma," Toni said and hugged her mother tightly. Afterward they got ready to head out to the reception to meet Pierre whom Beatrice couldn't wait to see. She had heard enough when Toni told her what he drove and where he lived. Toni had never caught a big fish like that and Beatrice had to meet him, maybe see if he had a friend for her. She still wasn't seeing Stephen although he called twice in four months and her and Marcus weren't doing anything except sweating her weave out every chance they got. But it was good, the best she ever had, so she stuck with it for now. But he was being cheap and she wasn't feeling that. She missed the glamorous life.

"Is this him coming this way if so he is *foine*, you hear me you better go bitch, you better go!" Beatrice said through clenched teeth. "Oh hell yes Toni, I see now why he was such a secret, *dayum bitch!*" Beatrice kept on. Toni couldn't take it, she burst out in laughter as Pierre approached them dressed in a cream suit with a peach tie to complement Toni's dress.

"Pierre, hi, honey, this here is the infamous Beatrice," Toni said, taking a place next to Pierre and holding his hand.

"I heard so much about you, Beatrice, nice to have finally met you."

"Same here, darling, I hope all good things?"

"Nothing but."

"Wonderful, and I'm assuming you're treating my sister here with the utmost respect?"

"Absolutely."

"Wonderful and I'm assuming that you know she keeps a special can opener to open up her special can of whoop ass on anyone who tries to disrespect her blatant or indirectly."

Pierre chuckled and looked at Toni. "I'll blame this on the alcohol," Toni said.

"Oh hell yes I am feeling nice, but I'm speaking the truth, right Toni?"

"Right, B, right," Toni said, uneasy. She felt something coming from Beatrice but she wasn't quite sure what it was. She looked around for Marcus whom Beatrice said was coming so that he could whisk her away and keep her occupied. He was nowhere to be found.

"Don't go getting all saddity on me now, I remember when you used to . . . *Loooooove them and lee-heeve them, that's what she used to doooo, use and abuse them*," Beatrice said, breaking out into her own rendition of Rick James and Teena Marie's "Fire and Desire."

Toni looked on in shock as Beatrice finished her verse.

"You done now?" Toni asked, half-serious.

"Anything you want to know about my girl here just ask me," Beatrice volunteered.

"I think I know all I need to know, but thanks, I'll keep that in mind," Pierre said politely.

"I'll be sure to tell you about her days as a wild woman."

"Wild woman, huh?" Pierre said and smiled uncomfortably.

"Pierre, you thirsty?" Toni offered.

"Yes, I'll have *none* of what she's having," Pierre joked but Toni was uneasy. "Beatrice, I'll be right back."

"Um, hmm," Beatrice said and walked away. Toni eyed her as she walked away and disappeared to the other side of the tent.

"You okay?" Pierre asked as he ordered a drink for Toni.

"Yeah, I'm good."

"No you're not, I know you're not upset about your friend. She is just having fun."

"I know her, though, that was totally out of character for her."

"Oh, really. Don't put too much thought in it, here, drink some of this and ease your mind," Pierre suggested. Toni decided to put her mind at ease and concentrate on her man. "You looking all handsome. Are you here with someone?" Toni flirted.

"Yes, as a matter of fact I am, so please excuse yourself, I'm not interested in your convo, miss."

"Oh that's cold." Toni laughed.

"Imagine that." Pierre laughed.

"Well, can we have a dance at least?" Toni said as she pulled him on to the dance floor.

"Now this . . . is my record," she said, swaying her hips to 50 Cent's "Lil' Bit."

"A little bit of this, a little bit of that . . ." she sang as she bumped and gyrated her hips. Soon a crowd formed around her and Pierre who was singing in her ear. "*Come on let me unbutton ya blouse just a little bit, not a lot baby girl just a lil bit,*" he whispered, turning Toni on.

"Go Toni, go Toni, go Toni!" the crowd started chanting. The DJ then switched the record to Beyoncé's "Crazy In Love."

"Oh you in for it now!" Toni yelled as the crowd

began yelling *Go Toni!* louder. She could see her mother standing on a chair with her wedding dress on pumping her fist in the air and blushing, chanting *Go baby, go baby!* Toni did her best Beyoncé booty-bouncing rendition as Pierre playfully caught a heart attack and clutched his chest.

"Don't be skurred!" she said, grabbing him by his tie and pulling him closer as the DJ switched to Cameo's "Candy." By then the crowd all came together and began dancing. "It sure does taste like candy," Pierre purred.

Toni blushed and turned her back to him, dancing seductively. Beatrice knew that this was Toni's song. No matter where they were, Beatrice and Toni always acted a fool together off of this song. Toni looked around for her friend and finally located her on the sidelines shooting daggers her way. She chucked it up as her being drunk and needing a second wind and made a mental note to go see about her once the DJ played something she could sit down to but right now she was enjoying her new man and had no time to cater to Beatrice's hissy fits.

Beatrice reached home at 3:00 in the morning and was stone drunk. She hadn't gotten this drunk since she was a teenager. Not only did Marcus stand her up as her wedding date but also Toni had the nerve to show up with a date and ignore her all night. She was pissed that Toni hid this man from her. *What else could she be hiding?* Beatrice thought. First things first, she had to call Marcus and curse him out for not showing up as promised. He didn't answer his phone so she left him a message. "*Hey, this is B, you motherfucka, why didn't you call me and tell me that you couldn't make it instead of standing me up? Huh? Bet if I was calling you to tell you I was feeling horny you would have made it here yesterday. It's okay, though, Marcus, I'll fix you, you will not hurt me again, got it? I am not the young girl you used to know, please believe me!*" she ranted, then slammed the phone down. Beatrice walked around her house aimlessly until she hit her toe, which enraged her even more. "Fuck, fuck, fuck!" she yelled loud as ever. "*Dammit* that hurt." She got up and wobbled over to her dining area and picked up the joint that had been in the ashtray wrapped in aluminum foil for four days, so it wouldn't get stale. She lit it and took a hard pull. Between the haze and Jack Daniels that she had been drinking all night, Beatrice was really inebriated now. She began sliding out of her dress with the joint still lit in her mouth. She undressed down to her thong, and lay across her bed staring at the ceiling. "I hate this place," she said out loud then decided to call Toni.

"Your mother was a pleasure to meet, she looks so happy," Pierre said as they entered Toni's building. The doorman smiled at them both. "You guys look nice, coming from a wedding?"

"Yeah, my mother got married!"

"Oh congratulations, tell her she broke my heart!"

Toni laughed at the old man. "I will be sure to tell her. You have a good night."

"Good night to you both." His eyes smiled.

While riding up in the elevator, Pierre stared at Toni mischievously. "What? Why are you looking at me like that?"

"You ever did it in an elevator?" he asked.

I've done it just about everywhere. "No, you?"

"No, wanna do it tonight?" he said, stepping closer.

"Bad timing," Toni said as they reached her floor. Pierre walked Toni to her door and having never been to her apartment before he waited to be invited.

"Well, good night," he said, trying desperately not to break his rule of waiting to divorce his wife first before sleeping with Toni.

Toni took a deep breath. "Why don't you come in?"

"I don't think that's a good idea."

"Why not, don't you want to come?" Toni asked seductively. Pierre couldn't help but notice how seductive and sweet she looked standing there intoxicated with such innocent colors on. The contrast drove him wild inside. Toni grabbed his hand and pulled him inside gently.

"Don't you find me attractive?" she said, pouting.

"Oh you know I do, baby."

"So why haven't you tried to make a move on me? It's been four long years for me and I can't take you touching me and not penetrating me anymore. The last man that made me wait turned out to be a faggot," she whispered.

"Oh, I'm no faggot, love, bet that. You want penetration?" he whispered.

"Uh-huh."

Pierre sighed deeply. "Toni, there is something I need to talk to you about and it's been killing me to hide this from you."

"You're not gay, are you?" she said, thinking about Jacque.

"On a stack of Bibles, no, hell no and if I was, being with you has turned me straight," he joked.

Toni did not laugh.

"I'm sorry, baby, I forgot, sorry," he whispered and touched her face.

"Do you have a deadly disease?"

"No."

"Then I don't want to know. I'm enjoying you so much and whatever it is can't be that bad, can't be anything worse than what I have already experienced in life. The one thing, though, that I have not experienced is being in love, for real, for once in my life and making love with the man that I am in love with, which is you."

"I'm in love with you too Toni, I swear to you I am."

"You said to me one day, that you wanted to make love to me, but you had to love me first. You love me now . . . you just said it." She smiled.

"You are so sweet, Toni, like a little baby girl. I love you and I don't want to ever hurt you."

"So don't. It's that simple. But you're hurting me by not giving yourself to me, right now. Pierre, take me, please," Toni said, undressing herself. Once she was down to her panties she began loosening his tie and unbuttoning his shirt. "*All I really need is a lil' bit, not a lot just a lil' bit*," Toni sang. As she unbuttoned his shirt, he began planting light kisses on her neck. The ringing of the phone caused a momentary pause, then they proceeded on with their necking. The phone rang continuously until Toni finally decided that it might be an emergency.

"Hello," she answered, frustrated, as Pierre began to button his shirt again. That frustrated Toni even more.

"Yes, B, what happened?" she said as she watched her man get dressed.

Beatrice paced her small apartment with hatred on her mind. Marcus had stood her up and Toni's new man was reeking of money. Beatrice could tell by his clothes, his cologne, everything about him spelled money. He had the nerve to be handsome and by the looks of things be smitten with Toni. More so Beatrice was pissed that Toni had never mentioned him. "What, she think she too good for me now 'cause she got a fucking man!" she yelled to herself in her small apartment. "Man, fuck this shit," she said, staggering over a pile of clothes. She stood in the mirror looking at herself as she waited for Toni to pick up. "Yeah, um, you up, can you talk?" B asked confrontationally.

"Go on, it doesn't matter now, what's up?" Toni said, not trying to hide the aggravation in her voice.

"Okay, I know you got a new man and all, but I don't appreciate you totally ignoring me tonight!"

"I was not ignoring you. I was just having a good time. I had no idea that I was your babysitter! Bigger than that, it was my mother's day, not yours. And where the hell was Marcus?"

"What are you getting all smart for, Toni?"

Toni looked up in the sky for the answer. "I'm not getting smart, Beatrice, what's up with you? You've been acting funny all night!"

"*Me* acting funny? No, honey, I think you need to check your damn self. You've been up that man's ass so much you couldn't even tell me about him."

"Wait a minute, B, you're serious, huh? Is this what this is about? Me having a man?"

"Oh honey, don't go there you know I couldn't possibly be jealous of that. I stay with a nigga on my arm!"

Toni sat back in the sofa and rubbed her eyes out of frustration then rubbed her chin as if she had a goatee. She had nothing to say to Beatrice tonight. She was drunk and feeling a way so she was going to let B have this moment.

"You there?" B yelled.

"Um, hmm, I'm here."

"I need to talk to you, I'm coming over."

"Now is not a good time," Toni said, sitting up.

"What, that man is there?"

"*That man's* name is Pierre, Beatrice."

"I don't give a fuck what his name is, is he there?"

"Yes he is, why?"

"It figures, that's why you're talking to me all brazen-like."

"Brazen? You know how I can get. I'm hardly being brazen, Beatrice. What's on your mind?"

"I told you I do not appreciate you ignoring me tonight. Is this how it's going to be from now on? You know when I have a man, I do not act this way with you, Toni. You had him to yourself all this time. Don't you think it's time to loosen your grip a little bit and remember those who put things to the side to cater to you when you were lonely?"

"Beatrice, what the fuck have you ever put to the side? I have never asked you to come keep me company no matter how many men you had. I'm always busy working and doing other things to be worried about something as small as not having a man. You gotta be kidding me, B? Look, I can't have this conversation with you right now. Drink some black coffee and call me in the morning. Okay?" Toni said, ready to hang up.

"What? Yeah, I'll call you because *I got your number*," Beatrice said and laughed.

"I'll call you tomorrow, B, get some rest, bye," Toni said and hung up. She stared at the phone for a while then shook her head.

"Everything okay?" Pierre asked.

"I don't know. I hope so."

"Well, I'm going to head on home now," he said, standing up. By now Toni had lost her desire to lose her celibacy to him anyway. The whole chasing a man down for sex was never her style. "You can sleep on the couch if you like," she offered drily.

"No, that's fine," Pierre said, still trying to fight off the temptation.

"I won't attack you, *trust me*, the feeling is dead.

It's late, you were drinking and I don't want you on the road like this so please take my couch, *please."*

"Okay, okay." He relented and kicked his shoes off. "But Toni, if you don't mind, no strings attached, can I lay with you and just hold you?"

"Hold me? I don't think that's a good idea. I'll see you in the morning. I make a mean French toast," she said, heading toward her bedroom.

"Yes, a woman that can cook!"

"Cook? Nah, I don't cook," she yelled from her bedroom

Pierre frowned.

"I throw down baby!"

He wiped the imaginary sweat from his brow and laughed.

"You just don't know!" Toni continued.

"Well, make me a believer, T!" Pierre yelled out.

"In the morning darling, good night," she said and slid under the covers hoping that Pierre came to hold her anyway even though she told him not to.

Pierre tossed and turned on the couch. He had to find a way to tell Toni that he was married and that his wife was not trying to give him a divorce. On top of that, his body craved for Toni so much. He stared at her bedroom door, hoping she'd come out the room in something sexy and just throw herself at him. But he knew Toni wasn't the type to come back after being rejected. He felt somewhat relieved but guilty at the same time.

He had to go home and talk to his wife and finally end this marriage for good because he was in love with Toni and he wanted her to be his wife. So with that, he decided that as soon as he was done eating breakfast, he was heading home to have a sit-down with his wife.

On Sunday morning, after Pierre had eaten his breakfast, he said he had things to do and ran out, which was fine with Toni because she wanted to get to Beatrice's house before she ran out for the day. Pierre dropped Toni off and promised to call her later. With that, Toni jogged up the steps and knocked hard on Beatrice's door. She knew her friend would probably be hungover so she had Tylenol and coffee in a bag as well as leftover breakfast. She looked at her watch impatiently, knowing that B had to be home. She knocked louder then pulled out her cellular phone. She called and got no answer. She jogged back out the building and looked up and down the block to see if Beatrice's car was gone. She saw no signs of it but it could be parked anywhere. She ran back up the steps and began kicking the door.

Finally she heard the slow clicking of the locks. Beatrice opened the door clutching her tiny robe closed. "What are you doing here?" she asked unenthused and yawned.

"Can I come in?"

"Now is not a good time," she said sarcastically.

"Beatrice, I need to talk to you, can I come in?"

"I said now is not a good time."

"I didn't come all the way here for you to tell me that, so let me in."

"I didn't ask you to come over here now, did I?"

Toni stepped back and stared at her friend. "Okay . . . you're right. Well, I thought that you might need this, so here," she said, handing her the bag of goodies.

"What is this?"

"Call me later," Toni said, turning away.

"Tone, wait, come in," Beatrice said, stepping to the side to let her in. Toni came in and sat down on the futon.

"Let's get right down to it. What was up with you yesterday?"

"I was just in a bad mood, that's all," Beatrice said as she took the items out of the bag graciously.

"So you take it out on me? I need more. Why did I feel as if I was being targeted? Did I do something to you?"

"Toni, you know what my problem is? I don't know if I could trust you."

"Me? You can't trust me? From where?" Toni said, pointing to her chest.

"You are very secretive, Toni. That makes me uncomfortable."

"How so? I never hid anything from you that could hurt you or help you. So why do you take it so personal when I've been this way since we were kids?"

Beatrice shrugged. "I just think that you're going to change now that you have a man."

"Since when have I changed for some nig—some man?" Toni said, stopping herself from using the "N" word.

"I just see a change."

"No, you're just single for the first time in years and since I have someone you're lonely now. If I was single you wouldn't be feeling this way."

"*Maybe,* but you still didn't have to take so long to tell me about him, I feel offended."

"I don't know why," Toni said and got up to fix herself something to drink.

"I miss Stephen," Beatrice blurted out. *Now we are getting somewhere, Toni thought.*

"You miss his money. You don't even love him or care about him in the least, Beatrice."

"You're right to an extent. I mean, I do care for him a smidge."

"Is it the rejection that has you feeling like this?"

"What rejection?" Beatrice said, glaring at Toni. *How does she just assume that I'm being rejected? This ho got a lot of nerve.*

"Oh, okay, so he calls you? My bad," Toni said, sipping her cranberry juice.

"All of the time," Beatrice lied.

"Well, I'm not going to tell you to get back with him because you're lonely. All I can tell you is it's not that bad. I did it for four years. Give yourself some time to get to know you and all that good stuff."

"I couldn't do it. Besides, I've been seeing Marcus a lot lately," Beatrice said, dismissing Toni immediately.

"I thought you only saw him two times?"

"No, I see Marcus *a lot*. He is trying to get back with me for the past couple of months."

"Is that right?"

"Yeah."

"So you jump out the frying pan into the fire."

"See, there you go, Toni!"

"Oh, let me guess, because I have a man now, I'm talking shit? You know good and well man or no man I never change, Beatrice, so cut it out."

"Whatever."

"Yeah, I got your whatever."

"How 'bout those Knicks, Toni?"

"How 'bout 'em?"

"Bitch."

"Your mother."

"Yours!"

"I know!"

"You want to go out with me and Lola this weekend?" Beatrice laughed and sipped her coffee.

"Where to? I'm not going to one of those uppity places you guys like to go to looking for rich men. I need some culture around me, some life."

"I'm not sure where we are heading. We just figured a girls' night out is in order to sit around and drink and talk."

"A pity party?"

"I won't call it *that* but she is having problems at home. She called me before you came and told me that her husband called her and said he needed to talk to her and that it's very serious. She thinks he is going to lay the law down on her today. She's been pussyfooting around and stalling on him long enough. He's not playing anymore. They have been legally separated for a year now. She didn't succeed in getting pregnant and she says he doesn't even come home anymore. She knows her time is running out because he canceled all of her credit cards but one and that one only had a ten-thousand-dollar limit on it."

"Must be rough to only have a ten-thousand-dollar card," Toni said sarcastically.

"She's still a woman, Toni, show her some compassion."

"You know I have no respect for gold diggers."

"Look, I would like for you guys to meet anyway."

"As much dirt as you told me about her? You think it's cool for us to meet? B, I can't sit around hearing you and her swap stories about gaming niggas for money and all that. I just can't."

"Toni, there are other things that we can talk about. Be nice."

"She has one time to say some stupid bimbo shit, one time!"

"She sucks as a wife or girlfriend, I can admit to that. But as a person, she is nice, Toni, you'll see."

"Whatever. Count me in, just let me know where we are going as soon as possible. So Marcus is back up in you, huh? What's his deal?"

"Well, he is single and I can honestly say he has changed a bit."

"Well, *he is* old as hell he needs to be a changed man!"

Beatrice laughed. "He is still so so fine."

"Humph. Is he still in Brooklyn by Ocean Parkway?"

"No, he has a house in Mount Vernon now," Beatrice said proudly, as if it was hers.

"Nice, nice, you ever been there yet?"

"No."

"How come? Where does he tap that ass at?" Toni joked.

"Well, he picks me up from work and we always go out, stay in Manhattan, run up in rooms, things like that. There hasn't been a need to come to his house yet because we are never out that way," Beatrice said, now wondering why she was never invited to his house.

"Oh, okay, well just be careful with him, emotionally. You know how he can get you all jacked up in the head and I don't want to see my girl hurt, okay?"

"I got this, it's just sex and fun between us, well, on my end."

"You sound like me years ago," Toni said and smiled.

"So, how's your book coming along?"

"It's coming. I'm doing the edits on it now. Oh, Quentin called me," Toni said, trying to suppress a smile.

"Quentin? What did he want? Where he been?"

"Nothing. He was just saying hello. He wants to hook up for dinner soon but I don't know."

"Oh really."

"Yeah. He asked about you too."

"Is that right."

"Yeah."

There was a brief pause between the two women so Beatrice picked up her coffee and sipped it to fill the space.

"Tell him I said hello."

"I sure will," Toni lied. Every so often she'd get a bad feeling about B and Quentin and would try to get a reaction from Beatrice.

"Oh, that's cool."

"Yeah, he says he wants to tell me something, a confession of some sort."

"A confession?"

"Yeah. I wonder what he could confess to me after so long. He said it's been bothering him for years."

"What day are you guys trying to meet up?"

"Most likely Thursday after work since I'm off on Fridays."

Beatrice sat in a trance, sipping on her coffee quietly.

"What are you doing today?" Beatrice said, changing the subject.

"Nothing. What do you think he is going to confess?" Toni said, keeping it going.

"Probably how in love he has been with you, I don't know," Beatrice said and got up.

"We *will see*. Anyway, I'm going to chill out here until I'm ready. You don't mind do you?" Toni said and kicked off her shoes. "Do I mind? Girl shut up, just cook something to eat."

"With what? You never keep food in the fridge,

trying to get down to a size dead. What you got in the fridge, some carrots and shit! I need meat!"

Beatrice was cracking up. "My headache is leaving now, thank you. I'm going to hit the shower and run out to the store, okay?"

"Ya better," Toni said, turning on the television.

18

Pierre drove home fast but cautiously, his heart pounding, determination in his eyes. He had had enough. He needed to move on. He was stuck in an unhappy marriage long enough and as if his wife was trying to get all she can before he gave her the ax, she was charging up fur coats in the spring, $500 shoes, $1,000 spa treatments, she was acting desperate. Thinking about her scheming ways, he grew more upset and began to drive faster. The bright sun was shining in his face as he drove. He pulled down the visor in his car and did something he hadn't done in years, he lit a cigarette. It was a nasty habit he picked up as a young man from his first girlfriend, Leticia. She was a raunchy ghetto girl that stole his heart with her rawness. Leticia was beautiful. She was a honey-brown sista who wore her hair in extensions with gold balls and wire-like things in it. She wore big gaudy gold jewelry and had an ass to die for. She was a New York girl that moved down south to *get away*. She smoked cigarettes and drank hard liquor. She trash talked and liked hanging out with the boys. She was sweet on the inside but growing up in the hood did something to her. She was always on the defense, was very cynical and only showed her true emotions behind closed doors. You had to fight with her to get her to show her vulnerability and soft side, which she only did when making love. She was a seductress. He thought about Toni and could see her being like Leticia when she was younger. Leticia knew how to take care of a man, her problem was she wanted to be one too. He thought about her and his heart went soft. He would always love her for the look she held in her eyes for him. But growing up in the hood, she had to be with someone tougher than Pierre was, a thug, just to find out years later that what she needs is what she had way back then. She just wasn't woman enough to see that yet. She called and tried to plead her case and although he understood, too much time had passed and he was already with a new woman named Monica who was looking for a meal ticket and left him after a year once she saw that his money wasn't being made as fast as he promised her it would. He didn't really hurt over her because she was something to do to get over Leticia. It hurt to see her go but he got over it quickly. Although the sun was not in his eye anymore, he still had the visor down just in case. He finished his cigarette, which he didn't enjoy and flicked it out the window. He eased back in his seat and began to drive at a saner pace. It must have been the thought of Toni crossing his mind that made him calm down. Traffic was heavy so he put on

CD 101.9 and took in some light jazz. Songs that
played reminded him of his wife when they first
met. She was talkative but not to a fault. He liked
her bluntness and personality. She was a fire-
cracker and the best he ever had in bed by all
means. *Where did that woman go,* he often thought.
Money sure does change people. He couldn't understand it. But it was his father who knew his
son was about to strike it rich and it was his father who never cared for his wife. He saw something in her eyes that Pierre had yet to see and he
urged him to make her sign a prenup. Pierre
couldn't understand why when he was only making $70,000 a year at the time but his father made
him do it with urgency. He didn't like city
women, said they were too conniving, too slick
and definitely too fast for his son whom he knew
was a good man like himself, a classy southern
gentleman. He said she had wandering eyes and
was easily distracted and back in his day that was a
sign of an unfaithful woman or a woman that can
easily be manipulated. His mother loved Leticia.
She said Leticia just needed time to grow and
Pierre knew that, he just didn't have time to play
games with his love and wait around for her to
sleep with all the bad boys, get worn out and hurt
up just to come crawling back to him so he could
clean up her mess. So many memories he had of
his hometown of Georgia, all good ones though
painful ones stuck out like a thorn in a baby's behind. By the time he reached home, it was already
going on 6:00 PM.

* * *

He parked his car and almost jumped out of it before it even stopped. He was perked up again. Thoughts of how his wife talked to him like he wasn't the breadwinner and sole provider of her, like he didn't take her from struggles and hard times and not that he felt she owed him something but she did owe him the respect of not being such a bitch to him when he took care of her and was a good man to her all across the board. With that, he called her name loud and clear when he walked into the house. He stopped when he smelled some kind of cooking coming from the kitchen. He let his nose lead the way as he walked through the French doors and saw his wife cooking, something she hadn't done in many years, in an apron and shiny red heels. She had taken her weave out and her hair was dyed a warm brown. She didn't have on any makeup except lip balm. He hadn't seen her in a week. Her hazel contacts were gone also showing her natural sleepy dark-brown eyes. He looked over to the table and his favorite dessert, homemade apple pie, was on the table. A pitcher of apple martinis were on the table also, along with two glasses. She walked up to her husband with a wooden spoon filled with turkey gravy and onions for him to taste. "How's that?" she asked and smiled as if they had just made sweet love the night before. He looked at her, as he tasted the gravy, which tasted delicious. It reminded him of *back then*. "Tastes nice, what's going on in here?"

"Give me a second," she said and turned down the oven. "Come on let's talk although I know what you have to say," she said.

She poured him a drink and cut him a piece of cake. "Before you say anything, baby, let me just say this. I know I have been such an ungrateful woman. But you need to know that I appreciate everything you have done for me and the life that you have provided for me. It hurts me to know that I hurt you, such a loving man. I just want to apologize for everything, for whatever it is worth," she said, half sincere.

"I appreciate that," Pierre said. Now he was softened, as she had never been this warm to him since he became rich.

"Now I know you want a divorce and I am willing to give it to you."

"What kind of games are you running here? And what happened to your hair?"

"I didn't want you to remember me as a cold weave-wearing witch. I wanted you to remember me as the simple, loving woman you married years ago. So on that note, I'm cooking for you like I used to, my hair is how it used to be, I mixed our *used to be* favorite drink, your favorite shoes . . ." she said, twirling her feet around, "and if it's okay with you, I'd like to make love to you just one last time . . . condoms, of course."

"I don't know about that," he said, as his mind was on Toni.

"It's been a long time for me, Pierre. Please, just one time. If you look in our bedroom, my bags are packed and I am ready to go."

"Where are you going to live?"

"If it's okay with you, I'd like to move into the apartment in the city."

"Which one?"

"The one on Central Park West, since it's paid for."

"I can't let you do that," he said. He had plans on moving Toni to that apartment since it was her dream but first he had to handle his wife.

"Why not?"

"I can't. You can have the other apartment in Soho."

She thought about that apartment. It wasn't nearly as glamorous as the one in Central Park but she knew that once Pierre said no, he meant it and right now she couldn't afford to be picky.

"Fine with me."

But, I knew she came with perks.

"I'll give you something to get you settled but what could you possibly need? You took a hundred grand from me, you have plenty clothes and shoes and accessories. You won't have any rent or anything to pay so what else could you need or want from me?"

"You are worth damn near twenty-five million dollars and you're not even sending me away with a million? What am I suppose to do?"

"You just withdrew a hundred thousand dollars from the account that you didn't even tell me about and you can return half of that shit you charged, that would be an extra fifty thousand. And had we made the children I asked of you, you would have had half of everything but you chose this life *not me*. Therefore I feel no sympathy. You're well off more than a lot of people. You'll be living in a town house that is paid for and furnished, you have clothes and jewelry to last you forever. All you have to do is find a job, *any job*, just to have an income."

"A job? Are you for real?"

"You had a job when I met you, right?"

"Yes and you told me to quit it!"

"No, I told you if you got pregnant you wouldn't have to work, ever."

"I *will* get alimony."

"No . . . you won't, that was part of the pre-nup, remember?"

Lola was livid. Here she was trying to scheme and it was not working. Then she remembered something her mother always told her. *You can catch more bees with honey than you can with shit.*

"You know what? This is not a money thing. I told you, I wanted to go out the same way I came in, Pierre. Dinner will be ready in about a half an hour. Let's just talk about the past, us, the future, the divorce, the good things and let's leave on a pleasant note, that's all I ask."

"That sounds good to me, except for the making love part," he said, thinking about Toni.

"Who is she?" Lola asked, fed up of Pierre being so adamant.

"There is no *she*," he said, changing the subject.

"Tracy told me some time ago she saw you with a woman. So who is she?"

"A friend that I don't even see anymore. There isn't anyone in my life right now." He was really surprised that Tracy told.

"I don't expect you to tell me the truth. But what does it matter now, anyway? It's over between us," Lola said and forced tears. Hating to see a woman cry, he got up and sat next to her and comforted her. Her hair smelled like VO5 like back in the day and she was wearing his favorite body spray by Gap. He fought off the old feeling that tried to resurface from under the pain and continued hugging her. She pulled away. "I better go check the food," she said and ran into the kitchen, not the least bit hurt, just pissed that her plan wasn't working. She didn't even want to sleep with him really, just another plan to make him weak and buy herself some time, hoping to soften him up. She checked the turkey and had a revelation that maybe she should poison him then dismissed that thought. She'd be a prime suspect that would eventually get found out. Jail wasn't her theme. She sucked her teeth and grew angry then put a sad look on her face and forced tears when Pierre came in and asked was she okay.

Thursday was Toni's favorite day of the week for many reasons. One was that it was her Friday since she only worked four days a week, two it was payday, and three it brought such an adrenaline rush to her. Today she was going out with coworkers, something she rarely did. But she was opening up, feeling good and she was in love. She hadn't spoken to Preston in days, only briefly as he had been busy and she was fine with that, she was still a woman that needed her space. Besides she had a job and a book to write. Laura, the office manager, a short redhead with freckles who drank like a fish was coming toward Toni grinning from ear to ear. Toni smiled and shook her head know-ing Laura was going to say something funny. "What are you laughing at already?"

"Nothing, what's going on boss lady?"

"Nothing, you all ready to go get shitfaced?" Laura announced.

"I am!" a coworker named Jerri yelled out then came from out of his cubicle.

"This place has no law or governing," Toni said and chuckled.

"You know damn well you get shitfaced at home, I know your type, all demure at the office and you're probably an animal outside!" a tiny blonde named Heather said as she continued to type something.

"I get down, I do," Toni admitted.

"Well then let's do it, today is Thursday!" Laura yelled.

"What a fine example for us to follow," a sister named Tamisha said. "Hey you," Toni said, ac-knowledging her.

"Hey Toni! Come on, we need to get to this place before it gets really packed, besides it's not often that Miz Toni hangs with us. We need to take advantage of it before she becomes a million-aire and forgets about us."

"I agree, let's go. How far is this place?" Jerri asked, grabbing his wallet from out of his drawer.

"Not far, we can walk a good ten blocks," Laura said.

"Walk? You are crazy, ah-ah," Tamisha said as the small office of people gathered at the front door.

"It's a beautiful eighty-four-degree day you

lazy black woman! Damn, ya'll are lazy!" Laura said. Everyone laughed hard because Laura had a black husband and three beautiful mixed children so no one took offense as she did this often.

"Your mother-in-law." Tamisha snapped.

"That bitch too, now let's walk dammit, office is officially closed!"

19

Green lights garlanded the lounge area with plants on every table. The staff dressed in exotic greens and browns, every drink was named after an animal or connected to wildlife in some way. Toni's drink of choice was called tequila tigress and she was working on her fifth one and talking up a storm as her coworkers enjoyed her jokes. They never saw this side of her and although she had a warm personality, she always kept to herself and didn't mingle after hours. She was always rushing home. "So wait, right, so the little boy comes home and says *Mommy, Mommy why do the kids at school call me werewolf* to which the mother replies, shut up and *comb your face!*" Toni said and laughed so hard she began to choke. Her corner of the lounge area was rowdy. Her party of six was drunk and having a good time.

"Where do you get this shit from?" Laura said, wiping her eyes. Toni shrugged her shoulders and continued to laugh.

"Aw man, I need some water, I'll be back," Toni said and got up to walk. She was wobbling and her vision was blurry but she didn't care because everyone in there felt the same way if not worse. She tried to sit on the bar stool and slid off and was caught by female hands.

"Dang girl you okay?" the woman asked, picking Toni up.

"I'm fine, well I'm drunk but thank you," Toni said and laughed. She was too embarrassed to look at the woman that helped her up or the surrounding patrons. "Let me get a bottle of water," she asked the bartender, who slid it down the bar to her free of charge. She winked and turned to walk back to her party.

"Miss City?" Tracy said. Toni stared at the tall woman that was smiling so hard Toni could see her wisdom teeth.

"Miss City . . . whatchyou doin' in here all drunk?" Tracy said and squeezed Toni tight and that's when it registered in Toni whom she was looking at.

"Tracy!" Toni yelled as they squeezed and rocked back and forth, upsetting other patrons who were trying to get to the bar. They continued to hug as they moved over.

"Tracy, what are you doing up here in the Big Apple?"

Tracy grabbed Toni's hand and pulled her over to her table to introduce her to her party.

"Y'all this is my friend Toni who I said I been trying to find since she left Virginia about ten years ago!"

"Hello," "Nice to meet you," and "Hi," came

from the guests. Toni waved, smiling hard at Tracy. She hugged her again. "What is up with you, girl?" Tracy asked.

Toni shrugged her shoulders and smiled harder. Tracy laughed and they hugged again. "I'm over here with my coworkers; let me introduce you. How have you been, Tracy!"

"So you're married to a sports agent? It figures with your long ass. You have on makeup and heels?" Toni said, looking her old friend up and down.

"Look at you all dolled up, you looks good too Miss City!"

"So do you Miss Country!"

"So, who is he and what is he doing for you?" Tracy asked.

"His name is Pierre and in a nutshell he is so good to me. He takes good care of my heart."

"Uh-oh,that negro sounds broke. Any time a woman says that that means that bastard is ugly and/or broke."

Toni cracked up. "No, he is handsome, makes a good living, has a beautiful home, and is a gentleman. One setback, though."

"He got a small thang? His breath stank?"

"No, he hasn't given me any and we've been dating almost a year."

"What?"

"Makes me think of Jacque."

"Jacque, dang that's a name I'd like to forget. You know before I graduated that fool became a full-blown homo, right?"

"What?"

"Yeah, he had women trying to kill him, bitches had they brothers and uncles up at the school waiting for him, it was wild."

"Well, that's what he gets for that down-low shit."

"Ya heard."

"So where you living now, Miss Ahmad Rashad?"

"Well, my husband's name is Ricky Shaw and we live in Long Island. He's good to me, Toni, real nice guy, nice family, values, and morals, all that good stuff, it's working out. Sep' fo he want chirren now and I ain't fixin' to give him any right now."

"I feel you, take your time cause *mama's baby, daddy's maybe*."

"Hell yeah, but um, I'm a homebody, don't have to work but I volunteer to help the homeless three times a week and sick kids in the hospitals."

"Yeah that's you, I can see you doing that; you're very kind."

"Well, let's exchange numbers, what are you doing Saturday?" Toni asked.

"Nothing."

"Me and my friend B, you remember B, right?"

"Yes, I never met her but I remember her name. Beatrice, right?"

"Yeah, well me, her, and a friend *of hers* plan on hanging out this weekend. Just a typical girls' night out, you want to come?"

"Sure! I have no friends."

"How about you come spend the night with me on Friday, we can catch up and then we can meet up with them later on Saturday. Is your husband cool with you spending the night out?"

"He will be once he knows I bumped into you. I talk about you all the time, ooh I missed you so much girl!" Tracy said and they hugged again.

"Cool, so I will see you on Friday night, you drive?"

"Yup, you?"

"Nope."

"Damn spoiled city bitch, get a car!"

"I know, I know! Soon." Toni laughed.

He was in full Mr. White mode at the office, running things, making money, doing what he needed to do to keep his lucrative banking business going. He sat at his desk in a zone, wishing he had a picture of Toni to look at since he had been avoiding her since he saw her last Sunday. It was a beautiful day out as it had been for the past couple of weeks, bright sun, clear blue skies, lovers meeting for the first time in spring or happy to be out from the cold. He spun around in his large gray chair and looked out the window while chewing on a pencil thinking about how he messed up big-time by letting Lola's conniving ass talk him into sleeping with her again. He felt guilty because it was good. He hadn't touched her in a very long time, almost a year or so. It had been three months before he met Toni that he stopped having intercourse with his wife. But somehow he managed to sleep with her and have mind-blowing sex, Lola doing things she used to do and things she probably just learned or always knew but tried to be too civilized in bed. He didn't know, he was just happy that he didn't get too drunk as to not use a condom. He couldn't be that careless. He even made sure there were no holes and that he threw them out himself so that Lola wouldn't do something crazy like take it to the fertility clinic or something. His main issue was that he slept with Lola—*his wife*—and still hadn't told Toni a thing. He broke his pencil at the thought and stood up, looked at his watch, then smoothed the creases out of his silk pants with his hands. He couldn't avoid Toni forever. He just needed to fix this thing with Lola. Half of her things weren't even packed. She hadn't moved out the next day as planned. She was in the house, cooking, cleaning, and definitely doing what needed to be done. Getting rid of Lola was no easy task by all means. She was adamant in not leaving, half the reasons were financial and the other half had to be love. No one could perform that good he concluded and if so, that's one sick person. He kissed Lola, went down on her, made passionate love to her, he missed her, and he felt guilty but not confused. He knew where he wanted to be—with Toni. He thought about his age, his future, and his life. Would Toni change too once she found out about his riches? He had a lot to lose. Lola wasn't that bad, he thought. No, you can't let Toni down. You'd never be able to think straight if you broke her heart. Preston needed time to think. He couldn't face Toni unless he had his facts straight. His cell phone vibrated, it was Toni—*again*, and this time she left a message. She was probably worried as he had his assistant screen his calls, he hadn't been in his New York City apartment all week, and now he wasn't answering his cellular phone. He hadn't spoken to her since Tuesday, today was Friday. He pressed one and it prompted him straight to his voice mail.

Hi, Pierre, um . . . I . . . hope you're okay, it's unlike you to not call or return my calls. Are you okay? Was it the breakfast? Hope you're not in the hospital sick, which I doubt [chuckle]. *Um okay so I guess you'll call me when you get the chance. I truly hope that you are safe first and foremost and if you are, I'm gonna kick your ass! Bye baby."* Her innocence and concern for his well-being before accusing him of wrongdoing made his stomach turn. He grabbed his suit jacket and walked out to get some air. "Ann, I probably won't be back, send all calls to my voice mail and you know who's allowed to call me on my mobile," he said to his sixty-year-old assistant on his way out.

"You betchya!" she said and continued talking on the phone.

Toni left the message while Tracy took a shower. She sat down on her bed and wondered what was going on. It was so unlike him to not call her. She picked up the phone and called him again, this time he picked up. "Preston, where the hell have you been?"

"Toni, baby, I have been catching up on all of this work, I've been sleeping at the office, I've been sick, I've been tired, I've been missing you, baby, can I see you today?" he said, trying his hand. Toni was not going for it.

"No! What do you take me for, huh?"

"Not a fool, I can tell you that. You don't believe me or something?"

"I don't know what to believe, I'm starting to think you're gay, if you ask me."

"What?"

"You heard me. You eat a nice pussy, Pierre, you do. But I need more. You have not touched me the way I need you to and I'm starting to get really annoyed."

"Now that's not fair, Toni, just because I am a gentleman that wants to take things slow I have to be gay?"

"You take things any slower and you're going to wind up back in your momma's womb! The hell? It's been almost a year! I expected six months. I mean, that's what I gave myself to get to know you. But a year? Either you're gay or you have a small dick!"

"Ouch, Toni."

"Ouch, Pierre for not calling me and having me worried about you. Let me make something clear to you. If you have any plans on pulling the okey-dokey trust me you will lose me. I have no problem pulling a Houdini."

"So I guess what your friend said is true, you're a wild woman, or used to be. Anything else I need to know?"

"What is wrong with you?" Toni asked.

Pierre was desperately trying to turn things

around but it wasn't working. "Nothing is wrong with me, when can I see you?"

"Since when do you start asking when can you see me, Pierre?"

"How about Saturday night?"

"I'm busy."

"Tonight then."

"I'm busy."

"How about you call me when you're not busy then," he said.

"Yeah, I'll do just that," Toni said and slammed down the phone. *Who the hell did he think he is? Okay, I see I have to let a little bit of the old Toni come out to play. You can't be a woman these days without some nigga bringing out the masculine side of you, which I have more of than I have feminine traits. Okay, all right, he wanna act like that?* Toni said out loud to herself pacing around, then she stopped.

Why are you getting yourself so uptight, Toni? Is it that serious? No, chill out girl, she said out loud again then began laughing to herself.

"Girl you trippin' off sherm or something?" Tracy said, standing tall with a towel wrapped around her watching her friend talk to herself.

"No, I was just thinking about something," Toni said, fixing her face. She walked past Tracy and smiled. "I am so happy that we bumped heads again!"

"Me too Toni, and your place is really nice, not that I expected different."

"Thank you but I'm sure this place can fit inside your house!"

"Naw, my place ain't all big and dramatic. I

like it that way. No need for all those rooms and stuff. We just have four bedrooms, two showers, an enormous backyard, porch, and four-car garage um . . . oh we have a kitchen and a half, an in-ground pool too."

"Dayum you living large and in charge honey. When I finish my book and Terry McMillan gets ahold of it, I'll be large and in charge too."

"Let me see some of your book!" Tracy said excitedly.

"Did you read the first one?"

"Yes I read it and whenever I tried to e-mail you or find you with the information on the back of the book it wouldn't go through! You know I'm not a reader I just read it on the bus one day and I liked it a lot, Toni. That shit was juicy as hayull!"

"Thank you, thank you. Too bad more people didn't feel that way because it flopped."

"That is all right. If you love doing it then keep doing it for you. That's when shit comes out right. So let me see this one here you got," Tracy said, taking a seat in Toni's working chair.

"Damn this chair feels good."

"His name is Idris, Idris Elba."

"You are so sick." Tracy laughed.

"Go on and read, I'm going to make some phone calls, you hungry?"

"Yeah, what you got? You don't have to go out of your way to cook or anything for me, it's Friday night."

"I have leftover chicken parmigiana."

"Oh okay, do yo thang then."

"And salad?"

"Yes, ma'am."

"Okay, coming right up," she said, snatching up her cordless to call B on the way to the kitchen.

Toni and Tracy got dressed while talking and laughing like teenagers. Toni's mind was on Preston as she turned from side to side, making sure her slacks were fitting her the way they should. Today she wore her hair in a choppy pixie, with sterling silver hoop earrings and donned all black with a short chocolate-brown leather jacket with a small Louis Vuitton fanny pack around her waist that Preston had bought for her. Whenever she mentioned something she liked or whenever he saw her staring at something too hard, he always managed to get it for her. Tracy was popping her gum country-girl style and sliding her feet into a pair of pale pea-green shoe boots with a kitten heel. "You know kitten heels is not for big feet right?" Toni joked.

"Yo daddy begs to differ," Tracy said not looking up but still squeezing her feet into her boots. Toni threw a pillow at her and walked into the kitchen to fix a drink. "Tracy! You want wine of something stronger?" Toni yelled out.

"Whatever you dranking is cool with me!" Tracy yelled back.

Toni looked at her barely-touched bar and decided on Alizé. "Haven't had this in a while," she mumbled and poured the Alizé into ice-filled goblets. On her way to her bedroom to bring Tracy her drink, Tracy met her halfway and took the glass, sipping it thirstily before saying something. "Doesn't this remind you of college when we used to prepare to go out?"

"I was just thinking that."

"So . . . whatever happened to that guy you were in love with?"

"Which one?" Toni laughed.

"You know, *the one*," Tracy said.

"Quentin?"

"Yeah, was that his name? The one that you left at home."

"He calls from time to time. I have his number. Tracy, can I confide in you about something?"

"You know you can, girl, what's on your mind."

"Well, you know that you are the only person I have ever told about the miscarriage and everything relating to Quentin, right?"

"Yeah."

"Well, it baffled me to find out that Beatrice knew about it. I never told her anything."

"So how does she know?"

"I don't know! One day she asked me about it and I denied it. But it's been on my mind for a while now and I need to know what she knows and how much she knows."

"So ask her!"

"I rather ask him. But how do you think . . . I mean, you know, how could she know?"

"Well, either Quentin told her or someone else."

"Like who? Only Mo knew and they didn't even talk so it had to be Quentin, my thing was why would he tell her those things?"

"Girl, I think you need to ask him then."

"I guess, but a part of me doesn't want to hear anything that might hurt me, you know?"

"Yeah, I know but I'm sure it's nothing as bad as you think it could be."

"I hope not." *'Cause B has been acting real funky lately.*

Beatrice and Lola were in Lola's black two-door coupe, driving to Queens to meet up with Toni and Tracy at a place called Jugernauts that Lola insisted was the best place for them to meet up. She claimed the atmosphere was perfect for socializing with girlfriends while listening to good music. She said the food was okay but the drinks made up for it. As she rambled on her Zagat opinion, Beatrice rode shotgun, thinking about her lifestyle with Stephen. She hated to be riding shotgun not being able to floss. With Marcus, he seemed so apprehensive with her and his generosity. Only on two occasions he had given her $300 that barely covered her rent, which had been raised to $750. She battled with thoughts of calling Stephen mainly because she knew Toni would have something to say. Toni, who had been jaded for some time had finally picked a winner. Or a winner picked her. Beatrice was relentless in either finding someone better or going back to Stephen. Marcus had her heart but he wasn't willing to provide for her the way she was used to and he didn't seem to care that she was upset about it, which made her want him more, as crazy as it sounded.

"Do you hear me?" Lola said tapping, B on the knee.

"Yeah."

"Well then, answer the question."

"Oh, what was the question?"

"What is on your mind?"

"Nothing, well my mother," she lied.

"Oh . . . how is she?"

"Fine I guess, I need to visit her soon."

"At least yours is still alive."

"On the outside," B mumbled.

"I hear that," Lola replied.

They pulled up to Jugernauts and from what B could see it was fancy, high-class, and bourgeois. Beatrice hoped she had enough money on her credit card or debit card to fancy such a place. She pulled out her cell phone and called Chase bank. "Are you calling your friend?" Lola asked.

"Um-hmm," Beatrice lied. The automated system informed her that she had $432.45 in her account. That would be good for tonight. She knew she'd spend probably more than half of that tonight and would only have about $100 to spare her for another two weeks. *This can't be life*, she thought as she sat at the table and waited for Toni and her college buddy.

"So, what is Toni like, do I need a warning?" Lola said.

"No, Toni is cool. A bit opinionated but cool."

"Oh okay, is she like ghetto or you know?"

"She's cool, now her college buddy I never

met, but they were very close and she just bumped into her the other day so she is bringing her."

"Oh okay."

"I'm here!" Toni said feeling bubbly off of the Alizé. She hugged Beatrice from behind around her neck as Tracy stood smiling, anticipating meeting Toni's best friend.

"Hey you finally made it, what took you guys so long, hi I'm B, nice to meet you finally!" Beatrice said warmly to Tracy.

"Same here, I heard so much about you I feel like I know you!"

Lola turned around after she heard the voices and deemed them to be warm. "This is my girl Lola," Beatrice said.

"Lola! Oh shit, Lola, this here is my cousin!" Tracy yelled.

"You guys are related?" Toni asked.

"Hell yeah, what is up, L?"

"Oh my god!" Lola said scooting out of the booth to hug her cousin. "This is your college buddy?"

"Yes! Would you look at that? Who would have thunk it, well let's sit down and talk!"

Tracy said. Lola and Tracy sat opposite Toni and Beatrice.

"Now this is a coincidence. How cool is this?" Beatrice said.

"So are you guys play cousins or fo' real?" Toni asked.

"Toni, this is my cousin from Penn State," Tracy said.

"Get out of here!"

"And I'm so sorry about Jacque. I could not believe he was gay!" Lola said.

"Small world huh?" Beatrice said, feeling left out. Nobody acknowledged her sarcasm but kept on talking.

"Well, let's order some drinks and celebrate!" Beatrice attempted again to bring the focus back on her.

"You just need a reason to drink, you lush, what the hell are we celebrating?" Toni said to Beatrice.

"Newfound sisterhood and friendships."

"True, hear hear!" Tracy said.

"You have to order the drinks first," Toni snapped.

"Oh this is going to be a long good night I can see it already!" Lola predicted.

After at least five drinks each from each woman, the girls were ready to go and decided that Toni's apartment would be the best place to crash. Toni invited the girls to sleep over since it was late and they all were too drunk to drive any further.

She blew up her air mattress and handed out blankets and sleep clothes to the girls then they all settled down into her living room where they sipped coffee and smoked joints.

"My husband is probably scratching the walls wanting me to come home," Tracy joked.

"Mine is probably scratching the walls hoping I *don't* come home," Lola said. Beatrice laughed,

Toni sipped her coffee, and Tracy tried not to comment.

"Why, you guys fighting or something?" Toni inquired.

"He used to love me," Lola started. "And if I knew then what I knew now I would have loved him too. I met him when I dropped out of college. I was working in a dentist office in the building that he worked in. I'll be the first to say that I always wanted the finer things in life and he looked as if he could provide it. Time went on and instead of loving him, I was loving what I thought he could give and when it wasn't enough I started to back off and that's when he asked me to marry him. His family never liked me much. His father is a nasty son of a bitch. He would look me dead in my face and not speak and if he did speak it was nasty."

"So you married him anyway," Toni asked.

"Yeah, I wasn't on the market like that. The men shortage was evident so I said, why not, at least he had a stable job. Then he asked me to sign a pre-nup and I'm like for what? You got a good job but it ain't all that. I mean I've seen the pay stubs he was bringing home about twenty-two hundred every two weeks back then."

"That's excellent!" Toni said. "So then what happened?"

"I found out that it was his father that made him do it. See, he has this thing against New York women."

"The typical southern-man mentality," Tracy spoke up.

"Right, so we got hitched at city hall and after a year or two I still saw no change in income, I was young and I wanted out. Then one day he said baby pack ya bags we are moving! We moved to Soho. The place was plush. I knew then he was on to something. He wanted babies now but I said no way, show me the money honey I wanna enjoy this shit! Now he's a multimillionaire and I was so caught up in his love for me I took advantage of him and the money. Now, he doesn't even want me anymore let alone love me and that hurts. I'm torn between just saying fuck it give me the loot and leaving or doing what my heart is saying, which is stay and be a good wife. He would never believe that I had any love for him left. He is done with me," Lola said somberly. Beatrice looked at her.

"Where is that cold bitch that I know? You are always going off about fuck him you are out to get yours. Who is this bitch before me?" Beatrice said.

"Girl you don't have a clue do you," Lola said, dismissing her.

"Well, my man is acting funny," Toni offered.

"How so?" Beatrice asked with her leery eyes still on Lola.

"Well, he pulled a Houdini, something he has never done in the entire time we've been dating, which is almost a year."

"You think it's because of another woman?" Beatrice instigated.

"I have trust issues, as most of us do. I don't know. I just know that I don't like it and told him if he did it again I'd be gone for good, B knows I mean that."

"Well, my husband has found someone, this I know. According to Tracy at least," Lola offered.

"I didn't say he found someone, I just said that I saw him with a woman."

"You also said he was singing about her when you saw him. I wish you would have gotten a good look at her."

"What good would that have done?" Toni said.

"Well, you know women always need to know what the other woman looks like for whatever reason."

"To get our feelings hurt, that's it," Tracy said nonchalantly.

"Whatever, you know how we get down. You should have rolled up on homegirl."

Tracy fanned her cousin off as Beatrice checked out Lola's new "hood lingo." Gone was the snooty bitch with the rich husband.

"He hasn't had sex with me in a year, well, not until the other day, actually we have been like animals for the past few days and I'm beginning to feel bad about using him," Lola said.

"Why? Fuck that. You were married to him and being a housewife is not easy, I'm assuming. You need to get paid for your services rendered," Beatrice said.

"Well, he is a good man, everything that a woman can ask for and sometimes when we have something good, we take it for granted," Lola said.

"Do you think that it's too late to get him back now?" Toni asked.

"Maybe, so now I'm just trying to get what I can from him just in case."

"Has he brought up the divorce again?" Beatrice asked.

"He asked me when I was moving out and I told him soon."

"Damn I thought you guys were going to make it," Tracy said.

"Me too but fuck it, what's done is done."

"Maybe you guys should just take some time and go away or something and really talk things over. This is a marriage, you know," Toni said.

"I don't know what I should do! Our anniversary is coming up. Maybe I should throw a party!"

"That would be nice," Tracy said.

"So you're not going to take the money and run? You're going to try to work it out?" Beatrice asked.

Lola shrugged.

"Why not? All the money in the world ain't gon' cure her loneliness and she fucked up, not him, so she might as well see if she can get him back. Girl let me tell you a few things you can do to win him over," Toni advised. Lola laughed and moved closer to Toni and the two women began scheming on how Lola could get her man back.

"My baby has a birthday coming up but it's too soon to be throwing niggas parties and shit," Toni said, causing laughter. "But Lola you go throw him a party, he is going to be open!"

Giddily Lola moved around on the air mattress. "Okay that's what I'll do! I'm going to win my man back, *my husband* because truth be told I probably won't ever find another man like him that will secure me the way he does. He is rich, he is a gentleman, he is nice, he is sexy as hell, he just has it going on. No baby mamas, no ex-girlfriends that he is in love with and I doubt he has met anyone and fell in love or anything like that. He loves me so much."

"You sure he still does?" Beatrice asked. She stopped Lola's wishful thinking. Lola sat and thought for a second. "All I can do is try. Besides my life will be better if I stayed as opposed to if I left. I thought I'd be good financially if we divorced but after talking to him, I won't be and I'll be damned if some new woman is going to take my husband and live my life!"

"She gon' rock them VVS stones if you let him go!" Toni yelled singing Beyoncé's "Ring the Alarm."

Tracy laughed and Lola gave her a high five. "Shit not my husband, fuck that shit!"

"Go get 'em girl!" Tracy said.

"I am, dammit!" Lola slurred.

"Well Toni, what advice do you have for me oh great one?" Beatrice said.

"Well you need to get rid of both of them cats you're dealing with. Marcus is a joke and Stephen is a jackass."

"That damn Stephen is something else isn't he?" Lola said.

"What is wrong with her man and why y'all in her face talking junk like she aint' here?" Tracy said.

"At least we ain't doing it behind her back! And that is not her man anymore," Lola reasoned.

"That doesn't make it right!" Beatrice spoke up. Everyone simultaneously sipped their drinks. Beatrice was upset. She used to have Lola on her miserable side now all of a sudden Lola wanted to get morals after talking to Toni and Toni now wants to be a housewife after being a mess all of these years. Beatrice made up her mind that she would go back to Marcus full time for now, and if that didn't work out she'd go back to Stephen even if she had to beg her way back and lie about how good it was.

The next morning, Chef Toni made a huge breakfast and the ladies all sat around and rubbed their bellies. "I can go right back to bed but my husband wants me home like yesterday so I need to get on the good foot!" Tracy said.

"Speaking of which let me call mine," Lola said, whipping out her cell phone. Her husband picked up immediately as he had been anticipating her call, he needed to talk to her.

"Hey baby. How you doing? I'm at a friend's house. You want to talk?" she said looking at all three women who were rooting for her. Toni nodded her head as encouragement. "I need to talk to you too. Okay so I'll be seeing you in about two hours, you know . . . traffic and all. Am I rushing home for bad news? . . . Okay, bye," she said and hung up.

"So, what did he say?" Toni asked excitedly.

"Well, he said that it wasn't particularly bad and for me not to worry," Lola said, smiling hard.

"Good, good, you two were made for one another," Tracy said.

"How sweet, let me call mine and make plans for today," Toni said.

"Hey you," Preston said as he stuffed his gym clothes in his bag. *Back-to-back phone calls, I am no player.*

"You sound better than before, how are you, I miss you!" Toni said.

"I miss you too. I guess you're not mad at me anymore?"

"Should I be?"

"I don't ever want you to be mad at me, Toni, ever. I never want to disappoint you or make you feel any kind of way about me. I know once that happens there is no getting the essence back. I'm going to the gym then I have some running around to but I want to see you no matter the time. Wait, let me scratch that, I need to see you, is that all right?" Pierre thought about how long his conversation with Lola would be and then he'd be on his way.

"Yeah that's fine. I got something I want to show you anyway so make sure you find your way to me tonight baby."

I'm going to attack him when he comes over, watch me. Having me wait all this time is he crazy?

"Get 'em tiger!" Lola said giving Toni a high five when she hung up the phone. Beatrice got up and went to the bathroom to contain her jealousy unbeknownst to the other girls.

"So Beatrice says you're really good at you

know, party stuff. Maybe you can help me?" Lola asked.

"Sure, I can do that. Let me get your numbers and we can talk about the themes and budgets and all that good stuff," Toni said.

"I think I'll throw the gathering in Soho, it would be convenient for everyone to get to."

"I agree," Tracy said.

"Oh I'm so excited about this now," Lola said, clasping her hands together.

"As you should be, good men are hard to find. I have me one so I might have to sacrifice some of my Toni laws for this one, he is a true gem," Beatrice heard Toni say as she came out of the bathroom. *Oh shut the hell up about him already!*

"You ready to roll, Lola?" B asked, coming out of the bathroom.

"Yup, ready, Toni, it has been a pleasure meeting you and cuzzo, I'll see you when?"

"I'm around now, I found my homey!" Tracy said.

"Cool, let's do this again," Lola said, giving out hugs and kisses. Toni walked up to B and hugged her. "Don't worry, we gone find you a good man!" Toni said and laughed. Beatrice gave her a phony chuckle and told her she'd talk to her later. Tracy walked out last as Toni held the door open. "Ms. City, I will call you later on, ya' hear?" she said, exaggerating her southern drawl.

"Yes suh, ise be here waiting fo my mayunn!" Toni said. Tracy laughed then blew her a kiss. Toni caught it and threw it back.

"Bye!" they all yelled from the elevator as she closed the door. Toni headed to the kitchen to clean up so she could relax and prepare for Pierre. They were making love tonight so she hoped he was ready.

Pierre was waiting for Lola so that he could talk to her. He had no idea what it was he wanted to say to her, as he was confused. Sex always complicated things, which is why he was responsible enough to abstain for so long. But after the last few days of sleeping with his wife, old feelings surfaced and Preston was now in deep trouble. He had to think hard. Lola was with him before he became rich but Toni was here now. He was in love with Toni but Lola was his wife and had been for years and truth be told he didn't want to throw her to the wolves. He pitied her dependency on him. He had to take things slow with both women now. His thoughts were interrupted by Lola who came in the house singing "Is It Still Good to Ya" By Ashford & Simpson. "Preston?" she yelled out. He was in the den dressed so that as soon as they were done talking, he could run out to see Toni whom he missed passionately.

"Hey, what's up?" Lola asked sweetly. She was making it hard for him.

"Nothing, have a seat," he said, standing until she sat, like a true gentleman. He pulled up a chair and sat directly in front of her with his thoughts running all over the place.

"So, what's on your mind?" Lola smiled as she held his hand.

"I love you, Lola, you are my wife. I am married to you, we took vows before God. I am a good southern man."

Lola smiled and put her head down.

"I don't know what to say or where to start so I decided to let you listen to this song," he said and got up. He went to the CD player and hit play. Lola had never experienced this with him before so she prepared herself.

Marvin Gaye's handsome voice filled the air. *You are my wife, my life, my hopes and dreams, for you to understand what this means, I shall explain.*

Lola's smile faded somewhat as she listened to the song, realizing what the song meant.

"Don't play me some damn song, Preston, like we are teenagers. What are you saying to me, Preston?" she asked.

"I don't know."

"Well this song clearly states how you feel, I mean . . . tell me, talk to me. I don't want to hear a song," she said, her voice cracking.

Pierre took a deep breath and stared into his wife's sleepy brown eyes and for the first time in a while he saw genuine love and pain; again his mind changed. "Come here, Lola," he asked her softly. She obediently rose from her chair and stood in front of him. He tapped his lap for her to sit on. She did.

"You hurt me by not appreciating the things I have done for you, by not holding up your end of the bargain as my wife."

"I know and I am so sorry, what can I do to make this right?"

"Give me time, time to see if this is what I want."

"I can do that but in the meantime, what do I need to do?"

"Appreciate me, feed me, love me, talk to me, be nice to me, be yourself, no more weaves and contacts, no more running the streets."

"What about a baby?"

"No babies, not until I see how far this goes."

"I can dig that."

Pierre tapped her leg softly, signaling for her to get up. She did. He looked down at her as she looked up at him naively. He hugged her tight. "Thank you for another chance, I promise I won't let you down," she said.

His heart hoped she would let him down, because he didn't want to hurt Toni by going back to his wife. He didn't even know why he was giving her a second chance when he really didn't want to.

Lola insisted that they make love before he left but he told her no, that he had things to do and didn't want to get caught up. She didn't argue, she obediently said okay and decided to relax. He would still stay at this Central Park apartment from time to time until things took a turn on its own. Although Lola hated the idea, it was Pierre's call and there wasn't anything she could do. She was just happy to be home and secure.

He checked his watch, it was 5:30 PM. He called Toni to inform her that he was on his way and might be at her house sooner than planned. She

was sounding sexy on the other end and he concluded that she might be sipping on something.
He couldn't turn her sexual advances down anymore. *What am I doing?* he asked himself as he
thought about Lola. *She doesn't love me, or maybe
she does dammit I don't know but I do know how Toni
feels*, he said and sighed hard. He planned on
going to her house to tell her that he was sorry for
how he acted previously and he would never do
it again. But with Lola back in his life, he couldn't
make any promises.

He parked in the garage next to her building
and headed to the lobby. His favorite doorman
was there. "Oh, you came at the right time!"

"Why, what happened?" Pierre asked, smiling.

"Well, your lady there had a houseful of
women and I'm sure they were justa dogging us
out!"

"You kidding me, how many?"

"Oh, about four of 'em all together."

"Is that right?" Pierre said, folding his arms.

"Yup, they came in stumbling drunk then I
guess they were too fired up to drive home so
three of 'em stayed, one of them was her longtime
friend, B. Never saw the other ones before. One
was real tall like a ballplayer, the other one cute
brown woman that had a mean walk on her,
phew!"

"Oh yeah you should have hollered at her!"
Preston joked.

"Yeah and get a heart attack, no thank you, my
wife likes me alive," he joked.

"Well thanks for the warning."
"Anytime, anytime."

Pierre's heart was beating rapidly as he got to
the twenty-second floor. He smelled something
outside of Toni's door. He put his ear to the door
but couldn't hear anything. He knocked loud.
Toni opened the door dressed in a long black silk
nightie with a thigh-high split. Her eyes were low
and her hair was in a pixie, a style he loved on
women but never seen her wear before, she had
on dark gothic-like makeup that made her look
smoky and insatiable. She smiled as he walked in,
leaned over and kissed her cheek. As he entered
the living room he could smell the aroma of jas-
mine. A bottle of Moët was on the table with
small juice bottles in case he chose to mix it; hors
d' oeuvres were on the table as well as strawberries and chocolate syrup. Preston's body grew
rigid at the thought of what Toni planned on
doing to him.

Toni sensed his apprehensiveness. "Have a
seat, relax. I hope you're hungry," she asked.
    "As a matter of fact, I am."
    "Good, I made curry shrimp, wild rice, jerk
chicken, and plantains."
    "Sounds delectable."
    "I was in an exotic mood today," she flirted.
Pierre felt his boxers get tight. Toni disappeared
then came back. "Listen, why don't you relax,
you look so tense baby. Come here," she said and

grabbed his hand. He was nervous. Toni was going to turn him out, *he felt it.* "Come," she said and led him to her huge bathroom. "Soak in there until I come and get you."

Pierre looked over to the tub. It was filled with floating candles and had a glass filled with champagne on the side. Lola had never done anything close to this the twelve years they have known one another.

"I'll leave you to your privacy, there is a double extra large robe and pajamas behind the door," she said and disappeared. Before getting into the water, Pierre took in the sights. Toni had gone out of her way for him and the night was just getting started. "Wow," he said as he slid out of his clothes. The warm bath soothed him immediately. He saw the Epsom salt under the sink and smiled. "Now this is how you treat a man," he reckoned and took a sip of his drink then closed his eyes to savor the moment.

20

Toni lit each candle with care and smiled. She knew Pierre was impressed with what he had seen so far and that is all she wanted, to make him comfortable. She kept the other bottle of Moët on chill and went to the kitchen to retrieve dinner. After making the plates and putting them in the dining room where they would have a candlelight dinner, Toni checked herself in the mirror and decided to change again. The black outfit was for introduction. She chose a pearl-white satin form-fitting teddy that stopped two inches below "the thing" as she liked to say and did the inevitable, she put on heels. *If I bust my ass, ooh! If I bust my ass,* she laughed to herself hysterically thinking about how far she was going as she had never gone to any lengths for any man. She did a sashay up and down her bedroom to see how comfortable she could walk in her heels and decided that she could pull it off. She even changed her makeup to something subtler as opposed to the dark sexy makeup she had on when he first came over. When she was done, she hit the joint one more time, sprayed the air with Febreze, and headed to the bathroom to retrieve her king.

She knocked on the door lightly and when she didn't hear a sound she peeked in. Pierre was handsome, lying peacefully in the tub with an empty glass next to him, eyes shut. He was humming a song that she couldn't quite make out but it sounded sweet. She watched him through the mirror. *I could get used to this.* "Baby, you done?" she asked softly. He opened his eyes slowly and smiled wide upon seeing her face. "I'm ready," he said. She helped him out of the tub and wrapped him in a large fluffy towel and dried him off. There he stood tall as this tiny woman applied lotion over every inch of his frame, finally placing her eyes on his manhood. *Nice,* she thought as she tried to act unimpressed, lotioning his shaft and his balls, he stood there and watched her tenderly. "Here, put these on," she said, handing him his pajamas. She disappeared and came back quickly with a pair of slippers. She put them at his feet and instructed him to meet her in the dining room. *Oh he has such a nice piece,* she thought and smiled extra hard to herself.

Silently they ate while Kenny G made love to their ears in the background with his instrumental strokes. Periodically they'd glance at one another then finally Pierre spoke. "I just noticed that you changed your clothes. You look . . ." he said and shook his head in denial. "Mmm, mmm, mmm, Toni, Toni, Toni, what am I going to do with you?"

"Take good care of me," she responded.

"Who cooked this, *you*?"

"Yes."

"This is delicious. I need to see you cook it to make sure you didn't order it."

Toni laughed softly. "I cooked it with TLC," she said.

He put his head down so that the guilt wouldn't show in his eyes, the eyes that Toni could read so well. "You okay?" she asked unassumingly.

"Fine, I just feel real good. It's been a while since I felt so good around a woman," he said with his head down, still eating.

You don't know what feeling good is yet.

"That's nice to know," she said.

"You have on heels?" he asked, eyebrows raised.

"Yeah, *you like*?" she said and lifted her nicely oiled legs straight up in the air like a gymnast. Pierre burst out laughing. "Lord have mercy!"

Toni cleared the dishes and put them in the dishwasher as Pierre made his way to the candlelit living room. He took the Moët out of the bucket of ice and popped it open and began pouring it into the two available flutes. "This is really nice, Toni, I have never had a woman treat me like this, thank you," he said sincerely as he handed her a glass.

"No . . . thank you, Pierre. You know, until you,

I was pretty much a loner and I put all men in one category, assholes."

Pierre laughed then got serious. He stared into her soulful eyes. She needed him to not be like other men and he wasn't . . . but Lola.

"But as far as I can see, you're nothing like other men or any man that I have ever come across. I want to thank you for being such a gentleman and an honest man. I have never experienced this feeling that I am feeling for you right now at this very moment," she said as her eyes began to tear. Pierre was kicking himself inside. *I can't do this, I have to go, I can't sit here and do this to her.* Toni grabbed his hand. "I love you Pierre and I am here for you. You got me," she said and placed his hand on her heart.

"I will die trying to show you that I am not like other men. I promise you," he said.

As the tears began to fall from her eyes he had to react so he pulled her face to his and kissed her softly on the mouth, no tongue. Then he kissed her forehead, her cheeks, her fingertips, her neck, her eyes, her nose, and her cleavage.

"I want you to take me and take your time, we have all night and it's been a while for me. Lay me down and take your time with me," she said as her eyes pleaded and her heart began to beat faster. "Can you do that for me?" she said, pouting and batting her eyes.

"I can do that," he whispered.

As soon as Toni's head hit the pillow her body got weak and her pussy got moist. Instantly she opened her legs, wanting to skip foreplay. The sight of him and what she knew he was capable of was enough to keep her moist. But Pierre was having none of that. Toe by toe he sucked softly not taking his eyes off her. Toni lay there rubbing her breasts, squeezing them and sucking them. "I like that," he whispered. Toni winked and continued pleasing herself. Slowly her hands traveled down to her private parts. She spread her shaved lips apart. "It's prettier than I imagined it," he said, releasing her feet and diving into her. Pierre teased Toni by blowing softly on her open lips. She could feel herself oozing, he was driving her insane. "Pierre, please, please just taste it a little bit," she begged.

"Like that?" he said, licking her clit soft and quick. Toni jumped at the impact of his tongue touching her.

"Do it again but this time suck on it for a while, please," she begged some more.

"Like this?" he said, sucking on her gently like a Laffy Taffy candy. Toni grabbed a pillow and put it over her face as Pierre sucked on her and licked the insides of her lips clean.

Squirming to get away from him, Toni backed up and winded up sitting on her knees. Pierre made his way toward her, his lips glazed from her love. Softly Toni grabbed his face and sucked herself off of his lips. "You taste so good baby how is it possible that a woman can taste so damn good?"

"Let me see how you taste," she offered, kissing him from his neck to his chest skipping his stomach and going right for this big brown muscle. First Toni stroked it and examined it. "This is very nice what you have here," she said, not waiting for an answer. She held his dick up in the air and began sucking on his balls, tickling them with the tip of her tongue. She heard him take a deep breath. "I haven't sucked a man in so long baby," she informed him.

"You got me now baby, have your way."

"Yes," she said, smiling, and headed back to his testicles, making her way to what she liked to call "the bridge," the small shaft between the testicles and the anus. With his legs up in the air, Toni placed both her lips on the bridge and began sucking it hungrily. "Toni!" he yelled out. *I ain't never have nobody touch that part of me*, Pierre was thinking. *She got my legs up in the air like I'm a bitch.* His pride wanted him to put his legs down but his body said no, let her do what she gotta do. Toni sucked his bridge while stroking his dick with her wet hand. Pierre was going insane grabbing the sheets and punching the bed.

Like a pro, she took the tip of her tongue and went in circles on the head of his dick. She swatted away his hands when he tried to grab her hair. Sucking on the head she let her saliva ooze down his shaft as she began stroking him and lapping it up.

"Toni I want in," he moaned.

She ignored him by continuing her head session. She could hear his toes cracking.

"Toni I'm about to cum," he announced. Toni put her finger up and motioned for him to come.

Pierre sat up and began stroking his dick while

Toni sucked on the head. "Right here baby you stayin'?"

Toni nodded her head yes and kept on sucking soon feeling the explosion of Pierre in her mouth. In one motion she swallowed what was his and rested her head on his lap for a second. Pierre was breathing hard and sweating. "Shit girl, shit!" he said, retrieving a condom from the end table along with the bowl of strawberries. One by one he placed a strawberry in the opening of her pussy, eating it down and sucking the rest out of her. Toni could not hold back her feelings.

His dick got back hard at the thought of what he wanted to do to Toni. "Come here," he demanded, chewing on the last strawberry. Toni laid on her back and spread her legs. Pierre took a finger and inserted it into her. "Damn you are so tight, damn!" He tried to stick in a second finger. Toni flinched. "Baby just give me you please." *Fuck this finger shit.*

Inch by inch he inserted himself in her while sucking on her neck and breast. Toni moaned with each inch he gave. She wrapped her arms around his head and pulled him to her bosom as he began to thrust his way inside of her. Soon he picked his rhythm up and began to grind in her nastily, his back snaking, his ass damn near touching the back of his head as he pumped in and out.

"This pussy is mine," he said as he got out from under her grasp. He held her legs up and began going in circles inside of her watching his dick go in and out. Toni's eyes were rolled up in her head and her eyes were tearing up.

Ayana Ellis

"Mmm hmm that's right baby, let it go, let it out, this dick feel good in you right?"

"Yes baby yes!"

"Turn over," he said, flipping her quickly like a rag doll.

With her back arched as high as it could go, Pierre placed a hand on each of her buttocks and spread her apart. Toni could feel the warmness of his tongue in her anus. She clutched the sheets as he sucked her clit from behind. Then she felt the burning of his tip trying to get inside of her again. "Keep your back arched," he demanded with such fierceness and a slap on the ass as Toni began breaking down. He held her up from underneath with his hand on her stomach and soon had himself inside of her. "Yeah roll that ass around in circles like that. Yeah baby I got you," he moaned as Toni caught his rhythm and made exotic noises throughout the night. *This shit is so good*, Toni was thinking when Pierre picked her up over his head and began eating her pussy in the air. *What the fuck?* She held onto his head as he didn't stumble or wobble. Strongly and sturdily he held her over his head and ate her raw then pulled her down without warning right on to his dick and began pumping. Leaning on the dresser with his hands he pumped up and down as Toni slid off and on making clapping noises. She held him around his neck and started going crazy, coming twice.

"You love me?" Pierre asked as he and Toni lay in a spooning position, his dick not having enough of her yet. He stroked her so slow it was almost as if he wasn't doing anything at all. Toni's pussy was so sensitive to his touch she shivered with each thrust. He kept his big hands on her stomach, his other hand on her forehead pulling her head back so he could kiss her. "You love me baby?" he whispered. Toni began grinding her hips nastily. Pierre let his hand fall from her stomach to her wet pussy where he began softly rubbing her clit as she gyrated slowly. They were making love.

"You so wet baby." He kissed her neck softly and turned her on her stomach where he slowly pulled himself in and out of her as if he was doing chin-ups. "I love you, I love you, I love you," Toni whispered slowly, surely, and seductively. "I love you too baby I do," he said, stroking her to climax. He could feel the explosion on his dick. "You extra wet now," he said, biting his bottom lip. "I need you baby," she purred as he nasty grinded his way to a climax of his own. "Yeah baby I need you too," he responded, collapsing on her small back, breathing heavily into her neck with all thoughts of Lola erased.

21

Today was suddenly so different from the other days. This morning they were different, feelings shifted, hearts were beating faster, more was on the mind, there was no longer you and I as the simple act of receiving pleasure has bonded two human beings emotionally, physically, and mentally. *The morning after* always changed things if not complicating them further. Toni lay there with her back to Pierre as he hugged her around her waist with his lips on her back. He was breathing steady and heavy, sleeping hard. Toni was up pondering, wondering, and thinking of many things, too many things to single out one. Her mind was just churning out thoughts of all sorts, racing against itself. She eased Pierre's hands off of her and slid out of the bed. She looked back at him. His eyes opened briefly. He smiled then slowly his eyes closed back again, his lips still smiling, then slowly the smile faded, his lips parted slightly and he was back asleep again. With that, Toni left the room and headed to her living room. She stood there with her long cream silk robe on and her hands on her hips looking around and decided to start cleaning the table. Her body was aching, she bent over slowly to pick up the empty Moët bottle and half-empty bowl of strawberries. She smiled when she remembered what they had done with the strawberries. She began to throw things out, put things in the dishwasher, wipe down her cherrywood table, vacuum, and play music all while thinking about last night and how incredible Pierre was. She smiled to herself and began to make breakfast.

The smell of bacon and syrup levitated Pierre out of the bed and into the living room where Toni was sitting there waiting for something to finish cooking as she sipped a French vanilla cappuccino, reading the paper and wearing gray sweat shorts and a wife beater. "Hey," he said and walked up to her. She answered him with a smile and put her cheek out for him to kiss. He did and sat next to her. "Food smells good, what are you making?" he said, wrapping his arms around her waist and curling up on the sofa.

"Omelettes, bacon, biscuits, silver-dollar pancakes."

"You say it like, *oh nothing a bowl of cereal*!"

"It's nothing to me, I love to cook," she said and shrugged it off. Thoughts of last night crept into his head and his manhood suddenly began to rise. He moved in closer to her. "As much . . . as I would like to wrap my limbs around you like an octopus, we have run out of all prophylactics, honey," Toni said as Pierre nuzzled her neck.

Pierre moaned and slid his hand up her shirt and began rubbing her braless breasts. Toni relaxed and took her glasses off and closed her eyes. Pierre nibbled at each nipple and rubbed her belly simultaneously. He then moved down to her lower region. Toni's legs automatically spread open like automatic sliding doors. Pierre got on his knees and propped her legs up. Toni's walls began to contract as he slid his thick tongue inside of her. "Mmmm" escaped her throat as he sucked and slurped.

"Guess what, we have one more, it was on the floor by the room," he said and smiled. Toni snatched it from him and put it on him herself. "Let's go!" she said and pushed him on the floor. She ripped his boxers off like an animal and eased herself down on his erection. He put his hands on her hips and began guiding her *his way*. She did what her body told her to do. His eyes were on her as her eyes were closed tightly. She was in pain but she was enjoying it. He could tell by her moans and her wetness. Her body was singing a sweet melody. It was feeling so good to him he hadn't realized how hard she was digging her nails into his neck and chest. Toni was reaching her orgasm, her eyes opened finally and she stared at him intensely, her lips were poked out and she was squinting. Her rhythm became steady and hard like the score in a horror flick when someone was about to die. Her music became louder and more aggressive. He held her stare, her eyes glazed over and turned coal black. She was grinding into him now and pulling her own hair with one hand while keeping her balance by digging her other hand into his neck. They continued the stare down. He held her hips tight keeping her *right there* and met her halfway with his subtle pumps, Toni held her stare even as orgasm reached her and she vacuumed his manhood up into her suction cup. The music her body played was deafening now. Her eyes became glossy as she pumped harder and harder down on him like he was pavement. He was turned on, impressed, intrigued, in awe, and amazed at her ability to keep a poker face while achieving such a torrential orgasm. When the last of her orgasm shifted her into a small five-second seizure, she took a deep breath, contracted her muscles so hard around him he could see her stomach cave in then she shut her eyes peacefully and exhaled.

Damn her lovemaking is like an orchestra, Pierre thought. He stared at her not wanting the sounds of violins, trumpets, harps, and pianos to end. But just like the end of any song, the music softened sweetly and faded out. She opened her eyes and smiled, satisfied like a child who finally got her way after begging a parent to go out and play. She made love with a force that no man could deem as being casual. Even if she verbally expressed a relationship to be casual, her body, her rhythm, her warmth spoke another language. And here he was being just like the men before him. He couldn't do it to her. He had to make a choice no matter who was going to get hurt.

Lola had been keeping in contact with Toni over the weeks as they prepared for Lola's husband's birthday bash. But Lola decided that she wanted it to be an anniversary party instead, so they pushed the party up from November 27th to October 26th. Beatrice was fit to be tied when she learned of the newfound friendship between Toni and Lola. Her attitude showed when Lola and Toni asked for her input while on threeway. "Oh I didn't think you guys remembered me," she said. Toni ignored her and Lola fell right into the trap. "Oh B, you know I didn't forget you, baby, cut it out, now what colors do you think I should decorate and do you think I should hire a stripper?"

"A stripper?" Toni and B said in unison.

"Now that would be hot," Beatrice said.

"Hell no not for an anniversary party, no!" Toni intervened. She could hear Beatrice sucking her teeth.

"Then it's settled. No stripper. Oh Toni, we are no longer doing it at our home because we need more room. I'm expecting at least two hundred people. I'm going to do it at the Roman Candle. My husband is very well liked there. They know him so I already made arrangements for that."

"Oh that's great, that is where I met my baby!" Toni squealed. "And B, did I tell you that he bought me a new bedroom set and a chandelier for my living room? A real crystal one?"

"No," B said.

"That's nice! Those are very expensive," Lola said.

"He is so good to me. It's about time, I've been long overdue, ain't that right Beatrice? And honey when I tell y'all the love making was the most intense shit in the world!"

"You finally got some from him oh goodie!" Lola said, clapping.

"Yes it was all that and then some we can't stop having sex. It's an all-day thing. At his job, at my job, in the car, home, wherever we go, Beatrice can you believe my drought is over girl?"

"Mmm, hmm," was all she said. Toni had long since picked up on Beatrice's shadiness but she was not going to let Beatrice be a killjoy so she ignored her further.

"Okay so next week is the big day, Toni bring your man and Beatrice bring whomever. Have you spoken to my cousin?" Lola asked.

"*Every day*, she'll be bringing her husband and I also told my mom and her husband."

"Wonderful, just wonderful!" Lola squealed.

"Yeah, break out the fucking confetti," Beatrice snarled and hung up.

Pierre's head was spinning, it seemed as if every day Lola had some type of gift or act of kindness for him. One day she was catering to him, the next she was dancing on tables, the next she was buying him chocolates or pulling out wedding photos and honeymoon pictures reminiscing. It was all too much too fast but he understood that she was doing all she could to keep him focused on her when all she was doing was confusing him. He was with Toni for the duration of the week then would go home to Lola some nights. One night she even popped up with a trench coat and heels at his Central Park place. He was thankful that he was there alone although he had just left Toni. So tonight, it was no problem to hang out with Lola as Toni had him tied up for some time. She didn't tell him where she just said she wanted to hang out with him and show him a good time. So he turned down Toni's request to go to a party that a friend of hers was throwing for her husband and told her that he'd be home relaxing and for her to call him when she was done partying. Although she was disappointed, she wasn't mad.

Lola dressed in a rose-pink cashmere halter top and pale pink slacks with the sling backs to match. Her hair was still honey brown in a bob but her bangs were cut straight across. Her lips were colored in "Kissed by a Rose" by Chanel and she happily put on her wedding rings and the necklace Pierre bought for her when he proposed many years ago. She looked beautiful Pierre thought as he watched her glamour herself up in her "dressing room." *She looks the same way she did when I met her.* She caught him watching but pretended not to see him. He was leaning on the threshold of the room watching her watch him. He leaned up and walked into the bedroom sort of looking forward to his night out with Lola. Lola knew how to have a good time. They partied well together. Lola came out of her room singing and headed to her bedroom to help her husband get dressed. He was wearing his favorite color, *beige*, with rose-pink Prada shoes with the belt to match. "Damn you look magnificent," Lola said and winked.

* * *

Stepping out in style as usual, the Whites jumped in Pierre's chauffeur-driven Bentley per Lola's request and hit the town. "Why the Bentley? This is only for special occasions." Pierre said as she poured Louis XIII in his bauble. "Today is special. Today we will celebrate our love, it's our anniversary!" she yelled.

"I know but don't you think we need to be low-key?" he asked. He wasn't too keen on celebrating his anniversary when he had another woman in his life. Or was Lola the other woman?

Toni pulled her show-stopping black dress out of the closet. It wasn't just any black dress. It was backless, had two splits on the sides and the hem stopped at the knee. The front was high cut so she wore long dramatic sparkling aqua-blue chandelier earrings with the shoes to match. She went out and brought a tiny clutch in sparkling silver that would go well with her earrings and shoes. Her hair was in her new pixie cut, resembling Halle Berry's hair in *Swordfish* and her heels were four inches. She felt good and looked good.

"When I see Pierre tonight he is going to go nuts! I will see him *after* the party for the after party," she said mischievously as she grabbed the keys to his BMW that he left for her to drive so she could get around.

Since Lola was out with her husband, Toni told Beatrice she would pick her up. "Mark is bringing me," Beatrice said.

"Oh, okay."

"Is Pierre coming?" B asked as she slid on her all-in-one royal-purple jumpsuit.

"No, I'll meet him at home, he's tired."

"Umph, I bet. He's too tired to accompany you to a party?"

"I guess so," Toni said, biting her tongue. "But anyway you sure Marcus is coming because I have Pierre's car so let me know now before I hit the road."

"You have his car? What? Well, yeah he's coming, that should be him at the door now so I'll meet you there," Beatrice said. *She is driving his Beemer?*

"Okay, bye," Toni sung and headed out the door.

Beatrice and Marcus reached there before Toni so they grabbed a seat at a table near the anniversary cake. Tracy was there as the hostess basically making sure everyone was having a good time, having enough to eat and drink. Lola was going to call Tracy when they were nearby so that she could get everyone into "surprise" position. Tracy walked up to Beatrice and hugged her. "Where's Toni?"

"She should be here any second, she left before I did."

"Oh okay," Tracy said and headed toward a group of people to show them to their seats. The DJ was playing Frankie Beverly and Maze's "Joy and Pain." People were around mingling, drinking, laughing, and talking. Some were talking about business, others were laughing, hysterically. The atmosphere was euphoric. The place was jam-packed. *Damn her husband must be larger than she said he was! There are some ballers up in here, they look like they are ballin' on an entire different level than what I'm used to. Damn!* Beatrice thought as she remembered how she made her way through the Benzes, Rovers, and Lamborghinis to enter the hall. Marcus, whom Beatrice hadn't seen in over two weeks was snuggled up under her, laughing and flirting unaware of the danger he was in. *Humph, yeah he see his competition so now he wants to be all up on me. We'll see if he learns to step his game up tonight or run from the competition like a coward.*

Toni walked in alone, and just as expected, her small dinner dress drew in a crowd of oohs and aahs. Everyone's head was turning causing Marcus and Beatrice to look to see what was happening. Toni walked in looking around and she spotted Tracy first obviously because of her height. They hugged and kissed as Tracy introduced Toni to her even taller husband then pointed to Beatrice and Marcus. Reluctantly Toni walked toward them mainly because she hated Marcus. She could feel Beatrice's uneasiness as Marcus gawked over Toni and how she bloomed and evened out her rough edges. She was elegant as she walked slowly toward them in her heels.

"Beatrice you are wearing that jumpsuit girl!" Toni said, happy to see her best friend. They gave one another air kisses but she could tell B was nervous. Toni decided not to spoil the night by entertaining the past and said, "Good to see you Marcus. You look well."

He smiled warmly and responded, "So do you."

Damn, she is rocking that little black dress. She always was cute in an around the way girl kind of way but my how she's grown over the years, look at that body! And she smells so damn good. I mean wow, I'm impressed.

"Thank you, can I sit here?" Toni asked of a seat next to B. *Look at the backside on her at that? She always had a little fatty but this is just downright ridiculous!* "Phew I need a drink," He said and excused himself from the table.

"Thank you for being cordial," Beatrice said.

"I am learning to just mind my business and not make too many comments on people and what they do. If you're happy then I'm happy."

"I appreciate that. Now, look at this woman over there with that funky green pants suit on," B said and pointed with her head.

"Looks like vomit," Toni said and chuckled.

"What color is that, *barf green*?" B said and they laughed harder. As the women talked and drank and basked in the ambiance of the night, Toni wishing Pierre was on her arm and Beatrice glad that he wasn't, the DJ abruptly stopped spinning records to announce that the "anniversary couple" was in the building. The room was filled with "ssh's" and "Cut the lights off!" throughout. Everyone was huddling together and Toni was thrilled when her mother tapped her from the side and hugged her. "Hey Ma, where were you?" Toni whispered as she waved at Thomas who had gotten closed out of the surprise circle by a bunch of giddy nostalgic women. "I was on the other side by the bar. Hey Beatrice baby."

"Hi Mrs. Wadley," B said, blowing her an air kiss.

Ms. Jolly smiled at B acknowledging her new name.

"T, where's Pierre?" her mother asked looking around.

"Oh, he couldn't make it."

Lola was smiling as they entered the two large steel doors of the Roman Candle. She knew everything was going to go as planned as meticulous as her party planning was. Toni and Tracy were of special assistance and she would thank them tonight on the microphone for giving her the heart-to-heart needed to get her man back and the desire to rekindle her marriage and throw this anniversary party. "Why are the doors closed?" Pierre asked as he pushed it open. It didn't budge. That was a sign for someone on the other end to press the button and unlock it. "This place looks closed. That's strange," he said and looked at his watch.

"It's only 10:00 PM on a Saturday at that. But look at all the cars outside."

"I don't know baby, try it again," Lola said. Pierre pushed the door open.

"Surprise!" his friends and staff alike yelled as confetti dropped down and the DJ started playing Tony! Toni! Toné!'s "Anniversary." Lola grabbed her husband and began dancing and smiling. "Remember this?" she said and tiptoed to kiss him while dancing. Pierre genuinely laughed and was surprised. As he leaned in to kiss Lola, he stopped smiling when he realized who was standing a few feet away from him in mid-clap.

"Honey, it's our anniversary, smile baby!" she said, grabbing his hand and pulling him through the crowd to meet her new friend as cameras flashed.

Toni, Ms. Jolly, and Beatrice stood amongst the crowd of partygoers with their mouths on the ground. The Jaws of Life couldn't move Toni from where she was standing. Beatrice stood next to her friend staring at her, waiting for her to make a move. Her mother folded her arms and Lola, still pulling her husband toward her new friends, stopped to introduce her husband to them. "Baby, you know Tracy, my cousin, and this is Beatrice that I talk about and this is Toni, they all helped me with the planning of the party!" she said happily.

Toni was still standing there with confetti in her hair and her hands clasped together from stopping in mid-clap.

"Pierre?" Toni said with much pain and agony in her words. Tracy looked at her. Lola looked at Toni.

"What's going on? You know my husband?" Lola asked.

"Tell me this is some sick joke or that I am dreaming or having a nightmare as a matter of fact," Toni continued. She felt something weird going on inside of her body. Her legs were getting weak and her speech was stutter filled.

Pierre was looking at Toni straightforward, his eyes never left hers.

"Why didn't you tell me you were married?"

she asked, ignoring the people around her. Right now all she saw was him and her, no one else mattered at this moment.

Lola chuckled nervously. "I'm sorry am I missing something?"

"Yeah like for real," Tracy said.

"This is the man that I talked about I was so in love with. *Your husband*," Toni said.

"What?" Lola said, letting go of Pierre's hand.

"What?" Tracy said, covering her mouth.

"Oh hell no," Beatrice said, folding her arms.

As partygoers stopped at Pierre and Lola's circle to say congratulations, they backed up when they felt the cold that surrounded the small circle of friends. "Wait, wait, wait one damn minute. Pierre is this the woman I saw you with that day?" Tracy asked.

"Yes," he said.

"Pierre, I want an explanation right now," Toni said, eerily low.

"Oh hell yes!" Beatrice said.

"Who the hell is Pierre? Why do you keep calling him Pierre?" Lola asked.

"I don't like Preston, so I call him by his middle name."

"Okay, okay, do we need to take this outside and talk about this further? I need to know right the fuck now what is going on here. I thought you and I were working this shit out and according to her you been having a passion-fucking-filled ball with her putting strawberries up pussies and whatnot. What the hell is going on?" Lola said.

"P, talk to me, tell me something, anything but please just don't sit there quiet and don't you fucking lie to me, either. What the hell is going on?" Toni said, searching Pierre's eyes for an answer. *This was not happening to me. I will not walk away from this and run like I did with Jacque, oh hell no, it's about to be on!*

Toni hauled off and slapped Pierre so hard the crowd dispersed and left the two of them standing in the middle somewhat isolated from everyone else. The DJ even turned the music down some. Toni began to cry against her better judgment, something she had never done for anybody let alone while hundreds of people were present. Her mother rubbed her back. "Pierre are you going to say something?" Ms. Jolly asked, looking at the man she thought was God's gift to her daughter.

"Everything all right?" someone walked up to Lola and said. Lola turned around and walked up the DJ, grabbing the microphone. "May I have everyone's attention please? Due to an unfortunate series of events I am sadly announcing the end of this celebration. Thank you all for coming out but this party is over, no questions please just disperse as quickly and quietly as possible, thank you," she said and headed back to the circle.

Pierre was standing there looking at the hurt and angry faces of four angry women. He had no idea how they all came about, how Tracy knew Toni and how Toni knew Lola. Then it clicked. Beatrice and Lola were friends and Beatrice and

Toni were friends. "I sat there night after night, telling your wife how to win you back," Toni mumbled, walking closer to Pierre. Her tears were falling hard and fast. Pierre stood strong and was willing to accept whatever was about to come his way. He hated that he broke a woman's heart, especially Toni. "I sat there and told her how to fuck you, how to cook for you, what to wear for you, when to give you space, when to comfort you. I told your wife how to get you back. Can you believe this shit? Can you?" *Damn she would never believe me if I said I was sorry. How could she understand my predicament? How would she ever know how much I love her and how would she ever believe that I am not like other men? I think I ruined her for good.*

"I opened up my heart to you," she said, walking closer. He put his head down.

"The first night we made love. I can't even put it in words how special that was for me. You ruined that for me. Five years and you just shit on me like this? Five years I kept my pussy to myself and you come into my life and do this shit to me? The first time we made love Pierre, you told me you needed me and that you loved me. I believed you. Damnit I believed you," she said, letting out a loud wail. Beatrice ran to her side and hushed her. Toni broke free with her face red and tear-streaked. "Get off of me," she snarled.

"What I want to know is when the hell were you going to tell me that you had someone else? All this talk about us getting back together and working it out and you had someone behind my back?" Lola yelled.

"Young man what I need to know is why would you do something so low," Ms. Jolly said, stepping between her daughter and Lola. "My Toni doesn't deserve this. No woman does, especially not my child."

"Ms. Jolly, I never meant for this to happen. I just need time to get my head together so that I could explain."

"You know her mother?" Lola yelled.

"He was at my wedding," Ms. Jolly said.

"Just give me a minute to explain myself," Pierre said.

"You mean so that you can think of a lie?" Lola yelled.

Toni stepped closer, this time she was right in his face, looking up at him as he looked down at her adoringly and painfully sorry. He wanted to hug her, kiss her, and beg her to understand.

She didn't say anything; she just stared through him with those dark cold eyes. He was feeling her loudness through her silence. Her pain was shooting through his heart. He was hurting for her. "Here are the keys to your car," she said, handing them to him. She grabbed his hand and dropped the keys in it.

"She was driving your car? How long have you two been seeing one another?" an out-of-control Lola asked.

"A year," Toni answered. Tracy put her arms around Lola.

Beatrice knew that Toni had so much to say but the words just wouldn't form in her mouth. Beatrice had been there years ago, in the same situation at an office party. She rubbed her friend's back as if that would make the words come out just as Toni did to her years ago. Toni just stood there feeling vulnerable, crying pitifully. That got Beatrice upset because she had never seen Toni cry or saw any traces of crying on her friend's face. Pierre wanted so bad to hold her and tell her what has been going on inside but he knew it was too late. He had made Toni cry, something he is sure no man has ever done. Lola stood there sobbing as Tracy let her go and walked over to Toni. She felt more sympathy for Toni because she knew of her struggles where as Lola had always been a gold digger and although Lola may have sincerely tried to turn her ways around it was catching up to her now. Tracy put her arms over Toni's shoulder and squeezed. "Pierre, I can't believe that you are this kind of person. I thought better of you as a man and just as a person. You have no idea the mess you made," Tracy said.

"I am ready to go home," Lola sobbed.

"Let this man say something. He standing there all night, quiet as if this isn't his doings, say something for yourself young man. Don't let him go so easy," Ms. Jolly demanded.

Pierre felt as if he had a cement brick on his tongue and a knife piercing his heart as he stared around the room to see who was there. "No need in being embarrassed now Preston, Pierre, *whatever* your name is. Toni let's go, there is nothing here for you," Beatrice said.

"Toni wait!" Pierre said. He finally moved up to Toni and grabbed her hands. She jerked them away and gave him the most evil look that he had ever seen come from a person, so he shoved his in his pockets, took them out, shoved them in again then settled on leaving them out again. "Toni I am sorry you had to find out this way about everything but you made it so hard for me to tell you."

"You could have told me the day you met me!" she yelled very loudly and unlike her normal laid-back self. It took everyone by surprise. "You had more than enough time to tell me dammit, why me? Why did you have to bring this shit to me? I am so tired of men being so damn inconsiderate at a woman's expense. Why do I have to continue to pay for your bullshit?" she yelled. Toni was losing her cool.

"Toni, calm down," Beatrice said.

"No, I'm not calming down dammit fuck this shit. I'm tired of being so strong. I'm tired of hiding this pain that sits right here," she said, touching her heart. "The pain that *you said* you would *die* trying to take from me. Remember that?" she asked Pierre of the night they made love for the first time and she expressed her fears and he told her what a good man he was and how he'd die trying to change her views on men. Lola was furious, she had no idea that he was in love with someone else, and so deep. She temporarily lost track of the fact that this was her husband and another woman as she listened to the pain Toni expressed and the genuine sorrow that her husband possessed for this woman.

"I waited to have sex with you because I wanted to get my divorce first. I didn't expect this to happen," he said.

"Am I supposed to feel better now? You could have told me from the gate that you were getting a divorce and left it up to me. Damn why me?" Toni was stomping her foot and punching her fist into her open hand. Marcus stood on the side holding Beatrice around the waist.

"I want you to understand what happened and *how* it happened. Please Toni just let me explain, give me a chance before you judge me," he pleaded.

"You lie to me, tell me you're tired that you don't want to come out, yet you come out to celebrate your anniversary nonetheless with your wife and you want me to let you explain? I outta smack the shit out of you again," she said, seething. Lola stepped in and stood in front of Toni putting her back in her face.

"I am your wife! And you're standing here pleading your case to some woman you met only a year ago? We have been together and married thirteen years and you're out here making an ass out of yourself over some other bitch?" Lola said, fuming.

Toni tapped Lola on the shoulder. "Lola I understand you are upset. I really do. But do not call me out of my name like I purposely had an affair with your husband. And don't call me out my name like I won't bust your ass!"

Lola gave Toni a look that said try me but at the same time said I apologize. It was Toni's call. Toni turned her head back to Pierre who was now looking at his wife.

"Lola I loved you so much but when we broke up I was not seeing anyone for a long time and a year ago, I met Toni, in this very room right by that bar over there. I have never loved a woman the way that I loved Toni and I am so sorry that this had to happen, I will make it up to you Toni. I want to be with you," he said, easing past Lola to get to Toni.

Everyone gasped. Lola walked up to her husband and attacked him, yelling and screaming. She was punching his back and kicking him.

"Why did you do that, you just don't get it! You think saying that is going to make me feel better? You fucked-up Pierre. You fucked up," Toni said and walked away. Pierre followed behind her.

"You can't just do my cousin like that!" Tracy said.

"Tracy, stay out of this!" Pierre yelled.

"Who the hell do you think you are?" Lola yelled running behind him. Tracy grabbed Lola. "Don't make an ass out yourself Lola, just let it ride right now," she instructed.

Ms. Jolly jogged ahead and stopped Pierre with her tiny hands so that Toni could get away. "Son, I think you have done enough damage for the night. Let my daughter go on about her business," she said in a no-nonsense tone that Pierre had no choice but to abide by especially with Thomas standing guard next to her.

"Ms. Jolly, I swear to you I didn't mean for this to happen. Will someone let me explain?" Pierre pleaded, desperately looking around for sympathy.

"I have heard enough bullshit in my own personal past, I don't need to hear yours," she said and turned her back. Beatrice rolled her eyes and grabbed Marcus's arm and Tracy stood outside holding Toni. Lola was crying on the side by herself.

Beatrice and Marcus drove home in silence after dropping Toni off. Beatrice had secretly hoped for Toni and Pierre's affair to end but she didn't expect for it to end so dramatically and she began to feel guilty at being jealous of her best friend's happiness. She didn't want it to end totally but she just wished that her friend wasn't so lucky, as twisted as it may seem. Marcus was going off a mile a minute about how he couldn't believe what had happened and how good Toni looked and how good his ex-girlfriend thought her book *Behind Her Smile* was. Beatrice was hearing none of it as she thought about how heartbroken her friend was but most importantly she thought about how Toni could no longer throw stones at her glass house.

A half an hour away sitting in a dimly-lit living room crying her heart out to God, Toni sat there wiping the tears away that seemed to come nonstop. She wiped and wiped and her head began to pound more and more. At this moment she couldn't even comprehend what had happened to her. She just needed for her head to stop hurting so she walked into her bedroom and lifted the sterling silver top off of the tiny Taj Mahal–shaped jar and pulled out a $20 sack of purple haze. She rolled the fattest joint that she had ever rolled in her life and drew a bath. As the water filled, Toni began to undress slowly because of the pain in her head and heart. Every inch she moved felt like it would make her head burst. Naked, pulling on her joint, Toni walked into her kitchen and poured herself a glass of water and took two Tylenols. She took a deep breath and pressed the bridge of her nose tightly to release some of the tension in her head while looking toward the ceiling. Slowly, she walked to the bathroom and saw that her tub was calling her name. She poured vanilla sugar bubble bath into the tub and foot by foot she entered the tub. The water was hot but Toni didn't care. No pain was worse than the one she was feeling inside of her right now. She held her cordless phone next to her, as she was sure someone would be calling her before night's end. She glanced at her clock; 1:13 AM *Yup, someone was calling me tonight.* She closed her eyes and took in as much yellow smoke and peace as she could until her first phone call came in.

"I shoulda took your ass to the bank, I should have been cheated on you but nooooooo here I am being a good wife, a good woman to you. I can't believe this shit!" Lola yelled all the way home as the chauffeur peeked through his rearview mirror periodically. "And if cheating on me is not good enough what you do? You go and you tell this woman, *in my face* that you love her and not me? What were you thinking?"

"The truth," Pierre said. Lola stared at him

blankly. "You know something Pierre, nothing good is going to come to you after this."

"Lola, it's *been* over for us. You think I could ever trust you after knowing that you only stayed with me because I struck it rich. You think I'm dumb? But no I didn't care because I loved you so much. And bigger than that . . ." he said, looking her dead in the eyes, "You think I don't know about you and Stephen?"

"Stephen? Who the hell is Stephen?"

"You think I don't know about Stephen? I know all about you and him and his woman Brandy, the little tryst you all had. Why do you think he and I don't talk anymore?" *How the hell did he find out?*

"Bet you're wondering how I know huh? Let's just put it like this, men are worse than women when it comes to jealousy and running their mouth and it got back to me sweety but again, I ignored it cause you're my wife. I chose him over your bullshit, I cut him off instead of you. I blamed myself for you stepping out, I blamed myself for all your shortcomings until I took the time to analyze shit and then I came to the conclusion that I was being played."

Shut your ole naive country ass up! You think this is the first time I played you out? You just don't know. . . .

"So you can kill that whole I've-been-faithful-to-you act. You're lucky I didn't tell your friend Beatrice that you were the reason behind her and Stephen's breakup and the way he treated her half the damn time. You used to tell him so many things, untrue things about her, just dogging her so he could dog her too."

Lola sat there in shock.

"Now when we get home I just want to rest and then in the morning it is official. I am calling my lawyer and we are getting a divorce. I will give you two million dollars to make you go away Lola, I want nothing more to do with you."

"You think you can just pay me off, you think that you can just throw money at me and make me go away?" Lola screamed.

Pierre simply answered, "Yes."

Pierre sat in his den in the dark sipping a hot tea with shots of brandy in it. All he could think about was the look on Toni's face and the sound of her heart hitting the floor as he walked in with Lola smiling like the proud husband he once was just to appease Lola when in fact he had Toni on his mind all night. Every time he looked at the phone he thought about calling her, but if he knew Toni well enough he knew that only a miracle would allow him to talk to her again so he did the next best thing, he called Beatrice.

"You still got it . . ." Beatrice purred to Marcus as he stood her up and made love to her from behind. "Yeah, you like that?" he asked.

Damn his bedroom talk is getting wack though, if he'd just shut up and do what he has to do, but nevertheless, Beatrice answered. "Mmm hmm."

"I know you do, I know you do, you ain't going nowhere right?"

"No."

"No who, say it! No who?"

"No El Capitan" Beatrice said. *Who the hell did he think he was? He barely has Spanish in him. His grandfather's mother was half-Spanish, that's it. I tell ya, you give a nigga good hair and they don't know how to act. El Capitan, I oughta kick his ass.*

"Say it like you mean it!" he yelled and banged her harder, so she did.

Upon reaching his climax, Marcus pulled out of her like something bit him and began to jerk his way to orgasm. Beatrice ran for the phone that continued to ring, leaving Marcus behind her panting and breathing heavily.

"Hello?" she asked, out of breath.

She heard the low baritone voice on the other end asking for her. "Who is this?"

"This is Pierre."

"Pierre? What do *you* want?"

"Beatrice. Look I know everyone is mad at me but I need to explain."

"No, no you do not need to explain anything, especially to me because I do not want to hear it. Lola should have took your ass to the cleaners like she planned because you're trifling, just like the rest of them!" she yelled.

Guess there is a reason why Lola slept with your man you're a real tacky bitch.

"Look, I just need for someone to hear my side of the story, someone who cares about Toni enough to let her know how I feel."

Beatrice laughed smugly. "You are something else. So if we love Toni enough, we will convince her to give you another chance?"

"I didn't mean it like that Beatrice. You know what I mean. Toni and I are soul mates, we love one another deeply Beatrice," he said softly.

"Right, right, I think I heard enough for the night, your best bet is to take heed to what I told you at the wedding. You don't want to see her wild side. She is probably opening her special can of whoop-ass for you right now."

"I don't care about no special can, I just need to talk to her before it's too late."

"It's already too late, she is not going to want to talk to you Pierre, Preston, whatever, okay?" Beatrice said nastily.

"Okay, all right. Well you have a good night Beatrice."

"And you sleep good if you can after the trifling shit you did," she said and dropped the phone because Marcus pulled her down on his face.

Toni was high as hell and feeling good and lousy at the same time. She floated out of the tub smiling as she thought about happier times when she was single and minding her business. Deep thoughts began to enter her mind. Thoughts of things she thought she smoked away. But that was the downside of smoking potent marijuana, it took your mind places that you forgot about. It was only right that at a time like this, Quentin entered her mind. She didn't fight the thoughts, she needed someone, anyone right now to occupy her mind, anyone but Pierre.

"Mo, when are you going to stop fronting and ask my girl Beatrice out?" Toni asked.

"When she stop acting so stuck-up. She's not even all that."

"She got some big knockers though!" Quentin teased. Toni doesn't remember why she got mad when he said that.

After the nighttime came and everyone dispersed, Mo offered to walk Toni home. "I'm going that way," Quentin offered so Mo went about his way without thinking twice. Once they reached Toni's building she gave him the usual hug and said she'd see him tomorrow. He held her extra long. She withered out of his grasp and headed upstairs.

Toni smiled at the innocence back then. It was so simple. So pure. She thought about Quentin's girlfriend Miriam and how much she complained about how she thought he was cheating, smoked too much reefer, didn't spend enough money but she loved him so much and to top it all off he had the prettiest dick she ever seen and knew how to use it. She talked about it until it heightened Toni's curiosity but she would never push up and never thought Quentin would. One day he just came to her house, not that it was unusual, but he always came with Mo or Mo with him, but when he came alone Toni was not alarmed. She had just woke up, brushed her teeth, and was on her way to the kitchen to make breakfast when she heard a knock at her door. She remembered looking through the peephole and seeing Quentin. She let him in, in more ways than one.

"Hi I was just about to make breakfast, you hungry?"
"Yeah, you spoke to Mo? Is he coming over here?"
"No not that I know of."

Then they ate and talked about the future and the past and the present and Quentin asked Toni about guys he had seen her with or heard of and she told him their status and he sat back and pondered how a girl so calm and collected have so much history and with that he became determined to be the one man, as he was the only one that she was friends with before relations so he knew he had a chance and too many nights had gone by where he'd dream about being inside of her to see how soft she was because the exterior of her was way too hard, which could only mean that she was soft inside and so after they ate and sparked up a Dutch and began to get high, Toni probably thinking about some other dude and Quentin wondering what she was thinking he stood up and walked to her then lead her up to him by her hands. He kissed her soft and the way she wrapped her arms around him only meant one thing to him, that she was waiting for this moment *and she was.*

* * *

After the smoke cleared *literally*, Quentin and Toni found themselves undressed, sweaty, smiling bashfully, laughing blissfully at their newfound love temporarily forgetting about Quentin's girlfriend and Toni forgetting about whoever the victim was at the time. And then Maurice knocked on the door and although they got fully dressed to answer it, Mo could smell sex in the air and he could see the secret on their faces and he walked in and said, *"I hope y'all know what y'all doing, we too cool for this man!"* and at that moment it dawned on them what they had done, but they couldn't stop and wouldn't stop until Toni got pregnant and Quentin skipped town.

Toni subconsciously picked up the phone and dialed Quentin's number.

22

He couldn't believe that her number was on his caller ID this time of night. *Not now!* he thought as he looked at the dark-haired beauty in his bed. But this was Toni, the love of his life so he took the phone into the bathroom and answered.

"Is this a bad time?" he heard her ask. Her voice light and trembling trying her best not to cry.

"No, I was sleep but this must be important," he said, looking at his clock. "Is all well?"

"No," Toni said and began to cry softly. She sounded like a lost child whimpering. *Toni? Crying? This must be bad.*

"T, you all right, do you need me to come over?" *This is my perfect chance to get her.*

"No, by the time you get here the moment will be lost and I'd be tired or sleep. We can just talk if you don't mind listening."

"I don't mind, you know I don't mind."

So with that, Toni rambled on straight for about ten minutes about everything that happened tonight.

"I don't expect a response, I just needed to tell someone. I am going crazy in here alone, high, hurting, needing, disappointed. I just don't understand why and how this could happen to me. I'm always so cautious and careful. I mean he didn't even show any signs of having anyone else in his life."

"T, damn you sure you don't want me to come over?"

I do, I do, just come and stop asking, come hold me.

"T, you there?"

"Yeah, I'm here."

"Aw, baby you sound bad."

"I feel bad Quentin. I feel so horrible that a man could do this to me."

"Talk to me baby, what happened?" he said, sliding down the wall and sitting on the bathroom floor.

"I need to know how Beatrice knows about *our* affair."

What the hell was she bringing that up for?

"What do you mean?"

"She made a comment to me about me being pregnant and all. So I need to know if Mo didn't tell and I didn't tell then who did and why?"

Quentin bit his lip, quickly the thoughts of him knocking on Toni's door and B answering entered his mind. "Toni isn't here."

"What are you doing here?" he asked her

"Watching her cable, mines is off, come in."

"Nah I'm good just tell T I came by."

"Oh what, we ain't peoples? You can't hang with me?"

"Yeah we peoples B but . . ."

"So come on in, I got some chocolate ty from up the hill."

Quentin's plan was to smoke with her and leave, hoping Toni would come in during the session. B failed to tell Quentin that Toni would be out all day at a writing seminar and wouldn't be back until hours later. Quentin was surprised at her gesture as she was always standoffish and hardly smoked and chilled without Toni being present.

"You're never this quiet when we are all around one another, 'sup with you?" B asked.

"Nothing. I'm just not used to you being so friendly."

He didn't feel right for some reason. His gut was bothering him, which meant something.

Beatrice pulled out another Dutch. This girl is trying to get me loose, he thought.

"Yo, I'm out B, I'll see you okay?" he said, standing.

"Come on, smoke this last Dutch with me then you can go," she insisted and so he did. "How harmful can that be?" she chuckled and got under the covers.

And so they smoked and talked and B put her guard down and wasn't so stuck-up and Quentin thought, she's kind of cool and then B thought got 'em! and then he told her about how much he cared for Toni and B was mad she hadn't pushed up sooner or told Toni to hook it up and was mad that Toni got him first but her feelings for him wouldn't change that quick and so she said "fuck it" and she pushed up and the chocolate ty took over his better judgment and right there on her best friend's bed, Beatrice slept with Quentin and conceived a child.

* * *

"Toni, can we talk about this tomorrow? I just want to hear about tonight."

Toni didn't like his answer, which meant that there was something to tell. She took a deep breath and said, "No, I need to talk about this now."

At all costs he avoided B until she spotted him and told him he would be a father and after telling her it was a mistake and that he couldn't do that to Toni she threatened to tell and he skipped in case B told. When he learned that she didn't he came back briefly only to be a man and to tell B that Toni was pregnant but B had aborted the baby and simultaneously Toni had lost hers. He hadn't seen Beatrice since. Yes it happened as children but it was one of those things that could never be forgiven once found out.

Toni, who was too high to press him any further, changed the subject on her own unknowingly by talking about Preston because he called in on the other end.

I have nothing to say to him but so much to say.

"I can't believe he did this to me, then again I am not surprised, after all, he is a man and men are the most—"

"Why you always gotta bash men Toni, you ever thought about the shit you've done to men *and* women?"

"Oh so now this is my fault? Some kind of karma? What have I ever done?" she yelled, ignoring the beep on the other end.

"Toni, I'm not trying to bring up anything or blame you but you dished out your share of heartbreak too."

"Quentin please okay? It was nothing compared to this shit right here. My heart is in a million pieces Quentin, do you understand what I am saying to you!"

"Well, let's talk about all of the men you dealt with that had wives, the men you just humped and dumped. I don't remember the names but I remember the stories."

"I was young! We are too grown for this kind of shit!"

"Age has nothing to do with it and you know it."

"I disagree. Pain inflicted upon a person at seventeen is different than at thirty."

"To an extent."

"Whatever Q. I didn't know he had a wife. And fuck karma okay? So don't even bring up no fucking karma!"

"I'm not trying to get you upset, it's just that . . ." Q spoke softly as to not remind her of Beatrice.

"I don't want to hear it right now. I need positive things not negative. I didn't hurt anyone back then but myself, I didn't hurt anyone!"

"You hurt Miriam."

"Miriam? No, *you hurt* Miriam!"

"She trusted you."

"She trusted you too!" Toni spit back.

"The other women, you didn't know so you slept with their men without a conscience. But you knew Miriam, she confided in you."

Toni couldn't believe what she was hearing. *Oh*

now you wanna be gentle Quentin? Now you want to act like you have a heart? You didn't have a heart when you left me pregnant or when you was sleeping with me, now it's my fault? You mother—

"You know what, I thought I could call you for support but I see this was a mistake. You take care Q," Toni said and hung up before she exploded into tears.

Damn T, I'm sorry I didn't mean to cause any further pain, he thought but decided to go to bed instead of calling her back. *I don't need her asking me about Beatrice anymore.*

23

For the past couple of months and consistently over the past couple of weeks, she watched Marcus as he stepped out as if he didn't have someone at home. He walked with the slim dark brown sista out in the streets like it was nothing. He met her after work constantly, took her to hotels each time they met up. She got pissed each and every time she followed him and saw them together, she'd call his cellular phone and it would either keep ringing or go straight to voice mail. But what pissed her off more than anything is when she'd call and he'd whisper and tell her a lie. Now a liar was one thing she could not take. *Black men, all of those bastards lie, they lie on job applications, they lie so they won't go to jail, they lie about their income, just natural-born liars,* she thought. But she was growing tired of him stepping on her after she had been so good to him. *I knew he wanted a black woman all this time, he just used me 'cause those bitches never have good credit and can't suck a dick to save their lives and look at the one he chose to step out with. Long weave, tight pants works in retail, ugh retail. She's probably one of those video girl reject wannabes black bitch! She's not even cute, she could be one of those manly-looking tennis player sisters, or a distant cousin of theirs. I know he loves me, but his heart is with the black woman. So fucking what I don't put a pound of salt in my food when I cook it, that's why they have those fat asses and high blood pressure now! Well before I leave him for good, I'm going to show him that not all white women are docile punks!*

Marcus

Marcus was the kind of man that you didn't want to get involved with. He was selfish, he was a user, and he loved what you could do for him more than he loved you as a person. That's just how he was and always been. He was charming, he knew how to feign love and although he may develop feelings for you it wouldn't be as deep as he would lead a woman to believe. Other than his mother, he had never sincerely given himself to another woman or loved another woman or respected one for that matter. So cheating on Zara with his ex was nothing, to him it was almost natural to do that. He reasoned that Beatrice knows him and therefore should know better than to put herself into him 100 percent and that Zara . . . well he just pretty much knew that Zara would do anything for him and stick by his side no matter what. If he was going to be the man that he was, he needed a woman by his side that kept her mouth shut and *stayed in a woman's place*. Beatrice just wouldn't do. She is a black woman that would pretty much go postal on him for any and every reason feasible. There would be no understanding if he came home late, spent the night out, asked her for money, didn't have any money, lost his job, asked for her to cosign anything, cheated, lied, peed on the toilet seat, forgot a birthday or needed space. He loved Beatrice but not the way he was leading her to believe, but what did he care, she should know better.

"She is just someone from back in the days,

something to do. I mean, Zara is cool and I care about her, but . . . she is not a sister," Marcus said as he reclined in his leather chair at home. His friend on the other end got quiet then answered, "So why don't you just marry a sister? Are you going to cheat on Zara forever? And what do you see in Beatrice anyway?"

"She got the bomb pussy, I won't lie," Marcus laughed.

"Why am I not surprised that you said that. Well she may have that but she seems way too shallow in my opinion and a little bit desperate at times, I mean according to what I've heard and seen over the years."

"I have a special place in my heart for her, I do, she is good people."

"Does she know about Zara?"

"Does she *need* to know?"

"Damn man what if she finds out about Zara? What are you telling her?"

"Well she just thinks that we are taking it slow and that she is my woman but if she finds out, I conclude, me knowing B that she will just be mad and pissed, it's not like I never broke her heart before, she ain't new to this. Besides she knows she isn't my woman."

"I doubt that M, I think you need to chill man. I mean Zara is a good woman."

"But she's not a sister!"

"So cut her loose then."

"I can't, I owe it to her to stay with her. She'll be devastated if I left her."

"You owe her big-time cause if it wasn't for her you wouldn't have half the shit you have now!"

"Why are you playing save the women, Jeff?"

"I just call it how I see it man. You're in your forties, it's time to stop playing these games and settle in, settle down or leave these women alone man. Leave that old school booty alone and do what's right."

Mark laughed at his comment. "Old school booty is the best booty! I will leave her alone eventually but right now it feels good to have two women both who love me so much, especially Zara, all at home, being a good woman, no questions, no suspicions, my homely chick then I have my wild woman too."

"Yeah white chicks is good for that, but still don't take advantage of that because eventually they all get hip to the bullshit and they get tired, some just take longer than others. Besides what kind of respect do you have for a woman that lets you do what you want? Me personally? I need my woman to tell me to shut the hell up and stay in the house sometimes," Jeff said, satisified.

"Not me, I don't want nor do I need any woman to tell me a damn thing! You try to control me and you will get dismissed."

Jeff took a deep breath. "If you don't take care of your woman the next man will, remember that."

"Who are you, the maintenance man? Let me find out I need to watch you around my women!" Marcus joked, too caught up in his ignorance to read between the lines.

Too late brother too late.

"Look man I gotta run. What are your plans for the night? What or *who* are you doing?"

"I'm doing B tonight, I already told Zara I'll be home late."

Good, I should be expecting a call from Zara then letting me know what time to hook up with her.

"What you getting into tonight?" Marcus asked Jeff.

Your woman. "Don't know yet. I'm going to make a few calls, I might go check my son, I'll know by the time I leave work, call me if your plans fall through."

"You wanna link up before I see B?"

"Sounds like you like B more than you lead on brother!" Jeff said.

"B is cool, my nasty lil' miss," he said, reflecting on a recent episode. "But that's it. She isn't wife material. Not in my opinion at least."

"Just call me when you leave work and we'll take it from there. I gotta go, my lunch hour is over."

"See that's why you need to be your own boss so you won't have to punch the clock!" Marcus boasted.

"Right, right. Later man," Jeff said and hung up.

Marcus hung up and smiled smugly. "Who says you can't have your cake and eat it too?"

"You know I'm getting really tired of Marcus and his roundabout answers every time I ask him where do we stand and who am I to him. He says

B you know who you are to me. For some reason it shuts me up but I know it's not the answer that I am looking for. You think he is trying to pull one over on me T? I mean because I love him and we have been seeing one another exclusively for a while now. I mean why is it so hard for a man to just say it, is it because they don't like to just admit and commit? Shit, I can't believe he and I are back together after so long. But you know what they say, if you love something let it go," Beatrice asked, talking a mile a minute as they pulled into the mall to pick up Christmas gifts on this cold November day. Toni, who had remained upbeat since her breakup with Preston was actually dwelling on him today at this very moment after being apart for two months, as Beatrice rambled on about the obvious. "T, you hear me girl, what do you think Marcus is up to?"

"The same shit he used to be up to B, a leopard can't change his spots."

"Damn I mean there is such a thing as being compassionately honest instead of brutally or bluntly honest T," Beatrice said and rolled her eyes. *Just because her man turned out to be a fraud why does she act as if everybody's man is doing wrong.*

"What is with you today? You okay?"

"I'm fine B, park in this lot right here. I want to go to the Ralph Lauren store. We can start from here and work our way down," Toni said, already opening the lock on her door and taking off her seat belt.

"It's cold outside Toni, I don't plan on doing too much walking. I don't know why we didn't just go to Saks and use my discount or Macy's. Why did we have to drive all the way . . ."

Why did I even bring this girl with me? She hasn't done anything today except run her damn mouth and complain. I know better next time.

"Well dammit we here! What sense does it make to complain, huh?" Toni barked.

"You're right, you are absolutely right." *You never have to worry about me coming out here or anywhere with your miserable behind.*

The women pretty much weaved in and out of stores quietly after that, only speaking when necessary. Beatrice pretty much had enough of Toni's shadiness so she grabbed her arm and turned her around causing Toni to pull away viciously and eye her up and down like she was crazy.

"You have something you need to say to me Toni? What is on your mind that you feel the need to come around me just to act like a bitch?" Beatrice asked as Toni continued to look her up and down like she lost her mind.

"First of all B, don't approach me as if you're a saint and like you haven't been giving me your ass to kiss. Everything is Marcus, Marcus. Marcus is not thinking about you!" Toni said but didn't mean to.

"Oh, okay, I see what this is about. When you and Preston were *on*, I needed to be easy and get a life, but now that you find your lover boy ain't nothing but a two-timing bastard like the rest of the niggas you left behind you want me to be alone with you again."

"Girl please, what are you saying?"

"You tell me!"

"Look, it's obvious that Marcus has something going on as usual, you need to open your eyes and recognize. I'm tired of hearing you ramble on about him like you don't know what he is about."

"No matter who I am with, you find something wrong with them. Who the fuck made you God?" Beatrice yelled, causing other shoppers to slow down.

"No, no matter who you are with something is wrong with them. I'm not finding shit. I'm not trying to be God, I'm trying to be a friend. Would you rather me just act like everything is cool when it isn't? Sell you a bridge and some land B?"

"Well do me a favor, don't try to be a friend anymore. As a matter of fact, finish up your shopping so I can take you home and get the hell away from you. I'm tired of your ass always talking shit like your life is so damn perfect or the men you deal with are so ideal, please."

"It sounds like you've been wanting to get that off of your chest for some time now. So since you're in the habit of playing confession, why don't you explain to me your relationship with Quentin."

Beatrice looked at Toni and began to walk. "Let's go, I don't have time for this shit."

"Yeah, I think you do. We have an hour-and-a half-ride home so you can tell me all about it," Toni said, calling Beatrice's bluff.

"What is it you think you need to know?"

"I want to know why you didn't tell me the deal back then. He told me but I want to hear it from you!" Toni lied.

The women got in the car and began to pull out

of the lot, all the while, Beatrice avoided Toni's dark eyes.

"B, start fucking talking!" Toni yelled, growing impatient now that it was evident that something had happened.

Beatrice took a deep breath and once they hit the Long Island Expressway she began to talk. "I didn't know you two had something going on. I secretly liked him. One day you were out and I was at your house watching your cable, puffing, doing the usual and he came by. I told him you weren't home, I took it as the perfect opportunity to let him know how I felt so I invited him in. He came in and we puffed some herb. Next thing you know—"

"No, I think you're leaving out a huge part, like the part where someone pushed up on someone."

"Well once the session started he began telling me about you and him. I don't really remember who made the first move but all I know is it happened."

"Right there," Toni said.

"Yeah."

"On my bed huh?"

Beatrice was quiet.

"So tell me about the baby," Toni asked of her own pregnancy. She wanted to know for sure if Quentin had told her. Beatrice, not knowing, foolishly confessed. "Well it wasn't until he came back to town that I told him I had an abortion and he told me that you miscarried, I was upset that you didn't tell me you were pregnant. I mean that is why he left, he was scared that I was going to tell you but I aborted the baby."

"You were pregnant?" Toni said, turning to face Beatrice.

"I thought . . . I mean, what baby were *you* talking about?"

"B, aw man B. Damn how could you do something like this?"

"Toni it just happened. That was so long ago."
Fuck, fuck, fuck!

"No, you just don't happen to fuck your best friend's man on her bed when she isn't home then get pregnant. Shit like that doesn't *just* happen!"

"Toni that was so many years ago, we were kids and he was not your man, he had a girl, remember?"

"We were eighteen years old! That is old enough to know right from wrong. And so what he had a girl, that's neither here nor there! I was dealing with him and you were my sister. You should have never let him in my house without me being there number one and once you found out about us you should have backed off, point-blank! That was just plain old foul Beatrice. So you hid this from me all of this time. What else did you do behind my back? You probably knew that Preston was married too and wanted me to look like a fool."

"I swear I didn't know Toni."

"I think . . . no *I know* that you and I need a time-out right now. I'm so mad at you I could kill you right now."

Damn, Beatrice thought as she gripped the wheel tight.

* * *

When Beatrice got home the first thing she did was call Lola with whom she was still friends with. She wanted to rant and rave about Toni and how she felt that Toni was being unfair and unreasonable as Toni gave Beatrice *the don't call me I'll call you* speech upon exiting Beatrice's car. Lola, who was happily housed in her Soho home, with $2 million in her bank account and newly divorced answered the phone singing. Gone was her hood hop, back was her snooty lingo.

"Hey!" she said.

"Hey, what are you doing?" Beatrice asked.

"Nothing. What about you?" Lola asked as she soaked in her small Jacuzzi.

"Are you washing dishes or something?"

"No, I'm in my Jacuzzi *dahling*," Lola boasted.

"Oh, well should I call you back?"

"Um, yeah, when I get out and get dressed I'll call *you* back. I'm going shopping first thing tomorrow morning, would you like to come?"

"Yeah, call me," Beatrice said and hung up. *I can't go shopping, dammit Marcus will not give me money the way I need and I don't have money to shop the way Lola shops. I can't go to Neiman Marcus and things like that. Marcus and I are going to have to have a talk.*

Jeff had given Zara information again on where she could find Marcus. As usual, he was meeting the brown-skinned woman and taking her someplace for them to rendezvous. She drove erratically in her friend's gray Durango, ditching her easily seen black Expedition to make sure she caught up with Marcus who left work early to *visit his mother*. According to Jeff, Marcus was going straight to Beatrice's house and was going to stay the night and tell Zara he fell asleep at his mother's. He knew that Zara would not question his mother because his mother did not like Zara and Zara was afraid of her. But as she followed Marcus in the cold, she realized that he was not going to New Jersey but heading to Manhattan. After following him for some time, she concluded that he was going to this woman's job. She was going to confront him wherever he stopped first, with pictures and proof of his infidelity. But then she decided it would be no fun that way, she didn't know if this woman knew that she existed but there was only one way to find out.

Marcus pulled into the underground garage. Zara parked two rows behind him. She knew that Beatrice worked on the sixth floor so she rode up in a separate elevator. She walked a good ways behind Marcus as he walked up to the register where the female there gave him a comfortable smile as if she knew him and nodded her head toward the direction of Beatrice's office. Zara pretended to shop and waited to see if he would come back out. After ten minutes, Marcus came out smiling and fixing his pants, no doubt looking like he had just received a blow job. That pissed Zara off. She watched him as he went to sit in the waiting area. He pulled out his cellular phone and called Zara.

* * *

Her phone began to vibrate. Zara stifled a laugh as she ran behind a rack of coats.

"Hello?" she answered jovially.

"Hi, baby where are you?" he asked.

"I'm in Long Island with my sister, why?"

"Oh no reason. Listen I'm going over to Mama's later so I'll see you tonight. I'll wake you up for a midnight snack, how's that?"

"Ooh yippee I can hardly wait!"

"If I didn't know any better I'd think you were being sarcastic."

"No, of course not but look, I have to run so . . . I'll see you later okay hon?"

"Okay, love you."

"Okay byee!" she sung and hung up. She watched Marcus as he flipped his phone off, fanned her away, shrugged his shoulders, looked at his watch, and then sighed. Zara cursed then made her way toward Beatrice's office and stood in a nook not knowing what her next move would be. Beatrice's office door opened and Zara got a good look at her. *Not bad looking, she'd be better looking without that ultra-thick horse's hair on her head. Her pants are way too tight and she has on too much makeup. Fucking bitch.*

Beatrice was gathering up her things then she got on the phone quickly and asked for another coworker, then said, "Okay I'll be over there in two minutes."

When Beatrice came running out of the office in a hurry without closing her door, Zara's mind began to race. Beatrice hurried past Marcus giving him the *five more minutes* hand then disappeared as Marcus watched her behind twist and turn away. Zara then ran inside of Beatrice's office.

"Marcus, honey let me just run into my office and grab my purse, I am ready," Beatrice said as she whisked past Marcus who was beginning to get impatient. Beatrice grabbed her oversized Dooney & Bourke bag and headed out to meet Marcus. "You ready?" she asked and looped her arms through his. Zara took the stairs and headed to her Durango.

They pulled out and seemed to be heading toward lower Manhattan. Zara lit a cigarette and put on lite FM as she waited for the light to change. Her phone began to vibrate. It was Jeff. "Hey you," she said.

"Hey what's up. Are you okay?"

"Yeah, I'm okay, I just put a nice package in her pocketbook but she hasn't opened her purse yet. I'm on Houston and Avenue A. I have no idea where these guys are headed."

"Let me call Marcus and I'll call you right back. What time are you coming home?"

"As soon as I see them to their destination."

"Fine, I'll call you back with the details," Jeff said and hung up.

* * *

"Marcus, can I ask you a question and get a straightforward answer? I mean I'd prefer an honest answer as opposed to a roundabout one," Beatrice started.

Why does this chick insist on prying into my brain about her status? What does she want from me?

"Go on, shoot baby!" Marcus said and made a left turn.

"You love me?"

"You know I do."

"So say it."

"What?"

"Say it then. Say you love me."

"Beatrice, you know I love you."

"No I don't. Not until you say it."

"Why is that so important to you honeybee?"

"Don't try that honeybee stuff Marcus, I need to know where this is going and *why* I haven't been invited to your home yet."

"My home? First of all, it just never panned out that way, secondly we both work in the city, moments away from your pad, *that* is why we haven't been to my house. Let's not act like I have something to hide."

"I didn't say that Marcus, but what about the weekends huh? Why can't I come spend the—"

"See this is the shit that drove me to the next woman last time."

"Oh don't go there okay, I am not some young chick you can run game on, so please, let's not go there."

Oh now she wanna use her head. Too late.

"I'm not trying to run game on you. You know me B, I don't like questions."

"And I don't like *not* getting answers, now I need to know where this is going?"

Nowhere, no damn where if you keep questioning me.

"Can you be more specific?"

Beatrice took a deep breath. "Yes, as a matter of fact I can. I need to know, am I your woman, that's first of all, secondly are you seeing other people and for how long."

"You are my woman Beatrice," he said as he stopped at the light. He looked at her for extra measure. "You are my woman."

Good, that's what I thought.

"Okay, are you seeing other women and be honest," she asked with less venom in her voice.

Be honest, she must think I was born five minutes ago. She is trying to run the oldest trick in the book on me, being honest to a woman? I may as well shoot myself now.

"No."

"I don't believe you."

"Too damn bad, are you going to arrest me now? If not I rather not continue this interrogation."

"I need to be taken care of better Marcus. You don't buy me anything, you don't help out with my bills the way you should. I mean I'm a well-kept woman I need my man to keep me kept."

Does this bitch think she's Tyra Banks or something?

"I feel you baby and I will try to do a better job at taking care of you." *Please, I got a woman, a mortgage, car note, and bills, I don't have time for this shit. Zara never asks for shit, if anything she gives me things not takes from me. Damn black chicks man. I gotta cut her off. After today I'm going to take a "business vacation."*

"You promise?"

"Yes I promise, what do you need right now?"

"I need your credit card."

"My credit card?" *She can't be serious. Did she just say my credit card? This woman is really tripping! My credit card? I need to laugh in her face.*

"What, is that outlandish?" *Let's see how much of a baller you think you are now, Mr. I-have-a-house-in-Mount Vernon, you should see my pool and I have a two-car garage and my salary is . . .*

"I'll take you shopping. What is it that you need?"

"I don't know yet. I'll just hit the stores with your card and get what I like. Problem?"

"Not at all, I'll give you my card tomorrow when I see you. The one I have on me now doesn't have a high limit. It only has five thousand dollars on it." *You ain't getting shit. Dream on sweetie!*

"I'll hold you to it," she said as his phone rung.

Marcus was relieved. "Jeff, main man, what it is?"

"Nothing, nothing, what's going on with you. You up with B yet?"

"Yeah, unfortunately."

"What happened?"

"Nothing man, I'm good."

"Oh, she's in your face now."

"Yeah, maybe later."

"Oh, well where y'all heading to?"

"Um, it's looking like B's house," Marcus said. Beatrice rolled her eyes and mumbled. *Make this the last time we go to my house, next time we are going to your house and who the hell is that anyway?*

He read her mind and mouthed "*It's Jeff.*" Beatrice waved.

"B said hi Jeff."

"Hey."

"He said *hey* B."

"Oh, she still over there in Jersey City?"

"Yeah, the pits."

Jeff laughed. "Okay man so you told Zara *what* this time?" Jeff said, laughing.

"You know, the ole mama routine. I haven't used that one in a while."

Jeff laughed again. "You spending the night out? Let me know 'cause you know she might call and have me call your mother. I need to get the facts straight."

"Right I didn't think about that. Well . . . you know the deal, do what you do best."

"Which is take care of *your* business . . . right?"

"Exactly."

"Cool, so I will see you or talk to you tomorrow. I got Zara covered if she asks."

"For sure," Marcus said and hung up.

Once Zara followed Marcus far enough to figure out where Beatrice lived, she made a U-turn and headed home to see Jeff. Since Marcus didn't plan on making her house a home tonight she called Jeff who was always willing and able to

take care of her needs. Zara was tired once she
came home so she immediately took a warm bath
and told Jeff to enter through the back door with
the spare key she had given to him over a year
ago. She sipped Merlot and began to cry at how
much she loved Marcus and how much he used
her and betrayed her heart and her trust. She guzzled what was in her glass and rapidly poured
another one as Jeff crept in. The sound of the bath-
water running let him know where she was so he
began to strip on his way to her. By the time he
reached the door of the bathroom he was naked,
standing there erect, waiting for an invitation.
Zara smiled. He walked in and slid in the tub sitting behind her. He reached for her washcloth
and began rubbing her soft brown hair and washing her neck, reaching around front to wash her
breasts. Zara leaned back against Jeff's wide chest
and got comfortable. He relieved her of the Merlot and drank her glass. "Do you ever feel as if
what we are doing is wrong?" Zara asked.

"I used to. But seeing how he treats you really
makes me upset. You're a good woman."

*Why does she always have to ask this? Dammit if
it's so wrong then stop!*

"Is it because I'm white? I mean, does he love
me or did he just use me?"

"You know the answer it's in your heart."

Zara began to weep softly.

"Don't cry Z. I'm here right?"

"Yeah."

"But you rather it be him."

"I love him Jeff. He is my husband!"

"He's no good. Can't you see that?"

"But he has been your best friend for twenty or so years."

"Zara, let me worry about that. You love me right?"

"I mean yeah I do!" Zara said and eased back down on his chest.

"I will do a much better job at securing your heart, mind, body, and soul Zara. I want to make you feel beautiful."

"You already do," she said. Jeff knew that once Zara got drunk and emotional, she would perform the best sex in the world on him. He was gearing her up to the climax.

"Then please, let's not talk anymore about Marcus. He's a womanizer and he will soon see what a big mistake he made."

"I feel safe with you Jeff, I'm in love with you." "Why can't you ever say it back? Remember when we first made love?" she asked upon his silence.

Jeff thought about the first time he and Zara connected. Zara had just begun suspecting Marcus of cheating and while he was out with Beatrice Jeff had come over unbeknownst of the situation. Zara was upset and Jeff comforted her. Zara asked Jeff to stay and to watch home videos of her and Marcus on vacation. She wanted to talk about the good times and maybe see if Jeff would give her some information as to why things were not working out. Jeff uncomfortably agreed. Zara put in an X-rated tape then headed to the kitchen before it started, to get Jeff something to drink. Jeff watched a good three minutes of the tape and loved what he saw. But he knew Zara would be ashamed so he took the tape out and told her that it wasn't working right and to put in another one. She did and they watched a tape of her and Marcus on vacation in Aruba. Weeks later, Zara came to his house crying hysterically after finding out for true that Marcus was cheating. Jeff let her in and the images of her, riding his best friend backwards while staring into the camera, rubbing her huge authentic breasts made him almost lose it. She cried and hugged Jeff and her lips brushed against his. He pulled away, Marcus was his best friend. Zara looked into his eyes. "I know you saw what was on that tape. So why don't you do what you've been dreaming of ever since that day?" she purred.

"Excuse me?" Jeff said.

"You heard me. I know you saw some of that tape."

It was then he smelled the alcohol on her breath. "Zara, Marcus is my friend, my best friend and you are drunk."

"If I was your girl and you were Marcus, do you think he'd sleep with me?"

Yeah, hell yeah, Jeff thought but did not say.

"I promise I won't tell. I'll even let you tape it and keep for collateral," she said and true to form she reached in her huge Dior bag and pulled out a small compact video camera. Jeff was going wild inside.

"You sure you want to do this?" he asked. Zara ignored him and stripped down to the bare necessities. It was déjà vu. Her body looked just like Beatrice's but a white version. Now he'd see if her sex was better. He briefly thought about Beatrice allowing him into her safe haven after Marcus left her for Zara years ago. Zara never knew about Beatrice. He had them both for many years until Marcus finally made a choice strictly for financial reasons. Jeff knew Beatrice only did it to hurt Marcus but how could she hurt him if he would never know? Beatrice was up front about it and that's what he loved the most about her. She called him up and asked him out for drinks, she said she needed to talk, her heart was aching. He came through for her, they drank, they talked and when it was time to go home, Jeff drove her home. Before getting out of the car she said, "Why can't he be more like you?" He felt her coming on, he put his head down, and she picked it up by lifting it with her tiny manicured index finger. "Look at me Jeff, I'm hurting inside, I need this pain to go away like right now at any cost. How much do you value your friendship with Marcus?" To which Jeff replied, "Very much." Beatrice lifted her shirt over her head in one quick motion and shook her weave back into place. "Enough to turn me down?" she purred. He could never forget how beautiful she looked sitting there in front of him in a black silk bra and blue jeans. "No Beatrice this is wrong. Let me walk you to your door." When they reached the door, Beatrice put on her poker face and insisted that she just wanted to talk. He believed her. They talked for about an hour and drank some more. Beatrice excused herself, he looked at his watch. 4:23 AM. *I gotta* go, he said to himself. He got up to say his goodbyes as he heard Beatrice flush the toilet and wash her hands.

He was stopped dead in his tracks by Beatrice donning an all-white lace thong leotard with a plunging neckline showing her lovely *girls*. He was turned on at how they stood so firm to be so huge. But he wasn't surprised, Marcus always bragged about them along with how good Beatrice takes it anally. "Come here Jeff, take the pain away," Beatrice said and stood in the doorway confident that Jeff would come, he did in more ways than one. He loved the way Beatrice smelled and the soft noises she made. "You're better than Marcus, damn," Beatrice whispered seductively in his ear. Her vagina was not as tight as he was used to with women but it was good just the same. She took it in every hole, didn't squirm away from his nine inches, she took it like a trooper and relieved him of all his juices and strength orally, she was a beast as small as she was. She even initiated the change of positions. And when it was all over, she put on her robe, took a shower, came out brushing her teeth, and asked, "You still here? I thought you would have left while I was showering." She was a bit annoyed but put a little playfulness in it. "Excuse me?" Jeff asked. "Jeff, I did this because it felt like the right thing to do, I may think differently tomorrow but by then it will be too late, the damage would be done already. It was good and although I was drinking, I knew what I was doing and I meant it when I said you were better than him. You really are." Jeff got up, got dressed and in his head he wanted to kiss her but the way she walked to the door ahead of him and opened it suggested that she wasn't feeling gentle like that.

So he walked out the door, as she smiled sarcastically and shut it behind him. He looked at his watch, 7:49. He had not seen Beatrice since. Zara interrupted his thoughts by straddling him. He'd been hooked on Zara's tightness ever since the first time, he loved her, but he'd never let her know.

"Maybe I should just go home!" Marcus barked before even getting out of the car. He was annoyed at Beatrice's constant nagging and desperation for a commitment. She was turning him off. "I don't have to beg any man to be with me Marcus, you got it?" *Coulda fooled me.*

"I didn't say that. Look can we just go inside?"

Beatrice calmed down a little bit when she thought about the loving she needed to get before her period came. "You lucky I love you boy."

"Boy? I'm a grown man, I haven't been a boy in over twenty years . . . *girl.*"

Beatrice laughed and dug in her pocketbook to get her keys. She eyed a small envelope that looked like it was holding a card of some sort. She opened the card as she walked slowly up the steps with an impatient horny Marcus walking behind her, rolling his eyes in his head. "Can you walk any slower B?" he asked.

Beatrice thought her mind was playing tricks on her. In her hand she held a credit card with the expiration date 11/06 on it. It had two names on it: Marcus Caban and Zara Altheim-Caban. It was an old credit card. *Who the fuck put this in my bag?* She dug further, opened the envelope and read the tiny note. *Guess it's safe to say that he is not*

worth the hell I will put you both through if you con-
tinue to deal with him. Lay off, he's married!

Beatrice could hardly contain herself. *Oh no not*
again. I can't go through this deceit and bullshit again.
Marcus baby please don't be married, please!

She turned around quickly causing Marcus to
bump right into her chest. He smiled, she pushed
him. "What?" he asked.

Not again, not again! Beatrice thought. "Marcus,
I want to ask you something and I need you to be
honest," she asked as calm as possible.

"What *now*, honeybee? You know what your
problem is? You worry too much, over nothing."

Beatrice ignored him and continued on. "Marcus, what reason do you have to lie to me about
anything? I've been knowing you for a good thirteen years now right?"

"Right," he said, rolling his eyes.

"So why didn't you tell me you were married?"

"Married? I'm not married! How can I keep
something *like that* away from anyone? You can't
hide a marriage B, not for a year."

"Some men have the gift, I'm telling you Marcus you have a gift for being a low-down dirty
piece of shit."

"B, you know something? I need to leave you
alone because you are a crazy insecure woman
and I don't need that shit in my life. I'm a grown
man you hear me? Not some little boy that has to
lie to get pussy."

"I'm sorry, you're right. I just get so insecure
sometimes Marcus. I've been hurt so many times
in the past, including by you."

"You have no reason to worry Beatrice, I'm not going to hurt you again."

"Okay, okay you're right," Beatrice said. She put the key in the door and walked in. "Tell you what, wait right here and I'm going to put on something nice for you okay? I need to make it up to you. I've been a bad girl all day."

"Okay but you can let me in so I can sit down and take my shoes off."

"No, um, um. I want you to wait right here. We are going to role-play."

"Role-play? Oh well in that case, don't be too long," he said, smiling.

"I got the perfect outfit for you. Give me three minutes," she said and closed the door. *Just enough time to boil some water.*

Marcus looked at his watch and grew excited at the thought of Beatrice wanting to role-play. *I got the best of both worlds,* he thought as he heard the door unlock. Beatrice opened the door with the chain on it. "I need you to read the card that I am about to push under the door. Read it and follow the instructions okay?"

"Anything you say your wish is my command."

Beatrice closed the door and slid the card under it. She looked through the peephole and once she figured that he read the note and saw what was left in her pocketbook she opened the door. He looked up at her but he proved to be too slow for the pot of hot water that was saturating his clothes. He let out a piercing, chilling scream. "You crazy fucking bitch!"

"Get your ass off of my damn doorstep before I make some grits stick to your ass next!" Beatrice yelled and slammed the door.

Marcus was hot, *literally*. He jumped in his truck and drove for a good ten minutes with his shirt off, yelling. He could feel his skin burning but not to the point where it might blister. It just burned like hell, the top of his head, his neck and the left side of his face was pulsating. By the time he reached lower Bronx he was numb to the pain. He looked at the note and wondered how Zara found out and how she knew where to find Beatrice and obviously him. He became angry and felt violated. Men had a way of changing things around especially when they were in the wrong. He was going to go home and put Zara in her place and let her know that she cannot follow him around like a detective. He had no intention on explaining his infidelity because *now it wasn't about that*, it was about Zara being a detective. He grew more and more angry as he thought about it, wondering how long she knew, how long she followed them and bigger than it all, why did she stay quiet and what she was doing in the interim. *Bitch wanna be sneaky? I'm putting her ass on time-out for a while*, he said as he pulled into his driveway.

Thoughts of Beatrice mixed with the pleasure he was receiving from Zara had Jeff erect to capacity. Him and Zara were insatiable tonight. They couldn't get enough of one another and with each stroke their love grew stronger. Jeff looked at the clock. *12:34. We have been going at it for the past two hours with no signs of slowing down,* he thought as Zara slid down his shaft and secured her hands under the back of his head. He grabbed her waist. "Ride 'em cowgirl," he said and tapped her buttocks lightly to get her started again. Zara threw her head back and did her thing. . . . *well.* Jeff closed his eyes and got lost in her love, so lost he didn't hear Marcus come in.

Marcus came through the door like a maniac looking for Zara. He headed straight to the bedroom knowing she'd be there sleeping as if she hadn't been out all day being a damn spy. He walked in and saw his wife. They hadn't seen him yet and at this moment Marcus had no idea who the man was in his bed as Zara's back was to the door. He stood frozen. Then walked up to the bed slowly. His wife was moaning, deeper, louder, and more passionate than he had ever experienced her do. This man, whoever he was, was giving it to his wife good. Marcus's mouth went dry. He couldn't move. Finally he couldn't take it anymore. The smell of sex was knocking him around in his own house.

"Zara!" he yelled. She had the nerve to ride for a few more seconds, obviously climaxing before turning around. "Marcus what are you doing here?" she said, still straddling the stranger with her head turned toward Marcus.

Marcus leaned over to see who the stranger in his house was.

"*Jeff*?" Marcus said and dropped his house keys. Jeff sat up and grabbed his boxers, throwing them on. Marcus looked from one to other not sure of what his next move would be. Zara didn't flinch, she didn't budge.

"What are you doing here Marcus? I thought you were spending the night at Beatrice's?" she asked as she slid into her robe slowly. Marcus still had his eye on Jeff.

"Why man. Before I kill you I need to know why?"

"Because you weren't on your job buster!" Zara said. Marcus reached out and slapped Zara across the bed.

"You dirty white bitch. You ain't shit!" he yelled then charged at her again. She screamed then yelled loudly. "You did this! This is your fault!" she cried.

Jeff began to get dressed. Marcus calmed himself down. "Jeff, you're my man. I'm upset that you did this in *my house* more than I am upset that you did this. Niggas over bitches right?" Marcus said, trying to hide his pain.

Jeff looked at Marcus then at Zara. "I think you guys have some things you need to discuss," Jeff said, leaving Marcus hanging.

"No, don't leave Jeff, we are in love, tell him, tell him that we have been in love for the past year! Tell him that you were the one telling me his whereabouts, tell him!" Zara yelled, red-faced.

Marcus glared at Jeff. "What?"

"I need to go," Jeff said, heading for the door. Marcus balled his fist and hit Jeff in the side of his head until Jeff returned the blows and an all-out knock-down, drag-out fight erupted.

24

Toni woke up feeling unusual today. She couldn't put her finger on it. Maybe it was being home alone on a cold winter day. Maybe it was the bright beautiful sun that she hid from behind her mahogany-brown blinds, maybe it was the neighbors giggling as they finished another round of lovemaking. Toni could never be the kind to not want someone else to be happy because she wasn't. Today was a day for acceptance, she reckoned. She realized emotion today. That's what the surreal feeling was. She was hurting. Today she sat at her computer, typing eighty words per minute, not knowing the words that her brain was forming, just going with the fallen snow that fell delicately outside of her window. She rationalized that she was crying for the character in her book as she sniffled and wiped her tears and that may be true but what she didn't know was that subconsciously the character she wrote about was she. And after that chapter was done, she effortlessly began to write a new chapter and wondered, *If only my life was that simple, to just turn the page and start another chapter.*

She was upset that Preston had not attempted to call her anymore. He hadn't tried hard enough. He was probably working things out with his wife. She started to call B to ask her but then she remembered how B had betrayed her and how she avoided Tracy and her mother's calls. Quentin called her once and offered his shoulder in case she was still grieving over her ex. Toni put her head back and took a deep breath. She was not just alone now but lonely. That's why she hated to love. It was a gamble, this person and feeling fills every second of your life and just like that it's gone, leaving you empty and broken. She turned down the urge to smoke a joint. *I don't feel like thinking.* And her stomach was too weak nowadays, probably her nerves, so she didn't bother pouring herself a drink. *I don't want to be dependent on any substances to get me through this.*

Thousands of miles away in Jonesboro, Georgia, a beautiful suburb, Preston stood in the living room of his father's C house and held a picture of his mother that his father kept on a mantle in a beautiful chromed 8x10 frame. His father came out of the den laughing at something his new wife of five years, Dora, said. "You okay son?" he asked with concern upon seeing his son's demeanor.

"No, not really."

"Toni huh?"

"Yeah."

"Well maybe you need a woman's perspective on things. What seems to be the problem?" Dora asked. Preston never really cared for Dora. He thought that she was way too young for his father. She was forty, looked twenty-nine, and acted nineteen sometimes. His father was sixty-one. He tolerated her because he knew his father was strong and could handle his own. If she wasn't right then his father would check her at the door but his father was getting old and couldn't afford to be picky with his companions so he settled in on Dora who quit her job the minute they married.

Something about Dora, though, didn't sit well although his father said she was all right. Maybe it was because she was not his mother and his dad had never gotten serious with another woman since his mother's death many years ago.

"I am in love with a woman, but I failed to tell her that I was married, she found out and now she's gone," he said, answering Dora's question.

"Why didn't you tell her in the beginning?" Dora asked.

"I didn't think it would go as far as it did. My wife and I were legally separated. Then time began to fly, feelings for my wife began to resurface, but I knew where I wanted to be. I just took too long to say it. I'm only human, I make mistakes, I'm a good man but how can I ever make Toni believe that?"

"That's a rough one. I mean have you tried to talk to her since she found out?"

"She won't take my calls and when I try to go through her best friend she tells me that Toni wants nothing to do with me. I call her best friend every day and she claims that she gives Toni my messages but she says for me to go away and to not show up unexpectedly at her home or job."

"What's going on with that Lola?" his father asked with distaste.

"Nothing new, about to run through the two million that I gave her. Sometimes I think about going back."

"Why, you done got a dee-vorce! You bet not go back to that trollop. You know I never ever liked that Lola girl. Her name alone sounds like trouble, like she is the Jezebel type."

"Is she that bad baby?" Dora asked as she put her feet on Mr. White's lap for him to massage.

"*Worse.*"

"Well Preston, all I can tell you is next time be honest no matter what you do. You may find someone you love or get along with more than Toni."

"I doubt it. You don't know Toni."

"I wish I would have gotten a chance to meet this gal you adored so much. You didn't have the best taste in women as far as their personalities were concerned. But she sounds like a true gem."

"She was, Pop." Preston said, allowing his shoulders to slump in defeat.

"Son, you got to get out of this funk now! If you love this woman, I mean deeply truly love need, want this woman . . . you stop at nothing to get her back. Nothing. Love is stronger than pride and if she truly loves you, she will eventually give in and give you another chance."

"Pop, she has been hurt, bruised, done in. She trusted me and I let her down. She really depended on me to take care of her heart and that was my intention. She has no idea what I was going through."

"It's hard for a woman to forgive when she has been through hell and finally after so long decides to try it again and gets betrayed. I'll be the first to tell you. But we are women, we understand men make mistakes. We just don't deal with the ones that used that as an excuse to keep fucking up. Now, sometimes all we want is a man to fight for us, prove to us that they were wrong and die trying to show us that they will protect us and never hurt us again, a man who needs our trust, a man who holds our emotions dearly and is delicate in all he does. A man that will take over, take charge and take care of us mind, body, soul, and wallet." She laughs. "But seriously, this woman has been hurt. Go after her, demand that she listen to your side of the story, she may push you away or disagree but she hears you and wants nothing more than an explanation that sounds reasonable, let her vent, let her scream, let her fight the feeling, let her pride take over and through it all you sit there and take it. Then wait for the right moment to move in for the kill and take over, knock her out with your devotion and love to her. Sometimes all we want is a man that will fight for us," Dora concluded.

"You hear that son? The woman of the house has spoken. So whatchyou gon' do?"

"Toni is tough, Pop."

"What? You 'fraid of some woman? Be a man and go get that woman!"

Still Preston shook his head. "You guys don't know Toni," he said.

"Well dammit if she's that hard then maybe you are better off without her. Don't no man want no hard woman. Strong yes, hard *no*."

"She's not hard like that."

"So what is it then, son?"

Preston sighed heavily.

"You waste too much time grieving over these women that don't give a damn about you son."

"Toni isn't like the others."

"What's her address? I need to take a trip to New York. These damn New York women always playing tough, always wanna be men. She ain't met me yet. Woman don't respect a man that ain't aggressive and about his business, I keep telling you that. Give me her information!" he demanded.

Like the good son, Preston handed over Toni's information. "What are you going to do with it?"

"Never you mind since *you surely* don't know what to do with it. And she better be all you say she is!"

> *You made a fool of me*
> *Tell me why*
> *You say that you don't care but we made love*
> *Tell me why*
> *You made a fool of me you made a fool of me*

Beatrice let the words to the song "You Made a Fool of Me' play over and over as she sat in her bed with her knees to her chest and her head down rocking back and forth. Her heart cried out but the tears would not fall. Stephen's words rung in her head. *Hell if you played your cards right you wouldn't have to work, but you just won't let this black woman independent thing go now will you? Following Toni. Is she buttering your bread?*

A knot formed in her throat. *I can't go crawling back to Stephen.* She looked around her small bedroom and thought about Marcus. *How could I be so dumb to trust him like that again? Am I that lonely that dependent on a man that I refuse to pay attention to the signs? Dammit!* She cursed herself as Me'Shell Ndegeocello's voice poured out of the radio like velvet butter *was I blind to the truth just there to fill the space. I never been to his home.* Her mind inadvertently ran across Toni whom she hadn't spoken to in weeks on end. *I wasn't wrong, we were kids besides I wanted him first,* she tried to convince herself. *Fuck Toni, Stephen is right, she is not in my caliber.* She got up and washed her face not realizing that tears had fallen until she looked in the mirror. *I need my hair done,* she said, pulling at the roots. *I need to get my hair done and my feet done and I need to go find my man,* she said and forced a smile. *I don't have to be alone and I don't want to struggle like my mother did. I'm going home to where I belong.* She washed her face as the words to the song of her life played in the background reminding her of the state she was in. *You made a fool of me.*

She walked over to her phone and picked it up. She had no idea who she was going to call. She wanted to call *someone,* she wanted to belong to someone, and she wanted to be strong enough or love herself enough to know that it was okay to be alone and that material things did not make a person. But she didn't have it in her. *I'm not like Toni, I won't accept loneliness and act as if it's okay.* She put the phone down and got frustrated. She called Lola. She wasn't home. She left her a message. "Lola, I need a favor, call me," she said flatly and hung up. The phone rung immediately. She assumed it was Lola calling her back. It wasn't. It was a man's voice. She immediately got excited. Her number had not changed in years. *An old flame maybe?* she thought as she tried to recognize the voice on the other end.

"Beatrice?" the voice asked, unsure.

"Yes."

"Hi, this is Preston."

What does he want?

"Yeah how can I help you?"

"I'm sorry to bother you, I just wanted to know if you spoke to Toni?"

"Every day, why?"

"Beatrice I really need for you to have her call me. I have to speak to her. It's been months and I need to talk to her. I can't get her off of my mind you know. I am so in love with her and I know you're her best friend and maybe you can just talk to her for me. I love her. Lola and I are done, we have been over and I know you know this. I made a mistake, I deserve another chance. Please Beatrice, help me."

"I spoke to Toni about you last night and she really doesn't want to be bothered with you Preston. Don't you get it?"

"No, I know she loves me I know she is hurting. Please have her call me, please."

"You're wasting your time *and* mine. I have to go. If Toni wants to talk to you she will call you. I have to run now. Tootles!" Beatrice said and hung up.

Toni doesn't know what to do with a man like him, neither does Lola. I would have had his children and forgiven him. I'd be set for life. Damn everything else.

25

It was January and the cold was brutal. Toni rushed out of her office building with her black tam on and black goose down coat and Timberlands. She charged through the forceful winds and ankle-high snow to get to the PATH train on Thirty-third street. The subway was slushy and crowded. People were trembling and sipping Starbucks. Toni squeezed her hands together under her black leather gloves. The PATH train came and Toni stepped on, swiping up a newspaper that someone left on the seat.

Once she got off the train at Journal Square, she stopped at a coffee shop and got a large hot cocoa, garbage bags, and bread then headed to the liquor store next door and bought two gallons of Hennessy. It was Thursday, her Friday and it was cold out. She had plenty food in her fridge and now she had drinks in case someone stopped by although no one had stopped by since her breakup with Preston in October. Things were pretty quiet and she devoted all of her time to her novel and even began working out in the gym that was located in her building. Before hailing a cab she jogged back across the street to the video store and picked up two pornos and *There's Something About Mary. I'm good now,* she said and laughed to herself. Within seconds she hailed a taxi and gave her destination. The cab drove for ten minutes before pulling up to her building. "Thank you sir, drive safe," she warned then ran into her building. Sammy, the doorman, wasn't there but a new guy stood before Toni. She smiled politely. "Hi, where's Sammy?"

"He took the day off," the man said, smiling. Something about him was familiar to her but she couldn't put her finger on it. "Your bags look mighty heavy. Can I help you?"

"Oh no, I'm fine but thank you. Besides you need to stay here and make sure no strangers come into the building!" she said, smiling and struggled to the elevator.

"I insist, please let me help you. See my name tag? My name is Vernon, I'll show you my ID, I'm no killer, I'm just being a gentleman," he said sternly and almost snobbishly. Toni didn't like him. "I said I'm fine."

He put his hands up in surrender. "You women are too independent these days. Let a man do his job sometimes," he scolded. *I am not in the mood for this shit,* Toni thought, ignoring him and getting on the elevator. Vernon hopped on the one opposite her and rode up to her floor. Toni got off first, heading to her door with her keys out then looked back when she heard the bell ring on her floor. As she put her key in the door, she looked down the hall one last time and saw nothing so she entered her apartment.

Once inside she put the items in her bag away, turned on the television and began looking through her mail. *He seemed like the type who would have written me a letter by now,* she thought of Preston. *Guess he has given up.* She decided that she didn't need a bath, that it was too cold so she put on her long nightshirt and fluffy slippers, put *in There's Something About Mary*, and poured herself a nice glass of Hennessy. Toni was enjoying her time alone and began to get upset thinking about how she let someone invade her privacy. *It's my fault,* she said and dusted it off. By the time she finished her third helping of cognac, her phone was ringing, it was Tracy. *She's harmless why won't I talk to her?* By the time she finished her thought, the call had already gone into voice mail. Toni shrugged her shoulders. *Fuck it.* She chuckled. She went into her bedroom and decided now was a good time to continue working on her novel. She sat at her computer and took a deep breath to clear her mind as usual. Her eyes came across a souvenir from a restaurant she and Preston visited. She picked up the tiny piece of crystal and stared at it for a while. The beautiful iridescent purples and pinks and blues fascinated her. *Should I call him? No, don't call him. You really don't want to hear what he has to say, besides if he wanted*

you he would have called or came over or something,
Toni reasoned then turned on her computer. "Shit
I got work to do."

Beatrice was through with Marcus. Her mind
was made up. She would never talk to him again
and would not open herself up to hear any excuses that he may conjure up as to why he had
not told her he was married. *Married, that son of a
bitch.* Beatrice could not deny that she was hurt
because secretly she yearned for Marcus to be the
one man. But he married someone else after all of
this time. Why not her? Was she not worthy of
marriage? *Who the hell do I have to be to get some respect around here?* Beatrice stood up in her office
and checked the thermostat, thinking about how
cold it was in her office. "Beatrice Washington
please dial extension seven-oh-seven-four Beatrice Washington." someone called over the PA
system. Beatrice picked up her office phone and
dialed out. "Yes," she asked.

"There is a young man out front. He says he's
your brother? I didn't know you had a brother,"
Javonna the cashier inquired. Beatrice was PMS'ing
so she didn't bother following her up. "What's his
name?"

"Joe."

"He said his name is Joe? Where is he?"

"In the waiting area."

"I'll be out shortly." *My brother Joe? Who the hell
could be out there . . . I bet you it's that damn Marcus.*
Beatrice fixed herself up and checked her

image in the mirror. Her ultra-long honey-blond ponytail hung to the middle of her back and her fake eyelashes were beautifully dramatic. Her darkest black Valentino suit that she happily found in a cleaner's bag in the back of her closet fit her like a glove and her silk turquoise blouse matched her shoes. She smiled at herself. *Gotta look good. You never know who is going to pop up,* she said out loud as she headed to the waiting area.

Jeff was waiting nervously as he spotted Beatrice walking toward him not noticing him. She was squinting her eyes and trying to figure out who he was. A frown of frustration crossed her face as she came to the conclusion that she had no idea who he was until she got within inches of him.

What is Jeff doing here? I haven't seen him since . . . since.

"Hi Beatrice, nice to see you," Jeff said and pulled Beatrice into a hug. Apprehensively she hugged him back. "Long time no see. How have you been?" he asked.

"Can't complain. So what brings you here?"

"I was in the neighborhood shopping for a female friend and I just wanted to say hi. That's all. You look good B, I haven't seen you since the last time I saw you."

"Yeah you look good too." *Real damn good.*

"Thank you. So how's it going?"

"I'm sure Marcus has filled you in on that."

"Actually I haven't spoken to him in some time. He and I are not on the best of terms right now."

"Is that right."

"I'm serious. Marcus is a . . . well you know Marcus."

What is he selling?

"So tell me something Jeff. Do you know his wife?"

Oh, I know her well. "Yes I do."

"I had no idea he was married until the other day. So she's white right?"

"Yeah. She's cool though."

"Is that right."

"Yeah. But I really didn't come here to discuss Marcus. I just came by to say hello. Are you okay, you need anything?"

"No, I'm fine. Living well, can't you tell?" Beatrice laughed smugly.

Jeff laughed at her. "You're still the same. Well you take care," he said but didn't budge.

"Something tells me that you came here for a reason. You mind telling me what that reason may be?"

"I told you. I'm shopping for a lady friend and decided to look you up. But I'll be going now. Take care," he said, leaning in and giving her a kiss on the cheek. He walked off, leaving Beatrice standing there touching the spot he kissed. "Jeff?" she called out to him for no particular reason.

I knew she'd call me back. He turned around slowly and stood still. Beatrice walked up to him. *What am I doing?* "Listen. I um . . . well, you want to go out for some drinks?" "The last time I went out with you for drinks you put it on me then put me out. I'm not up to that kind of treatment again," he said.

"I promise this time I won't put you out," Beatrice flirted.

"When and where?" Jeff asked, not hiding his excitement.

"You can pick me up from work Thursday, I get off at seven."

"I'll be waiting for you across the street in the Mani Café."

" 'Kay," she said. Jeff smiled then walked off. *Like taking candy from a baby,* he thought to himself. *I'll really fix Marcus's ass,* Beatrice thought and watched Jeff walk away. When he disappeared out of her sight, she headed back to her office to find a strange woman swiveling in her chair. "Can I help you?"

The woman stood up and smiled. She extended her hand for a handshake. Beatrice folded her arms and looked the homely white woman up and down. *Who is this bitch and what is she selling?*

Dressed in faded 7 jeans and a cream turtleneck, her long brown hair hanging to one side past her breasts, Zara stood in Beatrice's office.

"Hi, I'm Mrs. Caban."

"Who?"

"Marcus's wife."

What the fuck is this bitch doing at my job? Is this why Jeff came up here? Oh hell no. Why is this bitch here? I don't want Marcus anymore.

"How can I help you?" Beatrice asked, annoyed.

"Well you know why I'm here. My husband and I are having some *serious* problems, because of you."

"Oh yeah, and how so?"

"Well, for the past year or so he has been stepping out, staying out and acting out, obviously because of you. Now I just need to know one thing for sure before I leave here. You see, I didn't want to call you on the phone or send you a letter. I'm a woman. I take care of Marcus and I don't appreciate him hanging with the likes of you."

"Did you come here to attempt to insult me, or to find out information on your . . . *husband*," Beatrice asked sarcastically.

"Both. I'm here to tell you that I don't take lightly to women who invade other women's homes and marriages."

"What is your name?" Beatrice asked.

"Mrs. Caban."

"Your first name."

"Zara."

"Okay look . . . *Zara* what Marcus and I had was what we had, I found out about you and ended it. I have known Marcus for over ten years. In fact we were a couple years ago until he ran off with some homely white woman . . . no offense. I am done with him, I see he still hasn't changed. But good luck in trying to change a grown forty-year-old man because if it's not with me he's cheating, it will be with someone else. Funny, his best friend Jeff just came by to visit. If I didn't know any better I'd think you guys planned this."

"Jeff was here?"

"Yes, he was. You look startled."

"No, just wondering what he would be doing here." *Did Marcus have me followed?*

"I have to get going, is there something I can help you with?" Beatrice asked, arms folded.

"Stay away from my husband. That's all I ask of you."

I will beat this little white bitch's ass. Who the fuck does she think she is coming in my place of business demanding me around?

Beatrice stood there unfazed. "You know something. You tell Marcus that what he did has already been done. Tell him I said Jeff is something else and I found that out years ago."

Zara laughed nervously. "What does that mean?"

"Let me put it to you like this. It's not that serious with Marcus okay? I'll be seeing Jeff Thursday night. See? Just like that I moved on."

"What, so you were sleeping with Jeff too?"

"Hey shit happens."

Now I really have to set this black bitch straight. "So let me get this straight. You were sleeping with Jeff too?"

"Years ago when Marcus and I *first* broke up," B said fanning it off and walking over to her desk. "Excuse me," she said so Zara could move out of her way. Zara got up slowly and had thoughts of stabbing Beatrice. *So Jeff doesn't really love me, he was using me! He obviously has a rift with Marcus to be sleeping with both of his women.*

"I have nothing more to say, just stay away from my husband . . . you tramp."

"What did you just call me?"

"A *buh-lack* tramp."

Beatrice stood up and got in Zara's face. Both women were squaring off. "Listen you white-bread chickenshit. Don't get mad at me because your husband came back to what was right for him. I don't know where you bitches get off fucking with our men in the first place. You need to stick to your own kind!"

"Well if you black bitches spent more time taking care of your man and less time getting your tracks sewn in you wouldn't have this problem now would you?"

"Get ... out ... of ... my office!"

"Yes, your little office. You just remember I am not your average white chick, got it Shaniqua?"

Beatrice had enough. She hauled off and slapped Zara, which is exactly what Zara wanted. Zara ran out of the office screaming and calling for security. "Someone help me, this woman has assaulted me, help!" she yelled running toward the manager. Beatrice coolly walked out behind her knowing that she was provoked into the incident.

"What is the problem, Ms. Washington," her boss asked her coming out of the adjacent office upon hearing the commotion. Some customers and a few cashiers were looking on.

"This woman has been harassing me and I threw her out of my office," Beatrice said, standing tall and confident next to her boss.

"I will file charges against this damn place if action is not taken I mean it!" Zara screamed.

"Calm down, calm down. Both of you please step into my office."

"I am not going anywhere. I'll see you around, it's not over!" Zara yelled like a madwoman and ran toward the escalator. Mr. Shapiro, Beatrice's boss, eyed her. "I've been meaning to talk to you about some things anyway. I guess now is a good time to bring it up. Can you come inside my office in about ten minutes? I need to make some calls first."

"Yes sir," Beatrice said and headed to her office to wait.

". . . Notwithstanding your work, which has not been up to par. Are you having problems at home?"

"As a matter of fact, I am," Beatrice answered. *Out of nowhere you have a problem with my job performance. What a crock of shit.*

"I think that you need some time off. Without pay."

"You can't do that to me Mr. Shapiro!"

"I just did. Beatrice. I have been getting complaint after complaint about you and I honestly have been too busy to call you on it. But now you have some woman threatening to sue and I can't have that. She's threatening to come back and who knows what she will do. I think you need to take the time off. You have plenty of vacation time that you can use so you will get paid for that. Take two weeks off."

"But I don't want to use my time. I have things planned. Mr. Shapiro I do believe that your decision is unethical. Who says that there is any truth to the things you have been hearing?"

"Ms. Washington the fact that you have used your office as your private hotel on several occasions has not gone unnoticed. Other coworkers have complained of your lack of *tact* if you will on several occasions. Maybe you have taken advantage of the fact that I have been out of town or maybe you are abusing your authority around here. I don't know what it is or what you have going on but I will stand firm on this. I will not tolerate unprofessional behavior in my work-place, and what you do in your personal life should not spill into your professional life Ms. Washington. So instead of relieving you *perma-nently* and that's only because I did not see things firsthand, I will relieve you *temporarily* without pay or if you choose you can put in for emergency vacation either way, effective immediately I do not want to see you for the next three weeks, do not have me make it four."

"You said two before."

"Now I'm saying three, shall I make it five?"

"No sir but I can't afford to take vacation time or lose pay."

"You can't afford to lose your job either now can you?" he said matter-of-factly. *Why is he being such an asshole to me? Must be because I turned his ass down years ago. Does he still remember that?*

Beatrice decided to calm down and put on her charm. "Mr. Shapiro," she started slowly and gazed into his hard gray eyes. "What is it that I need to do to change your mind? I mean . . . clearly I am a good employee, I am reliable, pro-fessional, despite what you heard, I work hard and I get along with everyone. How can I get you to be a little more lenient on me?"

"Ms. Washington this conversation is over. Please excuse yourself."

Not to be outdone, Beatrice stood up, breast first and stood uncomfortably close in front of her boss, so close that he could smell her. Mr. Shapiro stood up as to not be lured in by her scent. She looked up at him then looked down at her breasts as a sign for him to look too. She looked back up at him and pulled her ponytail around front flirtatiously. "What is it Beatrice, do you have something else you would like to add?" he asked with a tiny hint of softness in his voice. Beatrice took the bait. She shrugged her shoulders like a shy schoolgirl and smiled softly. "I remember your interest in me years ago when I was just a salesgirl. You still got that eye for me?" she said, stepping closer. Her large chest was now on his chest. She licked her lips and flung her ponytail behind her.

"Okay . . . go on home, you'll hear from me tomorrow. I need time to think this through," the tall bald white man said. *Got em!* Beatrice thought and grabbed her pocketbook.

"Thank you Mr. Shapiro. I appreciate that."

"Yes, yes . . . good day, Ms. Washington," He said as she switched out of his office.

Just as promised, Mr. Shapiro got back to Beatrice the next day via Federal Express over night mail. The letter read:

February 4, 2004

Ms. Washington:

After much consideration and information, it has been collectively agreed that your assistance is no longer deemed necessary to our company. Despite the fact that you have been an employee of ours for the past six years, your indecency has been bothersome to several of our more dedicated and tactful employees.

Furthermore, you are hereby subpoenaed to court pending a sexual harassment claim filed against you by Mr. Shapiro, alleged to have taken place on Tuesday, February 4, 2004. Failure to appear in court on March 9, 2004, at 9:30 AM. Part 24, Room 312 may result in a warrant for your arrest.

Effective immediately, you are officially terminated due to dereliction of duty and a pending sexual harassment complaint and are hereby ordered to **not** return to the premises of your former employer. Your personal belongings will be shipped to you via UPS by two-day mail. You are also **not eligible** for unemployment due to the nature of your termination. Your identification card and keys must be returned to the address provided below by mail or personally, to the securities office located in lower Manhattan at 68 Changers Street, 4th floor. You will be charged with trespassing if you fail to comply and it will result in arrest and/or a $1,000 fine. If you have any questions, please feel free to contact our EEOC Department between 9 AM and 6 PM, Monday through Friday. Also attached please find your severance package. We would like to thank you for your time and we express our deepest sympathy regarding this unfortunate but necessary situation.

                    Sincerely,
                    Jack Pearson
                    Director of Employee Affairs
JP:ae

Almost in tears, Beatrice tossed the letter to the side to see what her severance package consisted of. She found a check for $2,800, which meant they only paid her for vacation days and her five sick days, tax free. Too shocked to cry or react, Beatrice stood there staring at the letter. She slowly lay down on her bed and shut her eyes softly as the burning hot tears slid down into her ears.

The new security guard was beginning to creep Toni out. No matter what time of the day she came in or out, he was there, watching and too eager to talk or comment on something she was doing. Today was especially weird for when she came upstairs after work, ten minutes later just as she got out of the shower, he rang her doorbell. She looked through the peephole annoyed then opened the door with chain on. He showed her his ID. "I do not want to do you any harm Toni I just want to talk to you."

Dammit I slipped. "Sammy told me to look out for you, that he took a special liking to you. He described you and gave me your name and apartment number. Told me to make sure nothing harmful comes your way while he is gone."

"Is that right?"

"Yes, may I come in?"

"Why?"

"To talk to you."

"About what?" *Where do I know this man? He looks familiar. Was he someone I hurt in my past? Who the hell is he?*

"I'm sorry, I don't feel comfortable letting you into my home. Maybe I'll see you when I come in from work or something. Have a good night," Toni said as politely as possible and closed the door.

Damn, she is rough, my son was right.

Toni sat on her couch replaying the past events in her head. "What is wrong with people in the world today?" she said and nervously chuckled it off.

Plan B, gotta use plan B, Vernon thought as he pressed "L" for lobby on the elevator.

Stephen was finishing up his dinner and reading the paper when he thought he heard someone knocking on his door. He looked up at his clock. It was 9:30 at night on a Monday. He wasn't expecting anyone and nobody really came to visit him unexpectedly to say the least. He got up from his dinner and headed through the house to his front door. He looked through the peephole. *What is she doing here?* he asked in disgust. He started not to open the door but then decided he needed to know why she was at his house this time of the night after being gone for over a year.

Stephen let Beatrice in and the first thing he noticed was that she looked a little different. She had put on some weight to his distaste and her hair was different, darker. He liked that. She obviously put on her best outfit to see him, a poor attempt in letting him know that she was doing okay. He stood by the front door and looked at her. "Hello Beatrice," he said and folded his arms.

"Hello Stephen, how have you been?" she said, smiling.

"You know me, always good, and yourself?"

"Just fine."

"Wonderful, what can I do for you?"

"I was in the neighborhood so I decided to stop by."

"Really, who do you know along these parts?" he asked.

"Lola."

"Lola, I thought her and Preston got a divorce and she lived in Soho?"

"How did you hear that?"

"Word gets around. In any event, you may as well come in and sit down for a couple of *minutes* before you take that long trek home. You thirsty?"

"No, I'm fine thank you." *Dammit girl sell yourself before he puts you out.*

Stephen sat at the table for a few more minutes with his back turned, eating his dinner then emptied his plate. He came into the living room sipping a huge mug of water and sat across from Beatrice.

She better talk fast before I put her ghetto fabulous ass out, I got shit to do, like sleep.

"Why haven't you called me?" she started.

Call you for what?

"Why haven't you called *me*? You're the one that walked out of here in a huff and never contacted me. I thought you were through with me."

Back at ya bitch.

"I felt disrespected."

"I don't know why. A woman as well-off as you *were* should never say no to her supplier. It's unheard of. Ungrateful."

Go on lay it on thick limp dick.

"You're right and if it's not too late, I'd like to make it up to you."

"Make it up to me? Surely you don't think you can just walk in here after so long and think you can just make something up to me. Besides there isn't anything you can do that I haven't experienced yet."

"You know what? I don't know what I was thinking coming here. Maybe I should just go," Beatrice said softly and got up.

"It doesn't hurt to try. You were very brave for driving all the way out here without calling. What if I was here with my woman?"

"You're right," Beatrice said, heading to the front door. Stephen came behind her and opened it for her.

Damn this nigga is a cold bitch!

"It was good seeing you, glad to know you're doing good. Guess you really didn't need me after all. Keep in touch."

"Likewise," Beatrice said and headed to her car quickly before she began to cry.

She backed out of his driveway strong-faced as he watched her and waved bye. She smiled and honked her horn once. Once she hit the expressway, the tears began to flow. She was missing Toni, Lola was too good for her now, Marcus turned out to be a nightmare, and Stephen didn't want her. On top of everything, she lost her job. Beatrice just drove and drove until she wound up at her mother's house.

Ava was happy to see her baby girl as she hadn't seen her in a long time. She opened the door smiling warmly as usual and invited Beatrice in. "Hey honey, what are you doing out here so late?"

"I'm having some problems, Ma."

"Problems? You okay?" Ava said stepping to the side, letting her only child in.

"No, not really. Did I wake you?"

"No I just got off of the phone with your Aunt Fee-Fee. So what's going on honey? You put on some weight. You look good. I was worried about you before."

"You look good too, Ma. I guess being single pays off."

"Who said I was single?" she said, winking.

"You got a man, Ma?"

"Several." She chuckled.

"Wait a minute, do tell! That's why you haven't called me!"

"Well your father been sniffing 'round but he done had enough of this here. It's time to spread sunshine in someone else's life you feel me? I haven't seen him in a while and I barely talk to him. He mainly calls to see if you're here or if I talked to you."

Beatrice was tickled by her mother's new attitude. "Anyway I have three men. One is Sarge, he's forty-five, an ex-marine, lives in Long Island, divorced, one child, and he is my *main* man. Then I have Cecil and Shawn. Both are in there mid-fifties, nice men, take me out, buy me things, and come by, spend time. But when Sarge is around? They gotta bounce."

Beatrice nearly fell out of her seat. "Well okay Ma!" she said and hugged her tight. "You look happy, it shows."

"Yes, I am doing *too fine.* But enough of me, what's troubling you baby?"

Beatrice decided not to damper her mother's spirits with her problems. It had been years since her mother had been this sincerely happy.

"Nothing really. I was thinking about buying instead of renting and my credit is jacked, I need a new car. You know, stuff like that. I couldn't sleep, I'm off tomorrow, Toni and I were hanging out and stuff so I just dropped her off at her mother's and came over here."

"Oh, okay how is she doing? She still with that fine man?"

"Off and on."

"And what is up with you? Who is the lucky guy?"

"No one right now."

"Marcus called here for you although that was so long ago, over a year."

"Yeah, I've been seeing him around but he's married so we are just friends." Ava knew better but didn't touch it. "You hungry?"

"Yeah, what you got?"

"Leftover oxtails, white rice, pigeon peas, and chocolate cake. My *mens* love my cooking."

"Ma you sleeping with all of them?"

"Yes, as a matter of fact I am."

"Mommy!" Beatrice said, laughing. "Ma, yuk yuk and yuk!"

"Please girl. Okay I am not *regularly*. Sarge yes, all the time *any time*. Um um um! But the other two? Depends on my mood, where Sarge is and the length of time in which I last had intercourse, but I am safe thank you, at all times. As a matter of fact, I haven't given Cecil any, he just you know . . . goes down there but I don't think I want to have sex with him. I don't like him like that but he comes around and fixes things, and he is good company. And they do not know about one another. All they know is I'm newly divorced and heartbroken so they are all trying to put their bid in for this fine seasoned woman." She laughed as she made Beatrice's plate.

"I hear that, Mommy. Where you meet these people?"

"Well Sarge is actually an attorney, he helped me with my divorce, I met Cecil by my job, and I met Shawn in church. You sure you're okay?" Ava said, stopping briefly to address Beatrice.

"Uh-huh, just tired, I been out all day. I may even spend the night here."

"How's um, Toni getting home?"

"I'll call her and see."

"Oh okay." Ava turned back to her daughter's plate and filled it with food. She handed Beatrice the plate of food and sat down across from her. "I do miss your father sometimes. We spent many years together. Breakups aren't easy. Marriage isn't easy, fighting temptation isn't easy. But I will tell you this. I wasted more time than I care to admit on your father and his nonsense. I should have left your father before you were born, then after you were born, when you were five, nine, fifteen. I had so many chances and reasons. But I got comfortable with him paying the bills, I didn't want to be a statistic, I didn't want to start over, I got immune to the things he'd bring my way that weren't any good for me. The last ten years of my life with your father has been the worst. You been out on your own and I could have left him then but I stayed and he played," she said, shrugging it off.

"So how do you feel? I mean dating all of these men."

"All because your father was here doesn't mean *I was*. I have been single in my heart and mind for years now. He was just here physically Beatrice. I wanted to go out and just be single and date or do whatever for a long time. I'm fifty-nine years old and . . ."

"And you look forty-three."

"Which is why my man is forty-five," Ava said, laughing.

"Well I am happy for you Ma."

"Me too, and I just want you to know that you don't have to give in to the pressures of being married by a certain time or having a man. It's overkill. Sometimes people need *me* time, time to just be alone, take up hobbies, do things, *see* things. Sometimes the pressures and expectations of what we need in relationships are too much to handle. There is nothing wrong with being alone but that is why through it all you pray and you never ever let go of your closest friends for a man. Men come and go. But when you leave the man you been with since twenty and you're sixty years old, it's hard and you'll find yourself alone. But then you have your best friend right there through it all." Ava knew bits and pieces of what was going on between Toni and Beatrice because Toni told her mother and her mother told Ava a little bit when they ran into one another. Ava didn't get the full story as they were both in a rush but she heard enough to know it involved a man and they were not talking. Beatrice continued eating her food in silence. She thought about Toni and how they have never gone this long without speaking. But stubbornly Beatrice refused to take the blame or feel guilty for something that happened so long ago.

The next morning when Beatrice was leaving her mother's house, she parked in front of the corner store to get a cup of coffee before she hit the road. When she was coming out she bumped into Mo. He didn't recognize her at first but she recognized him. "Excuse me," he said and walked around her. She turned and watched him then called out to him. "Maurice," she said. He turned and squinted at her. He walked closer. He began pointing and snapping his fingers trying to get his memory going. "Beatrice right? B?"

"Yeah, how you doin'?"

"I'm good, you look different, how you doin'?"

"I'm okay, hanging in there."

"How's my girl? I haven't talked to her in a little while."

"She's good."

"That's good, it's good to see you. What are you doing over here?"

"I was visiting my mother last night then it got too late to drive home so—"

"Excuse me," a voice behind her said as she was blocking the entrance of the store. Beatrice moved over without looking at the person. He walked up to Mo and told him to hurry up. "I'm coming man, look, remember B?" Maurice said.

Quentin turned around quickly. "Beatrice? Hey girl how you been?"

Oh lord this is the last person I need to be looking at right now. He looks wonderful . . . damn maybe I need to see him after all. Toni is already mad at me so . . .

"Long time no see Quentin. How's life been treating you?"

"I can't complain." *Damn, I haven't seen this broad since we were teenagers or something. She looks the same, a little thicker, she looks good.*

"How's T?" Quentin asked.

"I don't know, we aren't talking."

Why didn't she tell me that? Mo was thinking.

"What? You two not talking? Why?" Maurice asked.

"Let's just say our past came back to haunt us and one of us is not so forgiving."

Toni knows? Quentin was thinking. Beatrice gave him a look that said *yes, she knows.*

He put his head down.

"You two will be talking again, you know how women are," Mo said, fanning it off.

"Well I need to be going. Let me give you guys my numbers, maybe we all can link up in the future, you know, dinner, drinks, whatever."

The men began pulling out cell phones to record her number. Beatrice recited her numbers and took theirs.

"It was good seeing you both," she said, hugging Mo first then hugging Quentin, pressing her breasts up against him. "Call me," she whispered in his ears. His eyes held a questionable stare but one that said he'd call her soon. *I need to know what Toni knows. Then again, I don't have to be around Toni or Beatrice. I'm going to just leave it alone, it was long ago, we all need to move on. I don't have time for this.*

Beatrice waved femininely and almost flirtatiously at the two friends, then headed to her car.

"B looking good right?" Mo said and nudged Quentin.

"Yeah, she look a'ight, come on, we need to hit the road, it's getting late," he said rushing his friend to change the subject.

* * *

Beatrice was at her wit's end. Her rent was backed up three months, Toni still wasn't speaking to her, Lola had vanished, and last Beatrice heard she was hanging out with a bunch of white girls in Soho, shopping like it was going out of style. She was unemployed and lonely. She sat on her futon and cried for about three hours straight, nonstop. *I have to hit the ground in order to see my way up,* she said over and over and actually began to feel a little better for the moment. She hadn't any food in her refrigerator and she didn't even have any alcohol or herb stashed away to take away the pain a little bit. The only good news was that the charges brought forth to her from her old job was dropped so long as she didn't step foot on the premises again. *Where would I shop? I love Saks, it doesn't matter, I don't have any money to shop no way,* she thought. Her fingers roamed the telephone as she racked her brain trying to figure out whom to call. She had no one. *What have I done to deserve this? What have I done?* Beatrice began to cry again. Her phone rang for the first time in two weeks, immediately she snatched up the phone.

"Hello," she said, trying to sound cheerful.

"Hey, B, this is Quentin, you busy?"

"No, not at all Q, what's up?" Beatrice got charged up. She sat up in her bed and wiped her face.

"Nothing. You sure you're okay? You sound like you were sleep or something."

"No, I just woke up, but I'm fine, talk to me what's up?"

"Well, my conscience has been bugging me for

some time now. I just want to know how much Toni knows about, you know . . . our past."

"She knows everything Quentin."

"How did that happen?"

"She pried and pried until I finally told her. I couldn't hold it in any longer." Silence followed then Quentin whispered, "Damn."

"So this is why you guys aren't speaking?"

"Yeah, it's been about five months now."

"I'm sorry to hear that. I'm partly responsible. I should have known better, I should have known that my past would catch up to me. My mother always said what you do in the dark will come out in the light."

"Tell me about it. Look I have to be honest with you Quentin. When I saw you the other day, feelings that I thought I didn't have for you anymore resurfaced and right now, I am going through a really rough period in my life and I really need a friend. I do."

"What's going on B?"

Beatrice told him the events that had happened to her starting with leaving Stephen up until now.

"You feel like company?" he asked.

"I live way out in Jersey."

"Well maybe when I come over we can talk and go and visit Toni. I think we owe it to her to just apologize face-to-face and clear the air for whatever it is worth."

"Toni isn't trying to hear either one of us right now."

"That's why I said for whatever it is worth, even if it's us trying to do the right thing. It will be worth something later on."

"Okay, you have a pen so that I can give you directions?"

"Just tell me, I can remember."

It was awkward for Beatrice and Quentin to be laughing and having a good time without Mo and Toni. But Quentin noticed how bad Beatrice was looking and was trying his best to cheer her up and keep her in good spirits. In the month he saw her last, she had lost plenty weight, she looked depressed, her hair was a mess, and she just looked weathered. He even gave her a couple of dollars, bought her some groceries, a bottle of Grey Goose, and gave her money to do the laundry and get her hair done. He also told her he'd see if his mother had a spot for her at her job at Queens Hospital. As the night winded down, Beatrice didn't want Quentin to leave but she didn't want her vulnerability to put her in an uncomfortable and costly situation. Quentin showed no signs of wanting to leave as he flicked through the channels and sipped his juice. Beatrice yawned and stretched, trying to give signs that she was ready for him to leave. "Oh I'm going, I'm just waiting for a phone call. If I don't get it within the next fifteen minutes I'm leaving okay?"

"I wasn't rushing you," Beatrice said, ashamed.

"Sure you weren't."

"Well thank you for everything today Q, you didn't have to do this."

"I hate to see a woman in distress. It's not a good sight. Women are supposed to be nurtured, taken care of, protected. Anything I can do to help, let me know."

Beatrice put her head down, she was sad, she missed her best friend. "I miss her so much Q."

"So call her, swallow your pride and call her."

"I just feel so . . . I don't know, I just feel as if I'm going through hard times because of karma."

"Well in everything we experience in life, God has a lesson in it for us, we just have to be wise enough and open-minded enough to find it. So long as you learned a lesson then you'll be fine."

"She is the only friend I ever had, I never meant to hurt her," B sobbed. Quentin hugged her and before they knew it they were both fast asleep on the futon.

After much thought, prayer, and loss of sleep, Toni decided that it was time to make amends with her sister. She missed Beatrice and would have called her sooner but with the coming out of her new book she didn't have time for anyone except her mother. She was happy to be starting a new chapter of her life, a new year, newfound wisdom and she wanted and hoped that her best friend was doing well and in good spirits like she was. Tracy, who had proved to be just as loyal to her, was also another person she had made time for often. She filled Toni in on Lola and Preston and how they were definitely divorced and not together and that Preston had relocated back to Georgia but that did little to ease Toni's pain. She threw a copy of her new book, which was slated to hit stores a month from now, in her black tote

with intentions on giving the first copy to her
number-one fan, Beatrice. Toni had purchased a
car with the hefty advance she received and was
on her way to Beatrice's house to reclaim her
friendship. She wanted to put the past behind
and start anew.

It was Saturday morning and was very windy
out but not too cold. Toni's short crop was blowing every which way but the right way. She
jogged up the front steps to Beatrice's building in
a sexy fitting dark denim suit, tall stiletto heels,
and a bulky aqua-blue scarf around her neck with
eye shadow to match. Her large sliver hoop earrings blew in the wind. She ran into the building
and fixed her hair with her leather glove–clad fingers. She smiled as she knocked on the door,
knowing and feeling that Beatrice would be happy
to see her. She hoped her sister was home as she
had not spotted her car anywhere.

Beatrice and Quentin jumped up off of the
futon when they heard the knock. Since the futon
was right by the front door, the knocking startled
them. Quentin, who had just finished giving Beatrice cunnilingus, wiped his mouth and put his
sweater on. Beatrice pulled down her Howard
University T-shirt and went to the door. "Who?"
she asked. Toni decided not to say her name.
"Who?" Beatrice asked more angrily.
"Open the door," Toni said, masking her voice.
Beatrice looked back at Quentin and shrugged

her shoulders. Quentin, anticipating a man, stood up and came behind Beatrice to prepare to leave, as he should have done last night. His girlfriend was probably worried sick. Beatrice opened the door and was elated to see her friend but noticed Toni wasn't too happy to see her. Then Beatrice realized that Quentin was behind her. Toni dug in her pocketbook then decided not to give Beatrice the first copy and instead would give it to her mother. "I'm out," she said.

"No, Toni it's not what you think, please don't leave!" Quentin said grabbing her arm.

She pulled away.

"Now what? I don't want to hear it. Y'all just don't quit with this grimy shit do you?"

Beatrice let Quentin do the talking, as she couldn't think of something fast enough.

"Toni, come inside, we need to talk," he said.

Toni walked inside of the apartment and stood. "Make it quick, I gotta go."

"First of all let me tell you how I wound up here." Quentin told Toni everything from the meeting in the store up until now, leaving out the oral pleasure he had given Beatrice. "That's that. I swear."

"You have no reason to lie and I have no reason to care. The whole situation just makes me uncomfortable so I need to be leaving."

"Well I was leaving so, let me be gone. Toni I apologize for everything, I swear to God. I love you, I do. I'm sorry and I hope one day you can forgive us both. When and if you do, let me know. But nothing happened. We just fell asleep on the couch, look around," Quentin said.

"Swear to God," Beatrice threw in, looking sympathetic.

"You're sorry huh? Sorry for fucking my best friend on my bed when I wasn't home and getting her pregnant. Man, Quentin! You are so full of shit!"

"I'm gonna go now. But before I do I just want to apologize for what happened in the past. It was a mistake and I'm sorry," Quentin said, touching her arm gently. He looked back at Beatrice. "Beatrice keep ya head up ahiet?" he said then disappeared.

"Toni, I miss you," B said and put her arms out for a hug.

"I can't stand here and act like I believe the story Q just told me. It just doesn't sit right with me. I'm sorry B. I came over here with good intentions but after all this time, to come here at ten in the morning to find him here doesn't sit right with me. I need to get out of here, I'm sorry," Toni said, and walked out. Beatrice stood there in shock, her heart beating fast she ran to the window and saw Toni hop in her red 2007 Acura and pull off. *She has a new car?* was the only thing that Beatrice could think to say.

Preston's father tried his best to get close to Toni but just as his son said, Toni was tough and didn't let people into her circle easily. He gave Preston thorough advice, which was to step to the woman on his own and take rejection like a man if she turned him away or to leave her alone altogether and take the loss. From what he could gather about Toni he did say that he liked how she lived her life and that she was a beautiful woman in a tough, tomboy kind of way. "Reminds me of your mother," he said, oddly enough making Preston yearn for Toni more. But Preston insisted that his father stay and talk to Toni so with that Vernon stayed on more night and waited for Toni to come home. After much thought, Preston decided to pack his bags and head back to New York, to claim his woman.

"You do that son, you do that because if I can't get to her by tomorrow? I'm done here." His father cheered him on.

Toni dropped all of her bags and screamed that she'd kill him or call the cops if he did not get out of her house. The man stood up and put his hands up. "I am not here to hurt you," he said.

"What do you want!" Toni yelled but she did not move. The man laughed lightly. "I guess I should tell you who I am. I'm Preston Pierre's father, Vernon."

So that's why he looked so familiar!

"What do you want and how did you get into my apartment?" Toni said, walking closer to him.

"Sam let me in. He said please don't kill him but that he liked my son so much for you."

"Sam will get checked on this I don't give a damn who likes who. You could be a murderer."

"But I'm not. I flew all the way from Georgia for the mercy of my son. I had to see you for myself. I had to meet the woman that has my son in such a dampened mood."

"Okay, so now what?"

"He said that he had been calling your best friend every day to try to get to you and she keeps telling him you don't want him. Is that true?"

"My best friend and I don't talk but he said he calls her all the time?"

"Beatrice right? Yeah he calls her all the time she hasn't told you?"

"No," Toni said, pissed off.

"My son has made a big horrible mistake and sure you should be hurt. But forgive him Toni he is a good man with a big heart and he loves you. I know he does," Vernon spoke as Toni sat next to him.

He took in her skin, *flawless*. She was a "lil' mama" as they called the fine women back home.

"Mr. White . . ."

"Call me Vernon baby."

"Vernon, your son knows why I am having such a hard time to forgive him. I explained to him every detail of my life and my pain. This was early on and he should have broken things down to me then. Do you know how humiliated I was? I helped his wife plan the anniversary party! I told her what to do to get him back! Meanwhile I'm thinking he's in love with me and he's married? I'm sorry Vernon I am sure he is a good man but good men don't do what he has done. He hurt me more than any man that I ever knew because I believed in him, I trusted him."

Vernon sighed deep. He knew that his son was in a hard place and that there was no way to make Toni understand.

"I'm sorry that this had to happen to you. But I

know that my son has never loved anyone like he loved you and I know that Lola was never the one for him. He is a one woman's man and marrying her was the right thing to do because he wanted a family. When he realized that she wasn't the one, he legally separated from her. That's when he met you. He was not with her when he met you and was getting a divorce. Toni I hope that your heart heals soon and I hope that you are able to love again, just one more time. Love is about forgiving and caring. I'm trying my best to have you hear my son out at least, on your time of course. You mean after all this love and time you wouldn't even talk to him and hear him out? Are you that hard and that scared?" Vernon preached.

"As a matter of fact, I am, Vernon. That's just how I am, that's just how it is."

"Oh that's nonsense. What is there to be afraid of other than loneliness and you will be if you keep this up young woman," he said, standing up.

"My flight leaves tomorrow evening so I need to get on back to Preston's place in the city and get some rest. Hear my son out at least. Now you are someone I would love to have as a daughter-in-law. You got a nice place here, a good head on your shoulders. But loosen up, soften up lil' mama." Vernon winked and pinched Toni's chin. For the first time in a while she smiled.

It had been a long time since he had seen Toni or even spoken to her. His plan to get her back was lucid. If he didn't achieve that, he wouldn't remain in New York any longer. He had longed to move back to Georgia to a more simple life. Lola was the only reason he stayed so long. She hated the south. So with his mind made up, Preston headed to the newspaper stand to buy reading material for his two-hour flight. Needing a good book he walked toward the mystery section to pick up a James Patterson novel when the attention of a book caught his eye. The book was an iridescent black and silver mix with the title of the book small and directly in the middle, the author's name *Toni Jolly* in bold gold letters on the bottom. He purchased the book for $24.99 and immediately began reading it, the acknowledgments read, *Thank you experience . . . you are my best and only teacher*. Short, to the point, and strong, just like the author. Preston sat down and waited for his flight to be boarded and nearly missed the announcement as he was so engulfed in the book.

EPILOGUE

Dressed in black tuxedo pants, a black silk halter, and large diamond studs that she treated herself to also courtesy of her advance, Toni smiled hard as her fans, the many she didn't know that she had, lined up around the block to receive an autographed copy of her new book. Some of the faces were surprisingly people who lived in her complex that never spoke, coworkers, people from her mother's job, Beatrice's mother and a few of her friends, Beatrice's father, people from the neighborhood, her beautician along with her friends and family and a host of people that Toni didn't know. Toni couldn't stop smiling as she reflected on her life and the blessings she had received over and over again. She vowed to contribute a percentage of the book's earnings to a charity. Children and grandmothers were lined up to purchase two and three copies at a time. A young woman probably twenty-one or -two, touched Toni's heart the most when she spoke to her with teary eyes. "I bought your first book and I could relate so much to your character Carin. You helped me so much to just overcome the many obstacles I have faced in my life at such a young age. You are such a role model to me. Thank you," the girl said. Toni stood up and hugged the young woman, rocking back and forth for some time. "Keep your chin up. You are beautiful, don't let anyone deter you from your dreams and goals. You are in charge of your destiny."

"Thank you," the girl said, reluctant to let Toni's hand go. She wiped her tears and walked away a new person, Toni believed. *Lord this is my calling, to help young women, I know this now,* Toni said, as she remained standing because so many people were adamant about hugging or touching her in some kind of way. Toni looked down the long line and realized that she would be out here all day so she excused herself for a bathroom break. She purchased some water, gum, touched up her perfume and lip gloss, then returned to her seat. She took a deep breath then put on her smiling face for her avid readers. She signed her name in a book then handed it to the young woman in front of her, taking two seconds to realize that it was Beatrice. Not missing a beat or willing to devote any time to her, Toni smiled at her as if she was a fan and extended her hand to the next person. Beatrice walked away sulking. *The nerve of her to show up here wanting me to take time out to acknowledge her trifling ass.* And the surprises kept coming—Quentin, Mo, his wife, his sister-in-law, and daughter, along with at least twenty people from the old neighborhood showed up for support. Toni laughed, smiled, and hugged them all, thanking them for purchasing her book in bulk. Fifteen minutes later, her doorman showed up, then Vernon showed up. *Oh lord*, Toni thought but smiled anyway. "You are extraordinary," he said and took his copy without problem. He left a weird feeling in Toni. But no feeling was weirder than that of seeing Preston hand her his copy. Toni's eyes widened with emotion. Her heart began racing.

"Congratulations," he said, his eyes glossy. Toni didn't know what to say or do. She just stared at him.

"I miss you," he said very low.

She didn't know how to respond so she just smiled softly and handed him back his book after scribbling something in it.

"I won't hold up the line any longer. But I'm back in town, staying at my apartment on Central Park West and will be there all weekend waiting for you. No pressure, but if I don't see you or hear from you by Monday morning then I'll take it as you don't want to hear from me and I'll be going back to Georgia for good. Anyway, I'm proud of you," he said, snatching up a box containing fifty copies. "How much for this box?" he asked. His actions drew gasps and stares.

"That'll be about twelve-hundred dollars, sir," Toni said after punching it in her calculator. Preston pulled out his checkbook and wrote a check for $3,000 as his father lifted the box. "Have a nice day," he said and walked off.

Toni's book signing lasted until about 8:00 PM. She came home exhausted and couldn't wait to go to bed. When she entered her house she felt like she was in botanical gardens as dozens and dozens of her favorite flowers and some she had no idea what they were filled her living room. She searched until she found a card. *Toni, please come see me, love Preston.* Toni was moved but she had reclaimed her peace of mind, healed her heart, and moved on. She didn't need any interruptions; life was good to her lately. But she knew life would be better for her with Preston there and not just financially. She loved him so much and missed him and seeing him today confirmed that. She made up her mind to go see him on Monday. She didn't want him to go back to Georgia, not right now. She took time to move the flowers to one side of the living room so she could get by without knocking them over, then went to bed, sleeping all day Saturday, and running errands most of Sunday. By the time she got home, Tracy was on her machine asking her to call her and when she did she told her she wanted to take her out to celebrate her pregnancy and Toni's new-found success, Toni agreed.

To the only man I ever truly really loved. I miss you. Love T.

Preston read the inscription as his father drove him back to his pad in the city. "What do you think? You think she'll come around?" Preston asked his father as he closed the book.

"Yeah definitely. She thinks she's tough but she's not. She'll be back," Vernon said smiling. "They always come back.

* * *

Monday morning, Toni was heading to the city to sell books to coworkers who could not make it to her book signing when it dawned on her what she needed to do. "I forgot to call Pierre!" she said and stopped in her tracks. She jumped back on the train heading uptown but by the time she reached Pierre's apartment, the snooty doorman informed her that *Mr. White* was on extended leave from his residence and left strict instructions for him to not take or relay any messages to him.

"But you don't understand, I am a close friend of his and he was expecting me!" Toni said.

"I'm sorry ma'am but Mr. White is no longer residing here. He left town this afternoon leaving no contact information. I'm sure he'll contact you," the doorman said and returned to his reading. "Thank you," Toni said, feeling defeated. "Dammit I wanted to see him shit!" she cursed. She thought about him all the way to the train station. "I still have his dad's home number," she said, shrugging.

"Guess it wasn't meant to be."

She jogged down the stairs to catch the train, smiling at the woman buying a metro card who held a copy of her book. When the two women got on the train, Toni decided to stand next to the woman who was sitting down.

"Is that a good book?" she asked the woman upon noticing that she was halfway through it.

"Excellent, I recommend it to any woman to read. It's a nice, easy read. The author's name is Toni Jolly," the woman said, smiling.

"Thank you," Toni said, leaning up against the door of the train, smiling. *Thank you.*